"Was someone else injured in your accident?"

Gage gave a rough laugh. "A dozen other FBI agents and local cops were there. None was lucky enough to receive the same special attention. Why do you ask?"

Lisa shrugged. "While you were sleeping, I thought I heard you call out for someone named Charlie. I thought it might have been another agent who'd been hurt along with you."

His expression went instantly cold, so cold she shivered, regretting whatever crazy impulse had led her to bring up the subject. "I must have been having a nightmare."

She knew she should let it drop, but something made her push. "Is Charlie a friend?"

"Charlie was short for Charlotte."

He went on, his face without expression, his eyes focused on the curtains fluttering in the night breeze. "Charlotte was my kid sister. She was kidnapped from our front yard when she was three years old. We never saw her again."

Dear Reader,

The year may be coming to a close, but the excitement never flags here at Silhouette Intimate Moments. We've got four—yes, four—fabulous miniseries for you this month, starting with Carla Cassidy's CHEROKEE CORNERS and *Trace Evidence,* featuring a hero who's a crime scene investigator and now has to investigate the secrets of his own heart. Kathleen Creighton continues STARRS OF THE WEST with *The Top Gun's Return.* Tristan Bauer had been declared dead, but now he was back—and very much alive, as he walked back into true love Jessie Bauer's life. Maggie Price begins LINE OF DUTY with *Sure Bet* and a sham marriage between two undercover officers that suddenly starts feeling extremely real. And don't miss *Nowhere To Hide,* the first in RaeAnne Thayne's trilogy THE SEARCHERS. An on-the-run single mom finds love with the FBI agent next door, but there are still secrets to uncover at book's end.

We've also got two terrific stand-alone titles, starting with Laurey Bright's *Dangerous Waters*. Treasure hunting and a shared legacy provide the catalyst for the attraction of two opposites in an irresistible South Pacific setting. Finally, Jill Limber reveals *Secrets of an Old Flame* in a sexy, suspenseful reunion romance.

Enjoy—and look for more excitement next year, right here in Silhouette Intimate Moments.

Yours.

Leslie J. Wainger
Executive Editor

Please address questions and book requests to:
Silhouette Reader Service
U.S.: 3010 Walden Ave., P.O. Box 1325, Buffalo, NY 14269
Canadian: P.O. Box 609, Fort Erie, Ont. L2A 5X3

Nowhere To Hide

RAEANNE THAYNE

Silhouette®

INTIMATE MOMENTS™

Published by Silhouette Books

America's Publisher of Contemporary Romance

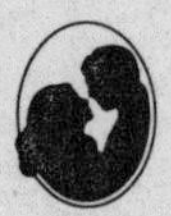

SILHOUETTE BOOKS

ISBN 0-373-27334-7

NOWHERE TO HIDE

This edition published by arrangement with Harlequin Books S.A.

Visit Silhouette at www.eHarlequin.com

Printed in U.S.A.

Books by RaeAnne Thayne

Silhouette Intimate Moments

The Wrangler and the Runaway Mom #960
Saving Grace #995
Renegade Father #1062
**The Valentine Two-Step* #1133
**Taming Jesse James* #1139
**Cassidy Harte and the Comeback Kid* #1144
The Quiet Storm #1218
Freefall #1239
†*Nowhere To Hide* #1264

*Outlaw Hartes
†The Searchers

RAEANNE THAYNE

lives in a graceful old Victorian nestled in the rugged mountains of northern Utah, along with her husband and two young children. Her books have won numerous honors, including several Readers' Choice Awards from *Romantic Times* and a RITA® Award nomination by the Romance Writers of America. RaeAnne loves to hear from readers. She can be reached through her Web site at www.raeannethayne.com or at P.O. Box 6682, North Logan, UT 84341.

Chapter 1

He had trespassers.

Two of them.

Dressed for jogging in shorts and a T-shirt, Special Agent Gage McKinnon eased open his front door just a crack and peered out into the small front garden of the house he rented.

What were they up to? He could hear them out there, laughing and whispering together, but he couldn't make out the words in the crisp high mountain air of the Park City summer morning.

He didn't think they were dangerous, but if he'd learned anything in his thirty-five years, he'd learned not to underestimate the female of the species. These two looked to be about three or four. One was slightly smaller than the other by a few inches and a little more round but besides that, they could have been twins. Same dark, curly hair, same flashing brown eyes, same little ski slopes for noses.

Where did they come from? And what were they up to?

He put his plans for a run up the mountainside temporarily on hold and watched them for a few moments longer. Ah, now he figured it out. Each of the girls had her pink nightie hitched up into a sort of basket, revealing small olive legs and matching Barbie panties. Into their makeshift carriers, they were both piling what looked like just about every single flower in his yard, roots and all.

Daisies, geraniums, purple lavender. They plucked some of each.

He didn't care about the flowers. They could have the whole garden, as far as he was concerned. But he had a feeling his landlady wouldn't see things the same way. In the month he'd lived here, she had been by at least three times a week to baby these and the even bigger garden in the back. He figured this wanton pilfering would *not* make her happy.

Gage opened the door wider and walked out onto the porch. The sun had barely crept over the horizon of the surrounding mountains with their wide ski runs, bare of snow now but still a pale contrast to the dark evergreens covering the slopes.

The early-morning air was cool. He hadn't spent much time in Utah since his childhood but it hadn't taken him long to remember that temperatures in these high mountain valleys could often dip below freezing at night, even in June.

These girls weren't exactly dressed for cool weather.

"Hey, what are you doing?"

Two dark heads whipped around as his voice sliced through the still morning. The smaller girl looked suddenly terrified, her eyes and her little mouth both open wide. She clutched her nightie with one hand and what looked like a stuffed monkey with the other as she edged slightly behind the other girl, who gave him a winsome smile that had most likely been her ticket out of far worse trouble than some plucked flowers.

"Hi, mister. We're picking flowers for our mama. Today is her birthday. She's old."

He bit his cheek at that piece of frank information and summoned a scowl. "These are my flowers. You should have asked me first."

The older girl frowned. "Mrs. Jensen said they were *her* flowers. She said we could pick a few for Mama's birthday."

Mrs. Jensen was his dour, taciturn landlady, who had yet to unbend enough to smile at him since he moved in.

She owned the house next door, too, he remembered, a virtual match to his small, wood-sided cottage on this row of old dwellings that traced their existence back to the days when Park City was a rough and rugged mining camp, not a high-society resort town.

He had found it odd that Ruth Jensen had surrounded his cottage with this lush, fairy-tale garden while leaving its twin to sit squarely in a bare yard of crab grass and empty flowerbeds but she explained that she'd only recently purchased the house next door and hadn't had time for landscaping yet.

In the last few days, he'd noticed the first signs of life over there—lights on at night, an older model Honda parked out front, a few toys in the yard. Looks like he was meeting some of his new neighbors.

"You're sure Mrs. Jensen said you could pick the flowers?" He had a tough time picturing her giving these little urchins free rein to romp through her beloved garden, but the older girl nodded vigorously.

"She said it would be all right just this once since today is Mama's birthday."

"Where is your mother?"

"She's still asleep. We're gonna s'prise her."

Their mother ought to be a little more aware of what her two girls were up to. She ought to at least put better locks on the door or something so they couldn't go wandering around town on their own.

"What about your dad?"

The older girl sent him a sad look. "Our daddy's in heaven. We miss him a lot."

Now what was he supposed to say to that? At a loss, Gage glanced up and down the street. The three of them were the only thing moving through the early morning except for a few songbirds flitting through the trees and a plump striped cat skulking across a yard.

This was a quiet neighborhood, but he knew that wouldn't make a damn bit of difference to a child predator looking for prey. Quiet neighborhoods in small towns were often more attractive hunting grounds than those that bustled with people. Parents could more easily be lulled into a false sense of security, thinking nothing could touch them here, that their children faced no threat more serious than the occasional skinned knee from crashing on their bikes.

But no place was truly safe. He knew that far better than most.

"My name's Gaby and my sister's name is Anna," the little girl confided into the silence. "I'm five years old but Anna's only three. She doesn't talk very much, but Mama says I talk enough for both of us so that's okay. My real name's Gabriella but Mama calls me Gaby because she says that's what I am. What's your name, mister?"

Their mother needed to have a serious talk with them about stranger danger. This little chatterbox had just handed him all the information anyone needed to earn their trust.

"McKinnon."

"You're nice, Mr. McKinnon."

"Uh, thanks." Not too many people said that about him. He wasn't sure he liked it. "You two ought to go on inside now. I think you've got enough flowers, don't you? And pretty soon your mother will wake up and start looking for you."

"Okay. Anna's feet are cold. This grass is wet and icky."

"That's what shoes are for," he pointed out.

Gabriella just giggled and even Anna gave him a shy smile, then they raced across the yard to the house next door. The older girl paused on the porch and waved at him, then they both slipped inside.

He watched to make sure they closed the door tightly behind them, then took off down the street toward the trailhead he'd discovered a few weeks before.

He ought to definitely have a talk with the mother, warn her about letting two cute little girls roam free where any kind of sick bastard could get to them.

He could tell her stories that would give the lady nightmares for the rest of her life. After ten years in the FBI's CAC division—Crimes Against Children—he had plenty of them to share. Hell, he didn't even have to dig into any of the cases he had worked over the years to scare her senseless. All he had to do was tell her about Charlotte.

He reached the trailhead and ran up the steep dirt trail faster than his usual pace, grateful for the physical exertion to take his mind off the sudden, searing memory of his little sister's cherubic face.

If he bumped into the girls' mother, he would warn her to be a little more careful with her daughters' safety, but he probably wouldn't go into details about either his cases at the FBI or about Charlotte, Gage thought, pushing himself even harder up the trail.

He wouldn't wish his kind of nightmares on anyone, even a woman who would let her daughters wander around at all hours of the morning.

On her twenty-eighth birthday, Alicia Connelly De-Barillas awoke to two horrifying realizations—she had slept through her alarm again and her daughters were standing by her bed holding two gigantic armloads of what had to be stolen flowers.

Allie groaned and propped herself up against the pillows, wishing she could hang on to the lingering remnants of yet another dream where the heartrending events of the past two years—particularly the last six months—had never happened. But like all her other dreams, this one fluttered away like dandelion puffs on the breeze.

''Hey, ladybugs.'' She paused and cleared morning gruffness from her throat. ''Where did you get those?''

''From the pretty flower house,'' Gabriella answered with her sweetest smile. ''Mrs. Jensen said we could pick some for your birthday.''

She supposed she shouldn't find that so surprising. Mrs. Jensen might look cold and forbidding on the surface but she had treated Allie and her girls with nothing but kindness since the day Allie had met her the week before at the garage Ruth's son owned.

She had become their guardian angel of sorts, the best of Samaritans. Allie had been desperate and frightened and so tired when she showed up at that garage just before closing with her car that suddenly wouldn't drive any faster than thirty miles an hour.

She had been trying to figure out whether she dared dip into her dwindling nest egg to fix the Honda—and to pay for a hotel room in this exclusive resort town—when Ruth had arrived to drop something off for her son. The older woman had taken one look at Allie trying to keep the girls entertained in that oil-stained mechanic's office through her exhaustion and fear and had for some unaccountable reason decided to take them all under her considerable wing.

Before Allie realized what happened, she had a job offer cleaning houses and a place to live in this small cottage.

She owed Ruth Jensen so much. The woman didn't know it but she had rescued them, given Allie the time and space she needed so desperately to figure out where to go from here.

Now it looked as if she owed Ruth for her lovely mishmashed birthday bouquet.

Anna smiled and held out her colorful armload to Allie. "Happy birthday, Mama," she whispered.

Allie's heart swelled at the rare words from her quiet daughter. She pulled the girls to her, flowers and all.

"Thank you! These are so beautiful."

"We don't have any money to buy you another present," Gaby said sadly. "I'm sorry, Mama."

She probably should have taken them shopping, Allie thought with a guilty pang. Just another one of the hazards of being a single mother. Until her daughters could handle money on their own, Allie had yet to figure out a way to deal with the whole present-buying experience when she was the recipient. It was a little hard for them to surprise her with a gift when she was the one paying for it.

"This is perfect, sweetheart. Absolutely perfect—exactly what I wanted. Let's go put them in water so we can enjoy them for a long time. After I shower does anybody want some super-duper birthday pancakes with chocolate sprinkles?"

Both girls nodded vigorously, their dark eyes wide with excitement. Allie smiled and quickly picked up the robe she had tossed over the old carved oak chair next to her bed, then led the girls out of her room to the kitchen.

After Gaby found a couple of canning jars under the sink for the flowers and they had arranged the bouquets to everyone's satisfaction, Allie sent them into the living room to watch cartoons while she checked her blood glucose.

It was exactly where it should be, but Allie was almost afraid to hope that things might be settling down. The last few months had been the best her levels had been in a long time. After Jaime's death the stress and fatigue of finding herself alone with two young children had taken a heavy toll on her. No matter what she did, her insulin levels had fluctuated wildly, culminating in that terrible day she had ended up in the hospital.

As she showered, she thought about the year that had passed since her last birthday. Twelve months ago she never would have guessed she would find herself fleeing from everything safe and secure in her life—her job, their house, her friends. She never would have been able to even contemplate her desperate fight to keep her daughters.

She closed her eyes and let the water sluice over her. She had made the right choice. The only choice. What else could she have done? Jaime's parents had been ruthlessly determined. Once they had been awarded joint custody, Allie realized it was only a matter of time before they found a way to take the girls back with them to Venezuela. They had the money and the resources to ensure she would never see them again.

She could hardly believe the warm, funny man she married and loved so fiercely could come from such cold resolve.

This was her second birthday without him.

One of those unexpected waves of loss washed over her and she clutched at her stomach. They didn't come with the frequency they had the first year, when she had barely been able to function, when just surviving each day—wading painfully through the ocean of grief encircling her—had been a monumental struggle of sheer will.

Jaime had been killed in a car accident just a month after her twenty-sixth birthday, a few days shy of their fourth wedding anniversary. Gaby had been three, Anna just over a year.

Where would she be now if not for that drunk driver on that rainy Pennsylvania road? Comfortable and secure and happy in the lovely life she and Jaime were building together. Certainly not facing this uncertain future, on the run with two young girls who deserved far more.

Allie scrubbed her tears away, then turned off the shower and wrapped in a towel. She gazed at her reflection in the mirror over the sink, at the woman staring back at her with big eyes and a choppy brown dye job.

She wasn't going to second-guess the choices she had made. This was her birthday, a day of celebration. She had her girls with her and that was all that mattered, the most wonderful gift she could ever need.

She still mourned her husband and always would, but over the past months the fierceness of it had faded from a raw, sucking chest wound to a slow ache in her heart.

She suddenly heard a knock at the bathroom door.

"Mama," Gaby chirped. "The nice man from the flower house came to see you."

Ack! Allie gazed frantically around the bathroom. The only thing she had to wear in here was a worn, threadbare robe. Since visitors at the front door of the small cottage had a perfect view of the hallway and bathroom, there was no way to slip into her bedroom for something else to put on without the man seeing her.

Left with no choice, she threw on the robe and ran a comb through her hair, hoping the nice man from the flower house was a kind, elderly gentleman who wouldn't notice her state of undress.

She hoped he wasn't angry at the girls for picking the flowers. But technically the house and its lush flower beds belonged to Ruth and she had apparently given the girls permission to raid them. Allie wasn't about to let some renter give them a hard time about it.

Prepared to defend her daughters, she tightened the sash on the robe and walked out of the bathroom.

Shock hit her hard in the stomach at the sight of the man standing by the front door.

Oh, mercy.

This was no kind, elderly gentleman.

The other nurses she used to work with would have said the man from the flower house looked very nice indeed, Allie had to admit. He looked to be in his midthirties, dressed in a smoke-colored suit, a crisp white dress shirt and a discreet navy tie. Beneath the suit, broad shoulders rippled with power and unyielding strength.

He was tall, well over six feet, with cool gray eyes and short-cropped dark hair that still looked damp, as if he had just stepped out of his own shower. A part of her mind registered that he smelled divine. Like soap and aftershave and just-washed male.

His strong, masculine features looked freshly shaved, and Allie was stunned by the sudden desire to run her fingers along the skin of that hard, tanned jawline.

Allie swallowed hard, disconcerted and a little frightened by the unwelcome tug of awareness. She didn't want to notice this man. She wanted to stay frozen forever in her grief for Jaime.

"Yes?" she said, uncomfortably aware her voice sounded cold, rude. It wasn't his fault her unruly hormones suddenly decided to wake up after two years of suspended animation.

If her neighbor was surprised by her unwelcome tone, he quickly concealed it. "Hello. I live next door. Gage McKinnon."

He waited for her to introduce herself and Allie scrambled for a moment to remember what she was supposed to say.

"Lisa Connors." She finally supplied the alias she had practiced, derivations of both her first name and her maiden name. "I believe you've met my daughters. Gabriella and Anna."

Since she hadn't been able to figure out a convincing way to persuade the girls they all had to use pretend names for a while, she had made the difficult decision to stick with their real names while they were on the run, risky though it might be.

"Yes. They were in my yard earlier. Actually, that's why I stopped by."

"Oh?" she said coolly. If he was going to yell at her daughters, she wasn't going to make it easy for him.

A muscle flexed in that strong jaw and he met her hostile gaze without a flinch. "I just wanted to give you a friendly warning to be a little more careful with them."

"Excuse me?" She stared at him.

"Your girls were outside alone in the neighborhood when it was barely daylight and not another soul was around."

"You were, apparently."

"Right. I was a complete stranger, but they had no problem striking up a conversation with me and telling me all kinds of details about their life. Their names, their ages, the fact that today is your birthday. That their father is dead. I know practically their life story."

Oh, no. Allie fought the urge to press a hand to her suddenly queasy stomach. Gaby could talk the bark off a tree. Her sweet, openhearted daughter simply didn't understand the meaning of discretion and Allie didn't know how to teach her.

If she didn't figure out a way, though, Gaby was going to someday let slip too much information to the wrong person, details that would identify her mother as a fugitive.

The girls thought they were simply off on a new adventure. Allie didn't want to frighten them by telling them this was all so deadly serious.

She turned back to the neighbor to whom Gaby had revealed so much. "All fascinating information, I'm sure."

He glanced over at the girls, engrossed in *Sesame Street,* then lowered his voice. "If I were some kind of child predator it would be very fascinating information. Once I had their names, it wouldn't take me long to completely win their trust. You should have a talk with them. Warn them to be a little more careful. In my opinion, girls that young shouldn't be wandering the neighborhood by themselves. You should never have let them outside without supervision."

"I was asleep!" she exclaimed.

"All the more reason to be concerned. Anything could have happened and you would have awakened to find your daughters gone."

"I can take care of my daughters, Mr. McKinnon."

"I never said you couldn't. I'm just bringing it to your attention. A mother who cares about her children's safety can't be too careful."

If you go into insulin shock again, anything could happen to those girls. A fragment of testimony from the custody battle slithered through her mind in a nasty whisper. *Look what happened last time. You were behind the wheel and nearly killed them all.*

If you love our granddaughters at all, you must see that your condition makes you incapable of caring for them on your own.

Oh, how those words had hurt. Irena and Joaquin had gouged at her mercilessly, again and again until even *she* had almost been convinced she was an unfit mother.

She had taken it from them in that courtroom—she'd had no choice—but she was not about to listen to the same kind of accusations from a stranger, even one who looked like sin and smelled like heaven.

She lifted her chin. "My children's safety is my own concern, Mr. McKinnon. I'll thank you to mind your own business."

His mouth tightened into a hard line. "This is my business."

He reached inside his breast pocket and pulled out a flat black leather case. He opened it and thrust it at her and Allie's anger changed instantly to a terrible, icy dread at the sight of the shimmering gold badge pinned inside.

Please, no. Somehow he had found her and now she would lose everything. She waited for him to break out handcuffs, but he only reached for the doorknob.

"I work for the FBI's Salt Lake City field office, Mrs. Connors," he said, his voice distant and cool. "I see hideous things done to children on a daily basis. You have two beautiful little girls. I would hate to see anything happen to them."

With that, he opened the door and walked out into the summer morning, leaving Allie staring after him with bewildered fear still pulsing through her in steady, unrelenting waves.

Chapter 2

"Mama, I don't want to go to Mrs. Cochran's house. I don't like her."

Allie paused in the middle of buckling Anna into her booster seat and gazed over at Gaby as unease coursed through her. "What do you mean, you don't like her? Since when? Last week you said you thought she was nice. She pushed you on the swing and let you have Popsicles and played Chutes and Ladders with you."

Gaby shrugged. "She's nice sometimes. Not all the time."

Oh, she *did* not need this. Everything had been going so well. Her insulin level was more stable than it had been for a long time. Her job cleaning houses, though a far cry from her work as a triage nurse at a busy innercity emergency room back in Philadelphia, gave her a steady income and more importantly, health insurance.

And she'd detected absolutely no sign that anyone had followed her.

The only fly in her particular ointment was her next-door neighbor. She had to admit, she'd suffered more than a few bad moments after learning she'd had the bad luck to move in next to an FBI agent.

After much angst, though, she decided she could risk living here for a few more weeks, just until she could pay off the car repair bill to Ruth's son. She would just do her best to stay out of his way and pray he would have no reason to connect the drab Lisa Connors to Alicia DeBarillas.

Avoiding the man hadn't been tough at all since he never seemed to be around.

Other than that stress of living next to Gage McKinnon, things had been going so well. She thought she had found the perfect caregiver for the girls while she was working, someone matronly and loving. Ruth Jensen had suggested an older, widowed neighbor of hers who took in children to earn a little extra money. Dora Cochran had come with other glowing recommendations and the arrangement had been working well, or so Allie had thought.

"What does she do that's not nice?" she asked carefully.

Gaby's little brow furrowed as she thought it over. "Yesterday she said I talk too much and told me to shut up. And she told Anna to stop acting like a baby on account of she started to cry after Mrs. Thompson turned off *Blue's Clues* so she could watch *Oprah.*"

The woman wasn't exactly beating them but she didn't sound particularly loving either. Allie gave a mental groan. What was she supposed to do? She couldn't dump her children off at a place where they weren't comfortable, but she had nowhere else to send them. She hated this. Absolutely hated it.

She had to work; she had no choice. Much of her and

Jaime's savings had gone toward her medical bills and legal fees in the last six months. Though she had received life insurance benefits after his accident, it had all been tied up in the custody battle.

Before she left, Allie had pulled everything liquid out of their accounts, figuring that if she was careful, she and the girls could survive for five or six months on her small nest egg, especially if she could find a job with health insurance to pay for her insulin. But she couldn't tap into that now. If they had to move on quickly for any reason, she would need that nest egg to fall back on.

She needed her job, but Allie knew she wouldn't be able to work a moment if she was constantly worrying about her daughters.

"Okay, honey. If you don't want to go back to Mrs. Cochran's, you don't have to. I'll figure something out."

Her mind scrambled to come up with some solution. Today she was scheduled to clean four vacation rental properties whose occupants had already checked out. Since they were vacant, she was sure Ruth wouldn't mind if the girls went along with her, just until she could find someone else to watch them. She would give her a call just to make sure, but she didn't think the other woman would have a problem with it. She had been more than accommodating so far and had treated her and the girls with a kindness that often brought tears to Allie's eyes.

"You might be able to come with me today," she told the girls. "I'll just need to check with Mrs. Jensen and get some videos and some toys and crayons from inside so you have something to do."

"Yippee!" Gaby cheered.

"'Ippee!" Anna echoed.

Allie headed back up the steps, then paused and looked over the hedge separating her rental house from its cheerful twin next door. Her neighbor would probably have something to say about a mother who would leave her daughters in the car while she ran back inside her house, even when it was only for a moment.

With a heavy sigh, she jogged back down the steps, opened the car door then unhooked the girls from their boosters. ''Come on. You can wait inside while I gather some things.''

She shouldn't care what some broodingly handsome, interfering FBI agent thought. Besides, the man seemed to have disappeared from the face of the earth. Probably undercover somewhere, she thought, sticking his nose into some other poor woman's business.

She had seen no signs of him over there since her birthday the week before when he had come knocking at her door, accusing her of being an unfit mother.

He hadn't really, she reminded herself. She had reacted far out of proportion to what had no doubt been well-intentioned advice. When she'd had time to cool down—and time for her terror to fade—she appreciated his warning and the reminder to be more careful with her daughters.

Later that evening over birthday cake and pizza she had reminded both girls about their family's safety rules. Don't ever talk to strangers; don't ever give your name to a stranger; don't ever take rides from strangers; report any strangers to an adult. She had to walk the same fine line every parent confronted, between scaring the girls to death and instilling a necessary sense of self-preservation in them.

They seemed to have gotten the message without destroying their natural gregariousness. The night before, Gaby had even started to strike up a conversation with a woman in the grocery line then stopped in midsentence and asked her mother if she knew the other woman or if she was a stranger, and if she was a stranger, could Allie please find out her name so Gaby could finish telling her about the baby kittens she'd seen outside the store?

She supposed she owed Gage McKinnon an apology for reacting so strongly to his advice, even though her own sense of self-preservation warned her she should stay as far away as possible from such a dangerous man.

But how could she apologize to him if he was never home? His late-model SUV hadn't been parked in the driveway since that morning a week earlier and his windows were tightly closed, even though a warm spell had hit Utah in the last few days. Not only had the windows not been opened but the curtains hadn't so much as twitched an inch in seven days.

She didn't want to be curious about his whereabouts but she had to admit she found herself watching out for his tall, muscular frame wherever they went. She didn't know if that funny flutter in her stomach at the idea of seeing him again stemmed from fear or anticipation.

She wrenched her mind from her dratted neighbor and focused on the girls. ''Find a few things to take with us today while I call Ruth, all right?''

She watched them go, Gaby chattering with excitement about all the things she was going to take and Anna trailing dutifully along behind, as usual.

Love for these two sweet children crept up on her and completely took her breath away, as it sometimes did. She would have died if she lost them, literally would have shriveled up and faded away into nothing. They were her heart, her soul, her life. Everything.

She wanted to hate Jaime's parents for what they had tried to do. At first when she had awakened in the hospital and been served with the paperwork petitioning for custody of the girls because of her condition, she had been both livid and terrified. For a long time her emotions had seesawed between fury and fear as the case had worked its way through the courts.

But now she couldn't manage to summon much emotion toward them but pity. Joaquin and Irena DeBarillas had failed miserably with their only son, had lost him long before he decided to come to the States to study medicine and had met and married her when he was a resident at the hospital where she worked.

Did they really think they could regain through their granddaughters what they had destroyed with Jaime?

Over her dead body.

She pitied them, knew they were lonely. But she would still be damned before she let them get their hands on her little girls.

Allie dialed Ruth's office number and waited through eight rings before hanging up. The answering machine must be busted again. She'd learned Ruth had little patience with gadgetry and didn't check her messages often anyway. She also didn't carry a cell phone, so now what was Allie supposed to do?

She had to drop by the office on her way to the first property anyway to pick up the master key. If Ruth wasn't there, she could always leave her a note, she supposed.

She went to prod Gaby and Anna along just as she heard the doorbell. For one crazy instant, she thought it might be her neighbor and her heart began a low, urgent drumming.

It wasn't Gage McKinnon, she saw as soon as she opened the door, but her employer who stood on the porch, thin and brisk and competent.

"Ruth! I just tried to call you. I'm so glad you stopped by!"

"Oh?"

"Yes." Suddenly she felt nervy presuming on her employer's kindness this way. But she also couldn't bear the thought of sending Anna and Gaby to a place they didn't feel comfortable, not when their life was in such tumult anyway.

"Um, I'm afraid Dora Cochran is not working out. Would you object if I took the girls with me to the houses I'm cleaning today since they're all empty? They can be very well behaved and won't get in my way or slow me down, I promise."

Ruth looked thoughtful. "I don't see why not. Actually, that's one of the reasons I stopped. I wanted to ask if you're interested in another job, one where you might not need day care for the girls."

"What kind of job?" she asked warily. She didn't necessarily enjoy cleaning houses but it paid the rent with a little left over, and Ruth hadn't asked any questions about her background.

"You told me you've had some medical training."

"Yes." She would love to find a nursing job but she would have to be licensed to legally work and she didn't know how to go about that while living under a false name.

"A renter of mine was in an accident last week. He's coming home from the hospital in a wheelchair the day after tomorrow but won't be able to get around on his own for a while. He asked me if I knew anybody who could cook and clean for him, run him around to physical therapy, that sort of thing. I thought of you."

"I'm not a licensed nurse in Utah, Ruth."

"I know that. A home care nurse will stop by to check on him, so you would only have to be around to help if he needs it. Pay's a few dollars more an hour than you get now and you could keep the girls with you.''

Excitement pulsed through her. If she were making a few dollars more an hour and didn't have to pay for day care, she could add even more to her small security cushion. And it would be so wonderful to spend all day with Gaby and Anna.

She was almost afraid to hope things could work out so well and felt a pang of guilt for benefiting from some other person's misfortune.

''What happened to the poor man?'' she asked.

''Job-related injury. He was hit by a truck. Crushed against a concrete wall, really, by a man he was trying to arrest.''

A terrible suspicion slithered to life, and Allie glanced over the hedge again at the cottage next door. ''He's a police officer?'' she asked with sudden dread.

''FBI agent,'' Ruth said, confirming her worst fears. ''You might have met him, since he just lives next door. Gage McKinnon. Tall, dark, good-looking.''

All her spiraling hopes crashed to the ground like a balloon shot by a BB gun. So she hadn't solved her child-care dilemma after all. She was right back where she started, without a good place for the girls to stay while she worked.

She wanted to weep from the crushing weight of her disappointment. ''I'm sorry, Ruth, but I'm afraid I'm going to have to pass on the job offer, though I truly appreciate you thinking of me. I just don't think it would work for me after all.''

Her landlady frowned. ''Pass? Why, that's just plain crazy. It's the perfect situation all the way around. If you wanted, you could even hire a teenager to watch the girls over here at your place and check on them through the day since you'd just be next door. I can give you some names.''

Maybe it would be the perfect situation, if the job involved caring for just an average person. But Gage McKinnon was an FBI agent. She hadn't worked this hard to keep her children with her—sacrificed everything for them—only to lose them in the end to Jaime's parents because of an interfering, inquisitive federal agent.

She couldn't tell that to Ruth so she quickly searched for a believable explanation. ''I don't think Mr. McKinnon and I would suit,'' she finally said, unable to keep the regret from her voice. ''We met last week shortly after I moved in and, um, had a few words.''

Ruth blinked at that piece of information. After a few moments she nodded. ''Your choice, I suppose. Too bad. You'd have been perfect, especially since you've been around hurt folks before. I'll try to find someone else, I guess. Shouldn't be too hard. One of my other housekeepers would probably do it in a heartbeat. It's pretty easy money. Much easier than cleaning toilets and making beds all day.''

Now that was a matter of opinion.

Allie thought of Gage McKinnon, all long limbs and lean power. Even if she hadn't been worried the sharp-eyed FBI agent would find out she was a fugitive, she wasn't sure she could work so closely with him, not when she couldn't manage to think straight around the man.

''I'm sorry, Ruth. I do appreciate you thinking of me, but I believe I'll stick to cleaning toilets and making beds. Speaking of that, are you sure you don't mind if I take the girls along with me today?''

Ruth shrugged. ''Don't see why not. As long as you're working on empty vacation rentals it shouldn't be a problem. I'll see if I can arrange your schedule this week so you work only vacant units.''

What would she have done without Ruth and her kindness? She couldn't even bear to think about it. ''Thank you.''

Ruth, as usual, shrugged off her gratitude. ''So what's going on with Dora?''

''Nothing, really. The girls can just be particular about what they like. They've decided they and Dora don't suit.''

''I'll try to think of someone else. Still, it seems to me the solution is right there in front of your nose. McKinnon needs help, you need a different situation for the girls. What better place for them than being with their mama all day while she works?''

Allie opened her mouth to reply, but Ruth cut her off with a shake of her no-nonsense graying head. ''Don't say no. Think about it. He doesn't come home from the hospital until day after tomorrow. You might change your mind before then.''

She wouldn't change her mind, Allie thought. She couldn't afford to, as much as part of her might want to. The stakes were simply too high.

Gage shifted in the back seat of an FBI Suburban, trying to find the impossible—a comfortable position. Just how the hell was he supposed to get comfortable when he had two thigh-length casts on his legs?

It was only a half hour drive from the University of Utah hospital up Parley's Canyon to his house in Park City. He could survive for that long. He had to if he wanted to make it back to his place.

No way was he going to recuperate in some rehab facility like the doctors at the university medical center wanted him to do. If he had to be cooped up somewhere for weeks at a time, he wanted it to be in his own space, surrounded by his own stuff. Not in some nursing home that smelled of stale urine and hopelessness.

"Everything okay back there?" Cale Davis, his partner of little more than a month, asked with concern from behind the wheel.

"Yeah." Gage tried not to wince as the Suburban hit a pothole, sending fiery pain shooting through his legs like twin comets.

"You sure? I can pull over if you need a breather."

"No. Just keep driving. I'm fine."

Neither Cale nor the other man in the front seat—Davis's temporary partner Thompson Lovell—looked convinced by his words but they didn't argue with him.

"Potter called while we were at the hospital," Cale said after a moment, referring to their boss William Potter, the special agent in charge of the Salt Lake City office. "Juber was arraigned this morning on attempted-murder charges, assaulting a federal officer and using his vehicle as a deadly weapon. Not to mention all the charges associated with his Internet child porn ring. There's talk about a guilty plea, at least to the charges involving you. Since a dozen Feds and local cops watched him pin you against that wall, I don't see what choice he has."

Gage groaned inwardly—and not only because the Suburban hit another bump in the road. He had no one to blame for his injuries but himself. He had been an idiot and now he was paying for it.

If he hadn't been distracted, he never would have made the greenie mistake of taking the shortcut between Lyle Juber's pickup and a cement retaining wall on his way to yank the man out of his vehicle and make the arrest.

His only excuse was that he'd been caught up in the

excitement of finally nailing the bastard. The case had been a long and ugly one, begun during his previous assignment in the Bay Area. He had trailed Juber here to Salt Lake City and continued building the case against him. Finally higher-ups determined there was enough evidence to make an arrest.

They'd found him in his hulking old pickup on his way to the grocery store. The guy had reacted like the cornered rat that he was. To the surprise of everyone on the team, he had resisted arrest with a vengeance.

Instead of calmly walking out of his truck with his hands up as he'd been ordered, he shoved the heavy truck into gear, crushing Gage against the wall, then backed into the other officers standing around with guns drawn.

Everybody but Gage had been able to dive out of the way. Because of the way he'd been positioned, Gage had ended up with one femur shattered in four places just above the knee and the other femur had sustained a clean simple fracture.

Juber hadn't gotten far before the tires of his truck had been blown out and he'd been taken into custody. That was small consolation to Gage, facing several weeks of sick leave and more of rehab.

Not to mention the humiliation of knowing he had screwed up.

He would have plenty of time to obsess over every moment of his mistake. But at least he would be doing it at home, not in some damn gray-walled hospital room.

The doctors thought he needed another week in the hospital but Gage knew he'd be a raving lunatic by then. He hated the nurses waking him every time he managed to drift off to sleep, hated the lack of privacy, hated the pills they shoved down his throat at every opportunity.

He could handle this, he thought as Cale at last pulled

in front of his rental unit. He had a home-care nurse coming to check on him and his saint of a landlady said she'd hired someone to help him get around throughout the day.

On the other hand, maybe he'd been a little too optimistic about his own abilities. By the time Thom and Cale helped him out of the Suburban and into the blasted wheelchair he was going to have to use for the next several weeks—until he could bear weight on his less-injured leg and start using crutches—his head was spinning and his gut churned as if he'd just climbed off a killer roller coaster.

He needed a painkiller but he hated the damn things. He closed his eyes in a vain effort to regain his equilibrium while Cale pushed up a temporary ramp that his landlady must have juryrigged into the cottage. He made a mental note to add a little extra to the rent check for all her work on his behalf since he had contacted her about his injuries.

"Do you have the key?" Lovell asked.

Gage thought about it and realized his key ring was probably still at his desk in Salt Lake City. He made a face.

"Guess not." The agent pulled out a credit card, ready to pick the lock, then tried the knob. It turned easily, putting Gage instantly on alert. Why was the door open?

Lovell opened the door and Davis wheeled him inside the living room. Gage gazed around, disoriented. He had been in the hospital for over a week. Had he maybe forgotten where he lived, given the guys the wrong address somehow?

No, this was his cottage. He recognized his furniture—the leather sofa and recliner he'd brought along from his previous assignment in San Francisco, the oak coffee table he'd made with his own hands the last time he'd visited his father's cabinet shop in Nevada, the big-screen TV he hardly had time to watch.

This was his cottage but what the hell had happened to it? He wasn't particularly messy but neither was he obsessive about housework. This place sparkled, without any dust or that closed-up feeling he might have expected after it had sat empty for a week.

There were fresh flowers in a canning jar on the coffee table and the whole place smelled of clean laundry and chicken noodle soup.

He was still trying to figure what dimension Cale and Lovell had wheeled him into when a beautiful woman stepped out of his kitchen like something out of his deepest fantasies.

She was lithe and curvy and wore nothing but an apron.

Chapter 3

He blinked at the vision in front of him.

She had short, wispy brown hair, blue eyes the color of mountain columbines behind small wire-rimmed glasses, and a figure that could make a man's mouth water.

"Oh! You're here!" the delectable vision standing in his living room exclaimed. "I'm so sorry. I was busy cleaning up in the kitchen and didn't hear you arrive."

Gage was vaguely aware of Lovell and Cale sharing a look before his partner stepped forward with his hand outstretched, a charming smile playing around his mouth.

"Hello, ma'am. I'm Cale Davis and this is Thompson Lovell. You must be a friend of McKinnon's."

She gave him a hesitant smile and shook his hand, then reached behind her to untie the strings of her apron. Gage was vaguely aware he was holding his breath, then he let it out on a disappointed sigh. She had shorts on underneath, he was rather disheartened to discover. Navy-blue shorts that skimmed the top of long, shapely legs.

"We're not really friends," she answered Cale. "We've only met once, just for a moment."

Through the pain beginning to pound through his legs like tribal drums beating out a message, Gage forced himself to look at her more closely. Now he recognized her. If he hadn't been half-dazed from pain and fatigue, he would have figured it out much earlier. "You're the lady from next door with the two dark-haired little girls."

She nodded with a wary look.

He must have been blind or crazy not to have noticed those high cheekbones and her full, delectable lips when he spoke with her before. No, when he had gone to her house to talk to her, he had only been focused on her daughters' safety, just as he should have been.

"Yes. I'm Lisa C-Connors. You met my daughters Gaby and Anna."

"The flower pickers. Where are they?"

"Playing in your backyard. Your *fenced* backyard."

Fences wouldn't mean diddly to someone who wanted to take two cute little girls. He was going to say something along those lines but pain again reached up with a mighty fist and yanked the words out of his head. He grimaced instead, suddenly light-headed.

Damn, he hated this.

"You must be exhausted. Let's get you into bed, Mr. McKinnon."

A quick, sensual image flashed through his mind, momentarily taking the edge off his discomfort. Bed. Not a bad idea. It had been way too long since he'd slid his fingers over soft, female skin—filled his hands with willing flesh—and he suddenly wanted desperately for that willing flesh to belong to the woman standing in front of him.

But then, he probably wouldn't be good for much with two bum legs, and he definitely didn't need Lovell and Cale looking on.

"A very attractive offer, believe me," he murmured through the soft haze in his head. "But I'm afraid I'm going to have to decline. Maybe another time, sweetheart."

Color flared high along her cheekbones. "Not funny, Mr. McKinnon."

"Sorry. You're right." He drew in a breath, feeling like both a jerk and a major-league wuss. He never thought he could be this wiped out by a couple of war wounds.

"How long ago did you take your last pain pill?"

He raised an eyebrow, wishing the simple movement didn't make his head feel quite so woozy. "Remind me again why any of this is your business. What are you doing here? This is still my house, isn't it?"

She frowned. "Ruth didn't tell you?"

"Tell me what?"

"She hired me to help you out while you recuperate."

"She told me she hired *someone.* I never thought to ask details."

Another wave of pain washed over him and he gripped the armrests of the wheelchair. Okay, at this point he was willing to forget about soft, willing flesh, as long as he could get horizontal for a few moments.

Lisa Connors stepped forward. "You need to be in bed. Let's get you settled."

He didn't have any energy left to argue so he let her wheel him into his bedroom, where he discovered the little elves had also been busy. His comfortably roomy king bed was gone, replaced by some steel hospital contraption just like the one he had just left.

"Where's my bed?" he asked, uncomfortably aware he sounded like a grumpy toddler in need of a nap.

"Ruth and I took it down and stored it in the shed behind the house. The home health-care provider sent this one over instead since the doctors said you'll need to keep your legs elevated a great deal of the time and this way we can raise the foot of your bed to facilitate that. With that big bed you had, there wasn't much room in here to move a wheelchair around and we thought this one will be much easier for you to transfer in and out of since it can be lowered to wheelchair level."

He liked his bed. He was a big man who needed space to sprawl around in, and these dinky hospital beds just didn't cut it. He didn't want to sound any more whiny than he already did, though, so he opted to keep his mouth shut.

He was distracted, anyway, when his neighbor lady took charge and helped Cale and Lovell move him from the wheelchair to the bed. He was relieved to discover the pain of the transfer was only agonizing instead of excruciating.

By the time he was settled, he was thinking he owed the doctors a huge apology. They were right, he was crazy to disregard their advice and insist on going home so early.

"You're a lucky man, McKinnon," Cale murmured to him after Lisa left the room to grab his pain pills and a glass of water. "I wouldn't mind being laid up for a couple weeks if I had such a sweet young thing attending to my every need."

A sweet young thing with two little girls and a chip the size of Montana on her shoulder, Gage reminded himself.

If he could hang on to any of the thoughts racketing around his head like a pinball in the middle of a record-breaking game, he could probably come up with at least a couple of reasons why it wasn't such a great idea to have her here caring for him.

Since he couldn't think right now beyond sinking into this bed and not waking up for a week, he decided he could always worry about it later.

She returned with the water and his prescription and handed him two of those annoying little white pills. "Here you go. Are you hungry? I made some chicken noodle soup. My grandma's recipe, with real homemade noodles. It might help settle your stomach from the pills."

Soup sounded delicious but he was afraid his stomach just wouldn't handle it.

"I'm fine," he said, taking only one of the pills and returning the other to the bottle. He hated this loopy feeling and the medicine only made it worse. A few more days and he'd be ready to chuck the whole damn bottle into the toilet.

"I think it would be best if we let him rest now," she told the other two agents as she bustled around him tucking in blankets, fluffing pillows, taking the glass of water from him to set on the bedside table.

She smelled delicious, he thought as she leaned over him to adjust the pillows once more. Like violets and sunshine.

"Sure. We were just leaving," Cale said with a smirk. *Lucky, lucky man,* he mouthed to Gage on the way out the door.

He didn't like bossy women, Gage thought as he watched them go. Even when their subtle spring scent made his mouth water. He closed his eyes as the pill did its magic and took the edge off his pain. No, he didn't like bossy women at all. That was only one of many reasons why having her here just wouldn't work out.

He made a mental note to tell her that as soon as he woke up.

Taking this job had been a mistake.

A huge mistake.

Her nerves jumping, Allie finished throwing together peanut butter and honey sandwiches for the girls in the FBI agent's kitchen. She didn't belong here. She should be staying as far away as possible from this man who could completely destroy her family.

If he recognized her as a fugitive, everything would be ruined.

She didn't know if Joaquin and Irena had reported them missing. Maybe they hadn't even realized she was gone yet since relations between them hadn't exactly been friendly since the beginning of the custody battle.

But eventually they would try to visit the girls and would find her empty house. Would they go to the police or hire a private investigator on their own?

Even now she could be a wanted fugitive with her name and description broadcast to every law enforcement officer across the country. Taking the girls out of Philadelphia without notifying them was probably in violation of a court order, no matter how confident Twila Langston was that the judge's ruling awarding joint custody to the DeBarillas because of her diabetes would be overturned.

Patient advocate groups were already rallying behind her cause, and she had been allowed to retain sole custody pending appeal. But she was fairly certain that custody arrangement didn't include the freedom to flee across the country without leaving a trace.

Maybe all this was for nothing, but she didn't dare take

that chance. Not after she had learned from the girls that Irena had taken them to get passport pictures taken.

Even if Jaime's parents could only win court-ordered visitation, they could still take the girls to Venezuela during one of those visits. Once in their own country, Allie knew they had the power and wealth to keep her from the girls forever.

Allie blew out a breath. If Joaquin and Irena had gone to the authorities, her name and description could be circulating among law enforcement officials even now. Her patient could have even seen it before he was injured.

She had been stupid to change her mind and agree to take this position. It was just too risky.

Fear settled cold and hard in her stomach, but she forced a smile for the girls and handed them the sandwiches, along with carrot sticks and a couple of cheese slices. "Here's your lunch. There's that nice table on the patio. Why don't you take your lunch outside and have a picnic so we don't wake Mr. McKinnon?"

Gaby and Anna grinned at the idea of eating outside. "Can we have juice boxes?" Gaby asked.

"Yes, I brought a few over from our house and put them in the fridge. Pick the kind you want."

She helped them carry their bounty out to the table in the fenced backyard then set it out for them.

"Mommy, can you have a picnic with us, too?"

She hesitated. Her patient might need her. But judging by the exhausted pain lines on his face when he first showed up with his friends, he would probably be sleeping for hours. Anyway, she should be able to hear him through the screen door if he called out for help.

"Let me go check on Mr. McKinnon, then I'll come back out and have lunch with you."

She walked back through the small house with its floor

plan similar to hers—two bedrooms, two bathrooms, a good-size living area, a small dining room and a comfortable, efficient kitchen. At McKinnon's bedroom door she drew in a steadying breath and pushed it open.

His chest rose and fell evenly as he slept, with the blanket she had tucked in so carefully earlier riding down nearly to his narrow waist now. The network of pain lines around his mouth were more faint now, she noticed, and he seemed as comfortable as possible given the two thigh-high casts on his long legs.

As she watched him, the fear in her stomach gave way to something far more treacherous. He was so gorgeous. Lean and dark, with sculpted features and that dangerous-looking stubble on his cheeks.

She shivered, hating this attraction stirring around inside her. She didn't want to notice how his lashes looked so long and spiky there against his skin, how his shoulders spanned nearly the width of the hospital bed, how his big hands on top of the blanket looked strong and blunt-fingered, capable of all kinds of delicious things.

She shouldn't be noticing any of those things, shouldn't be feeling this low sizzle of awareness. Not for any man, and especially not for this one, who could so easily destroy her.

Jaime had been gone only two years. Building lurid fantasies around another man's hands somehow seemed grossly disloyal to her late husband. How could she even think about having this man she didn't even know—and didn't particularly like all that much—touch her the way only Jaime ever had?

She had loved her husband fiercely. He had been her first and only lover, and their physical relationship had been rich and rewarding, filled with laughter and tenderness and passion. Maybe that's why she missed it so much, because it had been such an important part of their life together.

Still, missing the intimacy she shared with her husband didn't explain how she could have such an instantaneous response to this man she didn't know at all.

It was there, though, simmering under her skin with a steady, bubbling heat. His attraction wasn't diminished at all by the fact that he was lying in a hospital bed with two painful-looking casts on his legs. If anything, just that hint of vulnerability made him even more appealing.

She couldn't do this job. She absolutely couldn't—not only because he posed such a risk to her freedom and the girls' future but because of this, the low heat seething through her.

She would just have to tell Ruth she had made a mistake to take the job in the first place and hope her landlady would let her return to cleaning houses. If she started now, she could probably find a new caregiver for the girls by the end of the week.

She returned to the patio and found Gaby and Anna had abandoned their half-eaten lunches. One of the neighbors' cats had made the mistake of wandering into the yard to find a snack and he was far more exciting than peanut butter sandwiches.

The girls were chasing the bewildered animal around the yard, laughing with joy every time they came close enough to touch the cat, which wasn't very often.

"Kitty, kitty, kitty," Anna chanted, her chubby legs working hard to keep up with her older sister.

Just when Allie was about to open her mouth and tell them to stop tormenting the poor thing, the cat finally clued in that any morsels he might chance upon in this backyard simply weren't worth the trouble.

He sprang to the top of the redwood fence and sat

watching with an amused feline look while the girls hopped and jumped and squealed, trying in vain to reach him.

After a moment the cat tired of the entertainment and pounced down the other side into what was undoubtedly safer territory.

Unfazed by losing their prey, the girls flopped down onto their stomachs in the grass. Sunlight flashed off their dark curls as they laughed together.

''Mama, there are two ladybugs in the grass,'' Gaby called. ''Come and see!''

She joined them and bent at the waist for a closer look. ''I see four ladybugs.''

Anna frowned. ''No. Only two.''

''Let's count them.'' She pointed to the bugs with a grin. ''One and two.'' Then she pointed to her daughters. ''Three and four.''

Gaby giggled. ''We're not really ladybugs. We can't fly and we don't have black spots.''

''But you're *my* ladybugs,'' Allie said, tickling them both until they were shrieking with glee.

She had loved these last two days with her daughters, having them close while she and Ruth readied the FBI agent's house for his return. It had made her realize what precious little time she'd been able to spend with them since Jaime's death. She had been so busy sorting through his affairs, working twelve-hour shifts at the hospital, fighting the custody battle, struggling with her own health.

They were growing up so fast, right in front of her nose. Gaby should be starting kindergarten in the fall, which was just another thing to add to her worry list. How would they be able to stay in one place long enough for her daughter to complete the school year?

They couldn't stay here. She had acknowledged that

days ago. Without the FBI agent's presence in the neighborhood she might have been able to stay in Park City all summer, maybe even all year. But it was just too risky having him living next door.

That was one of the reasons she'd taken the job, so she could save a little extra to tide them over wherever they moved. That reason still held, she reminded herself. She could take a few weeks to work for Gage McKinnon while she made arrangements to leave. Surely she deserved a few weeks to simply enjoy her girls.

Besides, McKinnon wasn't working because of his injuries. If the authorities were looking for her, how would he possibly know? If he had seen her picture and recognized her, what difference would it make whether she worked for him or simply lived next door?

As to the attraction part, she could handle that, too. She just had to remember all the reasons why giving in to that attraction would be wholly, unequivocally disastrous.

Chapter 4

Geez, couldn't a guy get any sleep around here?

Through the thick fist of nausea and pain that had him in a chokehold, Gage blinked awake to the sound of girlish giggles carried through the window screen on the warm breeze.

They sounded like a couple of miniature laughing hyenas out there. Charlotte must have one of her obnoxious little friends over again. Did they have to titter and cackle right outside his window?

He was sick. Really sick. He couldn't remember when he'd ever felt so lousy. Was he dying? He figured he had to be pretty badly off or he wouldn't be stretched out here in bed in the middle of the day with pain racking his whole body.

Mom really ought to put her foot down and make the little brats play on the other side of the house so he could go back to sleep. He opened his mouth to call to her but couldn't manage to force the words through the sandpaper lining his throat.

Man, his legs hurt. He tried to remember what had happened to them. Did he crash on his bike or something? Maybe Wyatt tackled him when they were playing football in the backyard earlier. Why did everything seem so hazy and weird? You'd think a guy could remember why his legs felt like they'd been run over by the family station wagon.

He blinked as some fragment of memory came to him, but he couldn't move fast enough to pin it down. Before he could try to puzzle it out, Charlotte and her friend giggled again. A soft voice that didn't sound like his mother warned them to be quiet so they didn't wake Mr. McKinnon.

Mr. McKinnon. That was him. Weird. No. It wouldn't be Charlotte out there. He tried to clear the fuzz out of his brain. Couldn't be her. Charley was gone, had been gone for years.

Everybody was gone. Mom, Wyatt. Everybody.

So who was playing outside his window?

He'd have to figure that out another time, when he wasn't so damn tired.

The next time he awoke it was to a cool, dim room and the musical murmur of women speaking softly.

"I gave him a pain pill as soon as he arrived, about four hours ago. I offered him two but he only took one."

The voice was low, sexy, and he thought he could lie here in this dreamlike state and listen to it forever. He recognized it in some dim corner of his mind, but he was too hazy from the pain pill she was talking about to do anything about pulling the memory out.

"He's been sleeping since then," she went on. "I think

he might have surfaced a few times but never all the way and never for very long.''

''You ask me, the man's a damn fool to leave the hospital four days after breaking both legs.''

The second voice wasn't nearly as sexy as the first. This one was honey-coated barb wire. ''What's he trying to prove? I mean, come on. It's always the macho, good-lookin' ones, honey. They make the worst patients and the worst husbands. Believe me, I'm married to one and have nursed more than my share of the other.''

The first woman laughed. ''I'll keep that in mind, Estelle.''

''You do that. You do that.''

Still not sure he wanted to let these women, whoever they were, know he was conscious, he peeked under his lashes and saw that Estelle was a sturdy woman who looked about fifty. She had skin the color of warm caramel and dozens of rainbow-colored beads in her swinging cornrows.

He wondered who she might be and what she was doing in his bedroom, until he saw the bright pattern of her nursing scrubs and the stethoscope around her neck. Ah. The nurse from the home health company. Who was she talking to?

The other woman stood just out of the range of his vision unless he twisted around, something he wasn't sure he could do, even if he wanted to. Again, he thought he recognized the voice but couldn't quite place it.

''I really hate to do this,'' Estelle went on, ''but I'm gonna need to check his vitals. That's why they pay me the big bucks, to take care of stubborn cusses like this one who belong in the hospital but are too pigheaded to stay put.''

''I've been doing visual checks about every half hour while he sleeps. I've recorded all that for you.''

He managed to turn his head just enough to finally figure out who else was in the room—his very attractive next-door neighbor. Why had she been watching him while he slept? He wasn't sure he wanted to know, or that he wanted to delve too deeply into why that idea made him forget all about the ache in his legs.

''Something tells me you're no stranger to a sickroom,'' Estelle said. ''You seem to know your way around pretty well.''

If he hadn't been watching her so closely, he would have missed the way his neighbor's face froze for a moment—a funny, almost frightened look flashing through her eyes before those delicate features became a blank mask. ''I've had a little experience.''

''Good. I think you're gonna need it with this one. He's gonna keep you hopping. Hate to do it but to check his temp and blood pressure I'll have to wake him up. You want to do the honors?''

After a moment's hesitation, his neighbor nodded and stepped forward, her arm outstretched as if to shake him.

''I'm awake,'' he growled. He didn't want either of them poking at him or prodding him, not when he had suddenly discovered a much bigger problem than a couple of women who talked about him when he was supposed to be sleeping.

He needed to use the bathroom.

Severely.

Somehow he would have to figure out a way to heft himself into that wheelchair and maneuver through that narrow doorway while preserving whatever shreds of his dignity might be left to a man as helpless as a blasted kitten.

No way on God's green earth was he going to ask these two for help.

He sat up, ignoring the way the room whirled and spun. That's it, he decided fiercely. No more pain pills for him.

Right now he would have given just about anything he owned for a few moments alone in a room with that bastard Lyle Juber. Gritting his teeth, he managed to find the control to the bed and lowered it so he was on the same level as the wheelchair. He pulled himself to a sitting position then inhaled sharply as several dozen knives sliced at him.

"Hold on there, cowboy," Estelle said briskly. "Where do you think you're going in such a hurry."

"Bathroom," he growled. "You got a problem with that?"

The nurse laughed. "Only if you fall and break your arms to go with that matched set of casts on your legs. Let me give you a hand, there."

She quickly showed him the transfer board tucked next to the bed and instructed him on the easiest way to get from the bed to the chair.

"Lucky you've got all these muscles in your arms here," she said. "You're gonna need 'em the next few weeks while you can't use your legs."

He made some noncommittal sound, then wheeled into the bathroom. Once more he found himself grateful to his landlady for installing grab bars that hadn't been there a week ago. She'd thought of everything, he thought. Or maybe she'd had help from his neighbor.

"We'll leave the door open in case you need any help in there," the nurse called out.

"The hell you will," he snapped, slamming it shut behind him and driving the bolt home.

Everything took about three times as long from a

wheelchair, he was discovering. By the time he finished what he needed to do and managed to maneuver close enough to the sink and could run some water to wash his hands and splash on his face, he felt a little more human. He was weak as a baby, though, both from the pills and from his injuries. Just that small amount of effort tired him out.

When he unlocked the bathroom and wheeled back into the bedroom, both women were waiting just where he left them. The nurse wore an I-told-you-so expression on her face but Lisa Connors just looked worried about him. He didn't want to analyze why that soft concern in her eyes warmed him far more than it should.

He wanted to protest when the two women both stepped forward to help him transfer back from the wheelchair to the bed but he decided it wasn't worth the headache. To his chagrin, he was too relieved to be back in bed to work up much of a fuss.

While the nurse checked his vital signs, he couldn't keep his gaze from straying to Lisa Connors. She stood silently, taking notes as the nurse recited numbers to her. She looked cool and lovely, her eyes huge behind those wire-rim glasses. He couldn't quite place a finger on what it was about her that attracted him so much. Really, with that choppy short brown hair, most people would probably consider her on the plain side. But there was a delicateness, a fragility, about her that appealed to some deep place inside of him.

"Everything looks normal so far." The nurse set down the blood pressure cuff. "But you're gonna have to do a better job of staying on top of the pain. Take my advice and don't let it get out of control. You need to swallow two pills every four hours."

"No. No more pills."

Estelle stepped back and placed her hands on her ample hips. ''Oh, you are just gonna be a joy to work with, aren't you?''

''Look, lady, I'm not a junkie. I don't like being out of it and I don't want any more pills. I can tough it out with aspirin.''

Estelle and his pretty neighbor shared a look, then the home-care nurse shrugged. ''You want to be in misery, knock yourself out, sugar. We'll see how big and tough you feel in the morning after the pain has kept you up all night.''

''What do you need me to do?'' Lisa Connors asked.

''Just make sure you stick close enough to pick up the pieces. You sleeping over?''

''Oh, no!''

Did she have to protest so vehemently? he wondered, annoyed for some strange reason.

''I live in the house just next door,'' she went on. ''His landlady and I rigged up a system so I can hear what's happening over here even when I'm at home. It's just a baby monitor, really, but our houses are so close that it works just fine. All he has to do is call out and I can be here in a second.''

''A baby monitor?'' He couldn't keep his disgust out of his voice. As if he needed something else to make him feel helpless and infantile.

She gave him a lopsided smile. ''Sorry. It was the best we could come up with on short notice, without installing a whole intercom system.''

''It's a little invasive, don't you think? What if I don't want you spying on me twenty-four hours a day?''

Estelle snorted. ''Then you should have stayed in the hospital where you belong, at least for a few more days.''

Since he couldn't come up with any response to that, he opted to keep his mouth shut.

Into the silence Lisa Connors spoke again. "Once you can get along a little better on your own, we won't need to keep the monitor turned on. I have to admit, I feel more comfortable knowing I can keep tabs on you. What if you fell while you were trying to transfer to the wheelchair for a middle-of-the-night trip to the bathroom? I wouldn't have any way of knowing you needed me until the morning."

"That would be my problem, wouldn't it?"

"No. It would be *my* problem. I was hired to take care of you and I intend to do that. It's either the baby monitor or my girls and I can sleep in your spare bedroom for the next few nights. Which would you prefer?"

Definitely not the spare bedroom idea. The whole reason he fought so hard to come home was for privacy. He had lived alone since he moved out of his dad's place in Las Vegas for college. He was a solitary man, and that's just the way he liked things.

Besides, pain pills or not, he knew he wouldn't be able to sleep a bit knowing this woman, with her violet scent and her big blue eyes, was just in the next room.

When he didn't answer, Lisa Connors smiled. "Not in the mood for a sleepover? I'll confess, I prefer my own bed, too. So the baby monitor can stay?"

"I guess," he muttered. He hated the idea but this was another battle he couldn't quite summon the energy to fight.

"Good," Estelle said briskly. "Now I'm gonna leave my pager number. Lisa, you check those vitals every four hours or so. You notice any bleeding or anything that might indicate circulation trouble, one of you needs to give me a buzz right away. Doesn't matter which one.

Otherwise I'll check in with you tomorrow, cowboy. Don't you go out dancing, now, you hear me?''

''Ha-ha,'' he muttered. ''You're a real barrel of laughs.''

Estelle's raspy chuckle hung in the air behind her for several moments after she left, leaving him alone with Lisa Connors.

''Are you hungry?'' she asked after a moment. ''You didn't eat lunch. I can heat up some soup for you or make a sandwich if you feel up to some solids.''

Nothing sounded appealing to him but he knew one of the reasons that single pain pill had knocked him for a loop was his lack of appetite. He needed to keep food in his stomach, whether it sounded good to him or not.

''A sandwich would work.''

''Ham and cheese okay?''

He nodded.

''It will just take me a minute to throw something together. If you'd like to watch TV, I've hooked the remote to a cord tethered to the side of the bed there so you can always find it and there are some magazines here, too. I wasn't sure of your interests but I picked up several that my…my husband used to enjoy reading.''

He only looked at her, but suddenly she colored up like a sugar maple leaf in October. Odd for such a dark-haired woman to show color so clearly. He hadn't met too many women in his lifetime who could actually blush but the few he had met had been blond.

What had her so edgy? Maybe she didn't like this situation any better than he did. It was an interesting thought. He knew if he were in her shoes, he sure wouldn't enjoy baby-sitting a grumpy stranger for a few weeks.

For some reason the thought that she might actually be

as uncomfortable with this as he was made him feel a little better about the whole thing.

After a quick peek into the living room to check on the girls, still engrossed in one of their favorite videos, Allie hurried to the kitchen. She closed the door and blew out the breath she'd been holding, then pressed a hand to her fluttering stomach.

What was it about Gage McKinnon that sent her hormones into a tailspin? The man was lethal. Even stiff and bad-tempered from the pain, he had a raw, masculine appeal.

A wounded, grumpy soldier. He was obviously miserable and in considerable pain but he was standing firm on not taking the narcotics his doctors prescribed. She had a feeling despite Estelle Montgomery's predictions to the contrary, he wasn't going to bend on his objections to the drugs. He seemed mulish and hardheaded enough to stick with his convictions.

She couldn't really blame him for that, Allie thought as she buttered bread for his sandwich. A few times in her life she'd had to take pain medication and she had despised that out-of-control feeling.

He wasn't going to be an easy patient. Despite the sudden conviction, she had to admit that all her nurturing instincts kicked in whenever she saw him lying so dark and masculine on that bed. She wanted to take care of him. To smooth down that lock of hair mussed by sleep and adjust his pillows and distract him from the pain.

Something in his eyes called to her. He seemed lonely, somehow. Lost. As if he'd been wandering alone for a long time and needed somewhere safe and warm to rest for a while....

She heard her own thoughts and rolled her eyes. Right.

The man was a tough, hardened FBI agent. Maybe she was projecting her own problems onto him.

What was the matter with her? She had a job to do here and it didn't include mooning over her patient. This was a good opportunity to make a little extra cash to add to her precious escape fund and she couldn't blow it just because Gage McKinnon left her all soft and tingly.

She would do her job and do it well, Allie chided herself sternly. She would make the poor man as comfortable as possible given the circumstances. That didn't include letting him unsettle her.

Keeping a tight rein on her thoughts, she finished fixing the sandwich and arranged it on a plate along with some carrot sticks and potato chips. After she added a glass of milk and one of the low-sugar oatmeal cookies she had made earlier in the day, she carried the tray down the hall to his bedroom.

She paused in the doorway when she spied her daughters standing by Gage McKinnon's bed, Gaby in the lead and Anna hovering just behind her sister.

''Hey, mister, we colored you a picture,'' Gaby was saying, holding out a page ripped from a coloring book like it was a sacred pictograph. ''It's Big Bird and a rainbow. I did Big Bird and Anna did the rainbow. She doesn't stay inside the lines very well but she's only three. Hey, mister, what happened to your legs?''

Without bothering to wait for any kind of response, in typical Gaby fashion, her oldest chattered on. ''Do they hurt? I bet they do. My friend Gina at my old house broke her arm falling off the swings, and she had to wear a cast. She said it hurt a *lot.* She still used it to whack her little brother, Nicky. He was a brat. My mama called him a little pill. That's funny, huh? Hey, mister, where do you want us to put our picture? I bet my mama could find some tape.''

Something about the hard set of his expression warned Allie he didn't appreciate the company.

She stepped forward quickly, hoping to head off the abrupt answer she sensed brewing. ''Girls, it's very nice of you to try making Mr. McKinnon feel better with a picture. I think the best thing for him right now is to rest. Why don't you go color a little more? I'm almost finished here and then we'll be going back to our house for the evening.''

Faced with her no-arguments tone, the girls didn't quibble. Gaby skipped out of the room, followed by her Anna shadow.

When she and Gage were alone, she set the tray down on the rolling bedside table Ruth had procured and pulled it toward him.

''Sorry about that,'' she finally said to break the suddenly awkward silence. ''Gabriella can be a little overwhelming sometimes. She means well but I'm afraid she hasn't learned when to turn it off.''

A muscle tightened in his jaw. ''Don't you have anywhere else for them to go? A sitter or something?''

The sudden attack took her completely by surprise and for a few moments she could only blink at him. ''I...no. Not really,'' she finally said. ''I'm sort of between care providers at the moment. They're both usually very well-behaved. I...Mrs. Jensen and I didn't think you would mind them being here.''

''You were both wrong.''

She stiffened at his blunt tone. Well, that was plain enough. He disliked her daughters. How could anybody not adore her daughters? They were sweet and kind. Funny. Completely adorable!

Any warm feelings she might have been crazy enough to entertain for Gage McKinnon fluttered out the window on the breeze. The man wasn't a wounded soldier. He was grumpy and stubborn and mean tempered.

"I'm sorry," she said tersely. "I didn't realize you would object to the girls. I'll do my best to keep them out of your way."

"You do that, Ms. Connors."

She swallowed her sharp retort and nodded. He had a right to his solitude. A couple of preschoolers underfoot probably weren't the best medicine for someone recovering from a traumatic injury.

She would just have to do her best to keep them quietly occupied for the next few weeks. She could do that. Just as she could control her own unwilling attraction for her cranky patient.

Chapter 5

"Do you think you might need anything else before I leave for the evening? How about more ice water?"

Annoyance threaded through Lisa Connor's voice like a muddy irrigation canal making its torpid way through a field of alfalfa, and tension stiffened her shoulders and that stubborn little jaw.

He hated to admit it but he was sorry to see the soft compassion in those pretty blue eyes give way to cool, distant politeness behind her glasses.

He should have known she would take his comments personally. She probably thought he had something against *her* kids. They weren't really the problem. The little squirts seemed to be fine, although the older one certainly had a motormouth on her.

The truth was, he just had trouble with *all* kids.

Not that he disliked kids. He didn't. But he didn't have much experience with normal kids, the ones who were happy and well adjusted. In his line of work, most of the children he saw were battered and bruised, both emotionally and physically. Or worse, the ones who would never have the chance to grow up.

He had witnessed so many terrible things in his career with the Bureau. Child abuse, sexual molestations, kidnappings. Any possible way an adult could snatch away the innocence of a child. The agents who worked cases involving crimes against children had to maintain a mental toughness, a self-imposed distance, that others in the FBI didn't always understand.

Over the years Gage thought his skin had grown as thick as an elephant's hide. He wasn't good at letting anybody inside, especially not a couple of little girls who would hopefully never be touched by the ugliness he dealt with on a daily basis.

"Ice water would be good," he finally answered her question with wariness. He had a feeling she would just as soon grab that pitcher and dump the contents over his head. She didn't, though. Lisa merely picked up the pitcher with that same polite expression on her face and walked out the door.

The room fell silent after she left, and Gage tried to eat a little of the supper she had fixed. He still didn't have much of an appetite but he forced himself to chew and swallow several bites of the sandwich. It was good, he had to admit. Much better than the pablum they passed off as food in the hospital.

She was trying to make him as comfortable as possible under the circumstances. Maybe he shouldn't have come down so hard on her about her daughters hanging around.

He pictured the two little dark-haired girls. Anna and Gabriella. What were they? Three? Four? Whatever, they seemed to be fairly close in age to his little sister when she disappeared.

Maybe that was why he was edgy and uncomfortable around them—they reminded him too forcefully of Charlotte the last time he had seen her. No wonder he didn't like having them around. He didn't need more reminders of his little sister shoved in his face every minute. Especially when he had nothing else to do all day but lie in this damn bed and think about the past and the guilt that was as much a part of him as his bones and his blood.

"Oh. You're finished."

He glanced up to find Lisa standing in the doorway holding the pitcher of water. He'd been so engrossed in his thoughts he hadn't even registered that he had eaten the entire sandwich without tasting most of it.

"I should have realized one sandwich might not be enough. I'm sorry. It's been a while since I've fixed meals for a…for a man with a healthy appetite. Would you like another one? It would only take me a moment to fix it."

The spasm of grief that flashed across her face made him curious once more about her late husband. She obviously still mourned the man. "No, thanks. I'm good," he replied. "I'm afraid I'm still a few days away from a healthy appetite."

"I'll be sure to keep that in mind in a few days, then, and adjust your portions accordingly." She managed a smile—a peace offering?—and poured him a glass of water from the pitcher.

"It's almost six. If you don't think you'll need anything else this evening, I'll take Gaby and Anna next door and fix their supper and settle them into bed. I checked the monitor earlier and it appears to be working. If you need me, just call out and I can be here in seconds. Also, I've made sure the phone is right here attached to the side of the bed. My phone number is programmed into it and so is Ruth Jensen's, just in case the monitor doesn't work for some reason."

"I'll be fine."

Behind the lenses of her glasses, her eyes narrowed as she studied him, and he hoped nothing in his expression betrayed the throbbing pain that had suddenly returned to his legs with a vengeance.

"Don't be a hero, Mr. McKinnon. If you need anything, please tell me. I know how hard it can be to accept help—believe me, I know—but you've hired me to do just that until you can manage better on your own."

"I didn't hire you," he muttered, wishing she would just go away and leave him alone to tackle the pain.

"You're right," she said after a moment. "If you want to be technical about it, Ruth actually hired me. But she did so on your orders. We both know that right now I'm the only thing standing between you and that hospital room you just left. Please ask if you need something."

"Fine. I need something."

Her face lit up with an eagerness to help he would have found laughable if it didn't shine a warm light on a cold, empty place inside him. "Anything. What can I get for you?"

She was probably imagining he would ask for another pillow or even those blasted pills he hated so much. He almost enjoyed popping her devoted-nurse fantasy.

"My sidearm. It should be in a holster in the personal effects I brought home from the hospital. I want it close enough where I can reach it."

After a moment of shocked silence, she raised an eyebrow. "Planning on doing a little target shooting at the TV, are we?"

He shouldn't have to explain anything to her. It wasn't any of her business that he had acquired his fair share of enemies after more than a decade at the Bureau. She would call him paranoid if he tried to tell her that certain parties would be thrilled if word happened to trickle out that he was lying here helpless, unable to defend himself.

"Just get it," he snapped.

"I'm not sure this is a good idea. How do I know you won't accidentally shoot me in the night if I come over from next door to check on you?"

"I don't want or need you checking on me in the night. Don't come skulking over in the early hours of the morning and you should survive to collect your severance pay."

To his surprise she laughed at that. Her laugh was low and soft and reminded him of a high mountain stream, bubbling and clean. "You don't scare me, FBI."

Too bad. Things would be much safer all around if she had a healthy fear of him and the rough world where he usually lived. "Just get it," he repeated.

She paused for just a moment then crossed the room to the closet and found the white plastic bag from the hospital with the clothes he'd been wearing at the time of the accident.

He ought to just have her throw away the clothes, since he wouldn't get much use out of that suit now, not after the paramedics had to cut away his pant legs to access his injuries, he thought.

She rooted through the bag and a moment later pulled out his shoulder holster. As she carried it over to him with two fingers, he thought she looked like a prissy little girl being forced to hold a garter snake. "Where do you want it?"

Gage gestured to the rolling bedside table and she set it down gingerly, as if afraid it would explode. Under normal circumstances he would store it loaded. But with two curious little girls in the house—even two little girls whose mother probably wouldn't let them venture into his bedroom again—he couldn't take any chances.

He emptied the chamber and placed the bullets in the small drawer of the table, then put the weapon under his pillow.

As long as he could reach both the bullets and the gun, he didn't mind the extra safety precaution. He could load the Glock in his sleep. When he was satisfied everything was within reach, he turned back to Lisa Connors and found her watching him, her mouth prim.

"Should we come up with a secret knock or something so that if I have to come over in the night you'll know it's me and won't shoot first and ask questions later?"

"I'll know," he muttered. He didn't think he could mistake this woman for anyone else on earth, even if they were trapped deep inside the dank recesses of one of the abandoned silver mines that dotted the mountains around Park City.

He had a funny, uncomfortable feeling he would know her anywhere. How could he miss her? She smelled like violets, sweet and pure. For some strange reason she made him think of spring afternoons spent lying in damp new grass, plucking a handful of tiny purple blossoms he would clutch in his fist and present proudly to his mother, who would accept the gift solemnly, then grab him close and kiss his cheeks until he squirmed away.

That made twice in one afternoon he had thought of his mother. He couldn't remember the last time that had happened. Lynn hadn't been a part of his life for years, a conscious decision made by both of them. Why would he think of her now?

Probably the same reason men on the battlefield cried out for their own mothers in the midst of lonely darkness and fear. Maybe while he tried to cope with the physical pain of his shattered legs, some corner of his psyche wanted to reach out to the one person in his life who had kissed the sting of his early scrapes and cuts away.

Until they had all come up against a raw, devastating pain no amount of kisses could ever make better.

He jerked his mind away from that uncomfortable train of thought and turned back to his neighbor. "Make sure you lock the door behind you."

"I will. Ruth gave me a house key so I'll still be able to come over if you need me."

"Don't hold your breath."

"Estelle was right. You macho types do make the worst patients."

"I believe her exact words were the good-looking, macho types."

Her short wispy hair swung a little as she shook her head, exasperation in her blue eyes. But Gage thought he saw a hint of color brush across her high cheekbones. "That too."

She headed for the door. "I'll just wash your supper dishes and then we'll be out of your way so you can sleep again. I'm leaving your pain pills right here by the bed. Use them, Mr. McKinnon," she said sternly. "As Estelle said, if you don't stay on top of the pain, it's only that much harder to get it under control again."

She stood and reached across the bed for the dinner tray then carried it out of the room, leaving behind a tantalizing hint of the sweet, spring-like smell of violets.

Just past midnight, Allie sat up in bed again, hugging her knees tightly as she gazed at the glowing light of the baby monitor by her bed.

Stubborn man. Why didn't he have the good sense to take something for his obvious pain?

The monitor was just too sensitive. Sounds came through loud and clear. She could hear blankets rustling and the bed creaking under his weight as he shifted restlessly, and every once in a while she heard him mumble something low and tortured, then a sharp intake of breath that probably indicated he had moved wrong.

She had a feeling he wasn't really conscious. He never would have betrayed his discomfort if he were awake.

She knew she would never be able to sleep until she could be confident her patient rested comfortably. But shy of shoving the blasted pills down his unconscious throat, she didn't know how she would ever be able to accomplish that.

She had to do something, though. She wasn't sure she could take much more of this.

The hardest part of her job as a nurse had been seeing people come into her emergency room in agonizing pain and knowing there were limits to how much of that pain could be controlled. In this case she knew Gage would sleep far more deeply and comfortably if he would only take some pain medication.

He made another one of those raspy sounds in his throat, and she knew she couldn't ignore it any longer. With a sigh, she slid from her bed to the cool wood floor.

Pale moonlight shimmered through the curtains of her cozy little bedroom as she quickly threw on shorts under the T-shirt she slept in and slipped into her sneakers. After a quick peek into the girls' room where she found them both sleeping soundly, she grabbed her keys and walked outside, locking her house behind her.

The night was cool, scented sweetly from the hundreds of blooms growing next door. She paused on her steps to inhale some of that fresh air into her lungs. Something about the night reminded her of summer evenings on her grandparents' farm in western Pennsylvania with frogs peeping in the pond and fireflies flashing over the hay fields and a barn owl swooping silently through the night sky in search of prey.

She had never lived anywhere but Pennsylvania but she was finding she enjoyed life in the Rocky Mountains. The air was thinner and drier than she was used to and everything seemed to move at a different pace here but she and the girls seemed to have settled in.

For how long, she didn't know. If only she could shake this fear that hounded every stop, that left her anxious and uneasy.

Allie jerked herself back to her responsibilities and hurried up the steps to Gage McKinnon's house. After she found the key and unlocked the door, she stood inside trying to get her bearings in the dimly lit house. Before she left, she had turned the light on over the stove in the kitchen, but that provided the only illumination in the house except for the pale moonlight spilling in through the windows.

Now that she was here, she wasn't sure exactly what to do. She suddenly realized she couldn't just burst into his bedroom to check on him. Not when the man was a trained law enforcement officer who slept with an ugly black revolver under his pillow.

After a moment's indecision, Allie hurried to the bedroom door and knocked softly. "Mr. McKinnon? Gage?"

She heard nothing for several long moments, then a sleepy growl answered. "What?"

Maybe coming over here wasn't the greatest of ideas. He didn't exactly sound thrilled about the nocturnal visit.

"It's me. Al—" She caught herself just in time before

she blurted out the wrong name. "Lisa Connors. I'm coming in. Don't shoot," she tried for a joke, then pushed open the door.

"What's wrong?" he asked. In the dim light she could see that he had pulled himself up to a sitting position in the bed. His hair was messed and the muscles of his bare chest gleamed.

Oh, mercy.

She cleared her throat. "You were moaning in your sleep. I was worried about you."

He glared at her. "Worry about yourself. You're hearing things. I'm doing fine. Or I was, until a few moments ago."

Despite his insistence, she could see lines of pain around his mouth, and she thought he looked a shade or two paler than he had when she left earlier in the evening, but that could have been a trick of the moonlight. "You know you would have a more restful sleep if you took something."

"I'd have a more restful sleep if my nosy neighbor didn't come poking around, waking me up."

She deserved that, she supposed. "I'm sorry."

"You've done your job and checked up on me. As you can see, I'm fine."

There was clear dismissal in his tone but she wasn't quite ready to leave until she'd had some chance to assess his condition for herself. "While I'm here—and since you're up now, anyway—I would feel better if I could check your vital signs."

"Is that really necessary?"

"You met Estelle. Do you think either one of us wants to be on her bad side?"

He only grunted in answer, which she took as assent. After she turned on the low lamp by the bed, she found the equipment she needed on the dresser. He didn't protest when she shoved the thermometer in his mouth then wrapped the blood pressure cuff around his upper arm, trying fiercely to ignore the little sizzle of awareness that sparked inside her as her hands wrapped around his powerful biceps.

Her fingers quickly found his pulse at his wrist, a reassuring strong, steady beat, then she inflated the blood pressure cuff and put the stethoscope to her ears, conscious of him watching her movements out of those steely gray eyes.

By the time she finished touching all that warm, sexy male skin and pulled the thermometer from his mouth, she was feeling jittery, light-headed. Maybe she ought to check her blood glucose while she was awake. Or maybe she should just avoid touching Gage McKinnon in a moonlit bedroom in the middle of the night.

"You've done this before," he said after she noted his vital signs on the chart Estelle had left and returned the equipment to the dresser.

"Yes," she acknowledged after a moment.

"Are you a nurse?"

She thought about lying to him. But he was too sharp-eyed, too astute. He would know she wasn't telling the truth and would be suspicious as to what possible motive she might have for the lie.

"Yes," she finally said again.

She would have left it at that—better not to muddy things with unnecessary explanations—but he only waited, watching her out of those intent gray eyes, and she knew she had to add more.

"I'm not licensed in Utah yet. That's why I agreed to take this job, because technically I didn't need to be licensed for it."

"What were you doing until yesterday?"

"Cleaning rental units for Ruth."

She could see by his puzzled look that he was wondering why a registered nurse would be content scrubbing toilets and making beds.

"I guess it was a lucky day for you that I was stupid enough to get my legs broken then, wasn't it?" he finally said.

"Oh, yes," she said dryly. "You're a real answer to prayer."

To her surprise, he actually unbent enough to respond with a small smile. She blinked. It was only a smile. Nothing to get all twitter-pated about, even though he certainly didn't seem to have many of them to spare.

Still, she had to admit that simple, momentary lightening of his expression changed him from a stern, unapproachable FBI agent to a gorgeous, bare-chested male.

To cover up her reaction, she finally ventured to ask the question she'd been wondering about for the last hour, since hearing his unconscious mutterings on the baby monitor. "Was someone else injured in your accident?"

He gave a rough laugh. "Let me tell you something, sweetheart. When a suspect trying to evade arrest deliberately crushes you against a brick retaining wall with a three-ton pickup, *accident* isn't exactly the best word choice."

She winced at the mental image he conjured up. "Sorry. Was anyone else with you?"

"A dozen other FBI agents and local cops were there. None was lucky enough to receive the same special attention. Why do you ask?"

She shrugged. "While you were sleeping, I thought I heard you call out for someone named Charlie. I thought it might have been another FBI agent who had been hurt along with you.''

His expression went instantly cold, so cold she shivered, regretting whatever crazy impulse had led her to bring up the subject. ''I must have been having a nightmare.''

She knew she should just let it drop but something made her push. ''Is Charlie a friend?''

''Charley was short for Charlotte.''

Someone he had loved very much, she suspected, at least judging by the raw pain in his voice. She thought he would let the matter drop but after a moment he went on, his face without expression and his eyes focused on the curtains fluttering in the night breeze.

''Charlotte was my kid sister. She was kidnapped from our front yard when she was three years old. We never saw her again.''

Chapter 6

With a swift intake of air, her face went slack with shock. The woman didn't hide her emotions worth diddly. It was all there in her features—horror and compassion and disbelief.

"Kidnapped! How awful for you and for your parents! How old were you?"

"Twelve," he answered tersely, cursing himself for bringing the whole thing up.

He wasn't sure why he did. He never talked about it. Never. He was sure Charlotte's case history showed up in his file at the Bureau—the intensive background check done on him before he was accepted at Quantico would have turned up the whole grisly story. But none of his superiors ever brought up the kidnapping and he never volunteered the information.

So why tell Lisa Connors? A woman he barely knew, a woman he suspected had enough secrets of her own? Maybe because her columbine eyes had looked all soft and concerned and because it had been so long since someone had worried about him.

Or maybe because on some subconscious level, he still felt about as low as that imaginary garter snake he'd been thinking about earlier for the warning he'd given her to keep her daughters away from him.

Maybe he wanted her to make the connection he hadn't been able to spell out—that seeing her daughters, listening to their innocent laughter, was a painful reminder of the guilt he carried inside him over his sister's disappearance.

In the light spilling into the room from the bathroom he could see the brightness of unshed tears in her eyes. Damn, he hoped she didn't cry. Not over him.

"It happened a long time ago. I'm not sure why I would have said her name in my sleep. Like I said, I must have been having a bad dream."

He didn't like explaining himself and he especially didn't like feeling responsible for those emotions swimming in her eyes.

"Look, I appreciate you coming to check on me," he said gruffly. "But as I told you, I'm fine. I was sleeping and I would like to get back to it, if it's all the same to you."

She looked as if she wanted to say more about Charlotte—how could he expect otherwise?—but after a moment she followed his lead and let the subject drop.

"Are you sure you won't take something for your pain?" she asked.

That dead horse again. He sighed heavily. "If I do, will you leave me alone at least until the sun comes up?"

"Yes. If you take a pain pill, I promise I won't bother you again until morning."

"Great. Let's have it, then." He held out a hand and waited while she opened the prescription bottle and poured out two of the blasted things. She poured him fresh water from the pitcher she'd brought in earlier in the evening and handed him both.

Though he felt about as mature as a four-year-old, he concealed the nasty-tasting pills under his tongue and made a big show of pretending to swallow.

She bought it, apparently, because her features softened into a smile. "Anything else I can do for you before I go home?"

"Yeah. Turn off the monitor. To be honest, I'm not at all comfortable having you listen to me while I sleep."

"Agent McKinnon—"

"Don't you think you could call me Gage by now?"

"Gage, then. You need some way to reach me if something were to happen to you."

"I have the phone right here. Since one of those pills makes me loopy enough, I'm sure two of them will knock me into next week."

"Are you sure?"

"I like my privacy. That's why I left the hospital in the first place. How would you like it if you had to try to sleep knowing somebody was listening to your every move?"

Gage was relieved to see that soft compassion give way to exasperation. He could cope with annoyance far easier than he could handle tender-hearted sympathy.

To his relief, she crossed to the baby monitor and switched it off. While her back was still turned, he spit the pain pills out into his hand and hid them beneath his blanket with a maneuver that was as slick as it was sneaky, if he did say so himself.

When she turned around, he tried for an expression as innocent as he could make it.

Maybe he was spreading it just a little too thick because

she narrowed her gaze suspiciously. He thought she might be on to him but she only sighed. ''Has anyone ever told you, Agent McKinnon, that you could give lessons in stubborn to a whole barnyard full of mules?''

He managed a smile. ''Not in those exact words but I've been called worse.''

''Just make sure you remember who's to blame if you fall out of bed and end up spending a cold, miserable night on the floor.''

''Not you, of course.''

''And don't you forget it.'' With crisp, efficient movements, she reached out to straighten his blankets one last time, leaning close to him as she did and sending another sweet hint of that clean, honest violet scent washing over him.

In a demoralizing moment of self-discovery, Gage forced himself to face the horrible realization that maybe a warped corner of his psyche secretly enjoyed her fussing over him.

No, he just liked her. He could count on one hand the number of people he genuinely liked but there was something about Lisa Connors he found refreshing and decent. She represented a whole host of things that were missing from his life—things he never even noticed weren't there, like kindness, gentleness, compassion.

Beyond that, he had to admit he was physically attracted to her. With that short, wispy haircut and her delicate features and those big blue eyes, she reminded him of some kind of mystical creature out of a novel. A wood sprite or something.

If he didn't feel so lousy, Gage would have been tempted to check if that curved bow of a mouth tasted like violets, to skim his fingers over that skin to see if it could possibly be as soft as it looked.

If he tried, would she push him away or would she welcome him into her arms?

Gage cut off the crazy line of thought when he felt his body stir to life under the blankets she had just straightened.

"I need to get back to my girls," she said, deflating his fledgling interest faster than backing through a tire ripper.

She wasn't his kind of woman at all. As appealing as he might find her on several different levels, she had a couple of major shortcomings that would keep him from ever pursuing anything with her—two little girls.

He had a strict policy against becoming involved with women who had children, a policy he wasn't about to bend, even for someone as attractive as Lisa Connors.

"Right," he muttered. "Good night, then."

"Be sure to call if you need me."

"I will," he lied.

After she left, he pulled the pills from their hiding place beneath his blanket and tossed them into the trash, trying not to notice the soft, sweet scent that lingered in the air behind her.

Yeah, he might sleep better with the damn things. But he would be far more comfortable knowing he had all his faculties about him.

Besides, since she turned off the monitor, he could sleep free from the worry that he might call out the names of any more of the ghosts that haunted him.

"You can tell me the truth now, girl. How are you and our favorite grouchy hottie *really* getting along?"

Allie paused in the middle of pouring a glass of Estelle Montgomery's favorite diet soda after the home care nurse's daily check on Gage.

In the week since her patient had returned to his house and she had begun caring for him, she had come to savor these few moments with Estelle after a full day of tending to a churlish man who made no secret of the fact that he didn't want her there.

Still, as much as she enjoyed visiting with the nurse, she absolutely did *not* want to have this particular conversation with her.

"I...fine," she lied. "Just fine."

"Really?"

Allie debated her answer while she added a slice of lemon to the lip of the glass. She had a feeling Estelle could see right through her polite lie. She should just tell her the truth, that Gage McKinnon and his dark temper and gorgeous looks made her more nervous than a whole room full of yellow jackets.

If she entertained any misconceptions that their encounter that first night might have been the beginning of a wary friendship, Gage quickly quashed them. He didn't really complain about anything, he was just abrupt and brusque and deflected any of her attempts at conversation.

None of this could be easy on him. She could sympathize with him on that score. She always hated the times she had to be in the hospital, even though she'd been dealing with the medical complications of her diabetes since childhood.

Allie suspected Gage was used to being in the middle of the action, not sidelined to a hospital bed. He was probably going stir-crazy trapped in this small house with a woman he didn't know and two little girls he didn't want around.

Worse than his cool abruptness, though, was that disconcerting way he had of scrutinizing her out of those steely gray eyes until she was blushing and stammering and deathly afraid the man could look inside her and figure out all her secrets.

"He's challenging, certainly, but we're finding our way. Things have been better since I've given up trying to push the pain meds on him."

"Still being stubborn about that, is he?"

Allie shrugged. "One thing I've learned since nursing school is that sometimes the patient really does know best, even though we don't always like to admit it. If he wants to tough it out, I can't argue with him. He seems to be handling the pain his own way."

"By being as difficult as he can be."

Allie smiled. "Not really. He's quite undemanding, compared to some of the patients I've had."

Estelle glanced down the hallway toward Gage's closed bedroom door, then leaned closer to Allie with a conspiratorial smile. "You can tell old Estelle the truth now. Is the equipment below the covers as good-lookin' as what's above?"

"Estelle!"

Somehow the nurse managed to look as innocent as a baby kitten, even though her dark eyes snapped with laughter. "Come on, girl. It's an honest question. The man has been mightily blessed in the muscle department, at least what I've been able to see. I imagine you must have noticed when you've helped him take a sponge bath."

Her face caught fire and she knew she must be as bright pink as the scrubs Estelle wore. "I wouldn't know. He insists on taking care of his, um, personal duties himself. All I do is fetch and carry supplies for him. Water, washcloths, soap. That sort of thing."

"Does he let you at least help him wash his hair?"

Oh, heavens. She'd never even thought to offer help

with washing his hair. How had he been doing it on his own with just a washbasin? Probably not very well.

She couldn't believe she'd been so stupid not to ask if she could help. Heaven knows, the man would rather bite off his own tongue than ask for anything on his own.

He would probably love a good shampoo. The idea of burying her fingers in that thick, dark hair to lather and rinse him made her insides go jittery and warm. She sighed at herself. *Get over it, Allie!* The man was a patient. That's all.

"I'll ask him today if I can help with his hair."

"You want my opinion on how to handle that one, don't ask him anything. Just show up with a basin and shampoo. What's he gonna say after you've already dunked his head in the water?"

"'No way in hell.' And maybe 'Oh, and by the way, you're fired.'"

Estelle's chest bounced with her laughter. "Aw, sugar, the man's not crazy. He won't fire a cute little thing like you, especially one who can make chocolate chip cookies like my mama used to do."

She chomped on another one and Allie spent a moment wondering if she could indulge in one cookie. She did make a fine tollhouse, if she did say so herself. After calculating what she'd eaten that day and what her levels were the last time she checked she decided she could afford one half of one cookie if she ran a test strip after Estelle left.

"I imagine before he gets those casts off," the nurse went on while Allie broke one cookie in half and savored the rich, crispy treat, "the two of you will butt heads on more things than just a shampoo or two. Like my mama told me on my wedding day, just make sure you both know who's boss."

Allie laughed at Estelle's knowing look. "He *is* the one who pays my salary."

"Why let a little thing like that get in the way of making sure the man knows what's what? I'm only sorry I won't be around to watch the fireworks."

Allie frowned at the nurse. "You won't?"

Beads clicked in her cornrows as Estelle shook her head. "This is my last official visit. Mr. Sexy FBI Man is stable enough I don't need to check in every day unless he takes a turn for the worse. From now on the home health agency will probably just phone a few times a week to see how he's doing and to check if you need any supplies. But I want to hear everything you find out about our hottie, you hear me? I'll take you to lunch at the Barking Frog next week and you can unload everything on old Estelle."

Her sharp pang of regret made Allie realize how much she'd come to enjoy these daily chats with the nurse.

Estelle was the only close friend she had found since she left Philadelphia and she would miss her bitterly. She needed these visits. While she and Estelle shared a soda or a cup of tea, Allie didn't feel so very alone and afraid.

She hated this! She wasn't sure she had the personality for the transient, isolated life forced on her by Joaquin and Irena. She craved safety, stability. Firm, solid ground under her feet.

Friends had always played a vital role in her life and she hated knowing she was weaving connections—like this fledgling friendship with Estelle—only to inevitably watch them unravel when she moved on.

For the rest of their visit, Allie was subdued, depressed. After a few more moments, Estelle rose to go.

"Much as I'd like to stick around and have another few dozen of these cookies, I've still got to hit my last patient of the day. You think Sexy FBI Man is crotchety, you ought to spend a few minutes with Miss Annabelle Stephens. The woman's a hundred if she's a day and couldn't hear a nuclear explosion if it went off in her ear but that doesn't stop her from bitchin' at me nonstop from the minute I walk in the door. You give those cute little girls of yours a kiss for me when they get back, you hear?''

Allie nodded. Gaby and Anna had begun a daily ritual of playing at the park in the afternoon with a sixteen-year-old neighbor girl who tended her little brother and sister during the day.

The children had quickly become friends and the arrangement seemed to be working out well for everyone. Jessica Farmer was grateful for the extra spending money Allie gave her for taking the girls along, Gaby and Anna loved having other children to play with, and for two hours a day Allie didn't have to worry about them annoying Gage.

She certainly didn't want them underfoot while she washed Gage's hair, assuming he didn't jump down her throat for suggesting the idea.

After Estelle left, Allie gathered a washbasin and filled it with warm water, then found shampoo and clean towels from the laundry room. With her heart pounding in trepidation, she went to his room and knocked.

''Come in,'' he answered.

She huffed out a shaky breath and pushed open the door. Her patient was sitting up in the wheelchair she knew he despised, typing something on his laptop computer with ESPN buzzing softly from the television set.

He looked up, his gray eyes dark with irritation. ''Give it a rest already, Connors. Haven't I been poked and prodded enough for one afternoon by your friend?''

She almost backed out of the room, but at the last moment she straightened her spine. His hair did look a little dull. Besides that, lines of fatigue fanned out around his eyes. He was pushing himself far too hard, far too fast. He spent a big part of every day having her help him with the rehab exercises ordered by his physical therapist, doing them two or three times more often than the PT recommended. She knew some of the exercises were excruciating, but Gage refused to give in to the pain.

It wouldn't hurt him to relax a little, to allow himself to enjoy a bit of pampering. "Estelle made me realize I have been slacking in some of my responsibilities."

He frowned. "You're doing fine. Except you don't seem to know when to lay off and let me have a moment of peace."

She decided to let that slide. "I thought perhaps you could use a shampoo."

He finally looked up from the computer, his expression baffled. "A what?"

"You know," Allie narrowed her gaze, considering, "I think that wheelchair puts you just at the right height so we could use the kitchen sink. It will mean some tricky maneuvering but I think we can manage it and it will be much easier than using a basin."

"What are you talking about?"

"I was offering to help you wash your hair. I should have suggested it earlier in the week but it never occurred to me until Estelle asked about it. Trust me, the whole world seems a brighter and happier place when you have clean hair. I think you'll find you feel much better."

He looked completely flabbergasted at the idea, but then his gaze shifted subtly to the small mirror on the bureau. He cocked his head at his reflection then frowned at her again.

"I don't need a shampoo."

"Maybe you don't *need* it. But it won't kill you, will it? I promise, you'll feel better."

"You're going to hound me about this until I give in, aren't you?"

"How did you guess?" She smiled, remembering Estelle's words about letting him know who was in charge.

He sighed and typed a few strokes into the laptop then closed the lid. "Let's get this over with, then."

Chapter 7

Not sure exactly when his life had spun so completely out of his control, Gage let Lisa wheel him into the kitchen and arrange him in front of the sink. He really ought to be working up some sort of a protest. He didn't need another example thrown in his face to remind him how helpless he was that he couldn't even wash his own hair, for Pete's sake.

So why did he stay silent even as she draped a towel around his shoulders and handed him another for his eyes in case water dripped into them?

It couldn't be because he secretly wanted her hands on him. Absolutely not. No, more likely he went along with her only because he was too worn-out to argue with the immovable force that was Lisa Connors.

Besides, he had to admit, his head was beginning to itch. Why suffer one more misery on top of everything else if he didn't have to?

Behind him he could hear water run in the sink while

she tested the temperature. A few moments later the tone of the flow changed as she turned on the spray attachment.

"Can you lean back a little?"

Resigned to his fate, Gage complied, wondering as he did why her voice seemed to have slipped an octave. "Is that far enough?"

"It should be."

A moment later a spray of warm water hit his head. He forced himself to relax as she soaked his hair. He even managed to close his eyes instead of watching her with the wariness of a chained wolf.

Really, this wasn't so bad after all. She was right, it felt kind of nice. Restful, even.

After a moment it became better than nice. He had never realized what a sensual experience having someone else wash his hair could be. As she worked lather through each strand of his wet hair, he was suddenly uncomfortably aware of this woman who had managed to barge her way into his life.

How could he be anything *but* aware of her? As her fingers worked through his hair, she leaned over him to reach better, enveloping him in her clean, fresh spring-like scent until he didn't seem able to breathe in anything else.

If he turned his head just so, his cheek would brush against both of her high, firm breasts. He could nuzzle against her, could inhale the scent of her, could press his mouth to the warm skin of that enticing little hollow above her collarbone....

She cleared her throat. "I'm going to rinse now."

Her voice jerked him back to sanity. What in the hell was the matter with him? His body was stirring like some randy teenager's while he sat here fantasizing about a busybody nurse with a choppy haircut and secrets in her eyes.

Maybe she ought to just turn that spray to cold and stick his whole head under.

He drew in a deep breath, willing his body to settle down. In the loose cotton shorts he had to wear because nothing else fit over the casts, she would be sure to notice his arousal if he didn't do something about it.

With effort, he forced himself to recite Miranda until his body started to settle down. The fiercely secured distance seemed to work. By the time she washed and rinsed his hair a second time, he just about had everything under control.

"All done," she said briskly, her voice just a little too pert, and for one crazy moment he wondered if she might be as attracted to him as he was to her. No. Impossible.

"I brought in a comb and hand mirror," she went on. "I'll let you do those honors."

Feeling more clean than he had since the accident, he took them from her and combed his hair, aware of her observing him out of those big blue eyes. There was an oddly seductive intimacy in having her watch him perform such a personal act. It seeped around him like smoke swirls, threatening to erode all his hard-won self-mastery.

"Are you ready to go back to your room?" she asked when he finished combing his hair.

Even though he knew it was dangerous to spend any more time with her, he was coming to despise the four walls of that room. "I like the change of scenery. If it's okay with you, I'll just sit here for a moment."

"It's your house, Mr. McKinnon. You can sit wherever you would like." She picked up one of the towels and began to wipe down the counters on either side of the sink where water had splashed during his shampoo.

"Gage," he reminded her.

She made a face. "Gage."

With the counters dry, she knelt on the floor where more water puddled, probably completely heedless of the way her denim shorts outlined her very shapely rear end.

When she stood up, her shirt rode up a little and for the first time he noticed the small black electronic unit clipped to her waistband.

"Are you expecting an important page?"

Her gaze met his, confusion turning the columbine a murky blue. "A what?"

"A page. Why else would you wear a beeper clipped to your belt?"

The confusion in her eyes cleared for a moment and she looked down at the unit with a small laugh. "It's not a beeper. It's an insulin pump."

She pulled her T-shirt up a little more, leaving the distinct marks of wet fingerprints on the pale blue cotton. As she revealed a small strip of bare flesh at her abdomen he could see some kind of medical-looking tube inserted into the skin just above her waistline.

"You're diabetic?"

Her shrug was casual. "Since I was ten."

"That must have been rough when you were a kid."

She folded the wet towel and set it aside, then leaned back against the counter, her expression thoughtful. "Yeah, it had its moments. The year we found out I had it was a hard year all around. I was diagnosed two months before my mother died of kidney failure. I can tell you, that's a terrifying thing for a ten-year-old girl—losing your mother from the same disease you just found out you share with her."

He could picture her as a ten-year-old, sick and scared and grieving for her mother. A wave of sympathy washed over him and he was astonished by how strongly he wanted to comfort that little girl.

"Must have been tough on your father, too," he murmured.

Something hard and bitter flashed across her features. "Oh, I'm sure it gave him many sleepless nights in bed beside the new wife he married three months after my mother died. The sweet young thing who didn't want the burden of dealing with a sickly kid who was in and out of the hospital that first year."

A muscle worked in her slender jaw. "My maternal grandparents raised me after my dad remarried. I haven't heard from him since he cheerfully gave up any visitation rights around the time his new wife delivered a pair of healthy, nondiabetic twin boys."

He had seen plenty of cruelty to children during his years with the FBI but he never ceased to be amazed at how a parent could display such blatant inhumanity.

Gage studied her, anger for the pain she had suffered thick and fierce in his chest. Even with two broken legs, he wanted to find her father and kick the bastard's selfish, thoughtless ass.

After a moment she blew out a breath. "I'm sorry. I must sound like a bitter old hag."

"You don't. You sound like someone who's had a rough time, that's all." Besides, no one with a brain in his head or blood pulsing through his veins could possibly call her old or a hag.

"Ten is a pretty pivotal age for a girl. I fought and bucked against the restrictions of diabetes like a horse tied out in a hailstorm, sneaking junk food every chance I got and hiding out in the barn whenever it was time to check my BGs—blood glucose."

For some reason, he found it heartening that she grew

up on a farm somewhere, surrounded by animals and growing things. He hoped she had found some measure of solace living with her grandparents.

"I can't blame him for it," she went on, "but I've often thought that maybe if I had received a little more understanding and support from my father, I might have accepted my diagnosis more easily. I was a teenager before I was finally able to take control of my disease."

"It's still under control, I guess?"

"Not always but for the most part. It's much easier now with the pump than when I was a kid and had to do the whole needle thing."

"How does it work?" he asked.

She crossed the kitchen to the table and pulled out a chair beside him. Again she pulled her shirt up enough for him to see the insulin pump just above her waist and the line into her creamy skin. "It's pretty cool, actually. I only have to stick myself once a day when I change the catheter site. It stays in place all the time and is programmed to deliver the correct dose of insulin at preset times. I can also deliver a bolus if I need it. I still have to keep on top of what I eat and how I'm feeling but it's become just a part of life."

"Keeping up with two active little girls must not be easy with a complication like diabetes."

"I do fine with my daughters. Just fine."

The abruptness of her tone took him by surprise, as did the chill suddenly creeping across her blue eyes like a quick frost covering a flower garden.

Why such a testy subject? he wondered. Had somebody in her past implied otherwise? The husband, maybe? No. She seemed to genuinely grieve for the man, whoever he might have been. Gage couldn't imagine a woman as devoted to her children as Lisa Connors would have much patience with a husband who raised questions about her ability to care for them.

"I never said you didn't," he said mildly. He should have left it at that, but some streak of curiosity made him push the issue. "Still, I'm sure you must be worried about your daughters and their future if something should happen to you. Especially with their father gone."

He immediately regretted the comment when the coolness in her eyes was replaced with fiery-hot fear.

"Of course I worry! Sometimes I can't sleep for the worry eating me up inside. How could I not worry, when I saw my own mother die by inches in front of my eyes? I can't bear the thought of putting my own girls through that."

"Lisa..."

She went on as if she didn't hear him. "I work hard to keep my diabetes under control, mostly for them. For Gaby and Anna. I exercise, I eat what I'm supposed to, I check my blood sugar obsessively. I won't let it win, damn it. I'm a good mother. The incidental fact that I have diabetes has nothing to do with that. Nothing!"

Man, somebody sure did a number on her. Was her passionate response a result of her own father's cruelty, he wondered, or something else? She had scars, deep ones.

With no motive other than comforting her, he instinctively reached for her hand. "You're right. I didn't mean to imply you're not a good mother. I'm sorry I brought it up," he murmured.

Her hand fluttered in his and her cheeks colored. She made an embarrassed sound. "It's not your fault," she said after a pause. "You just happened to push one of my buttons. The big red one that launches me on a full-fledged tirade. I'm sorry I went off like that."

He recognized the emotion in her eyes for what it was—fear that she couldn't protect the ones she loved. Since he knew all too well the raw guilt that came from failing in that department, he had nothing but sympathy for her.

"If it makes any difference, I've seen a lot of rotten parents in my years with the FBI and you definitely don't qualify. From what little I've seen of them, your girls are smart and happy and well-adjusted. You must be doing something right."

She gazed at him for a moment, her high color fading a little, then she gifted him with a radiant smile. "I think beneath that cranky exterior lives a very kind man, Mr. McKinnon."

"Don't kid yourself."

She laughed and squeezed his fingers. Her hand was a small, warm weight in his. Subtly, slowly, the mood between them slid into something else. Something glittery and bright and charged with tension.

Despite his best attempts at willpower, his gaze landed on her mouth, those sensual lips that gave him far too many ideas he knew he had no business entertaining. As he watched, her lips parted slightly and she sucked in a small breath, awareness blooming to life in her eyes.

He wasn't conscious of leaning forward to kiss her until he was inches away from her mouth.

He couldn't think about all the million reasons why kissing her was a lousy idea. Her girls, the secrets he sensed in her eyes, the fact that he didn't need a complication like Lisa Connors in his life right now. None of that mattered. All he could focus on was stealing a taste of that soft, inviting mouth.

She watched him with wide-eyed shock but made no move to back away. Instead, her lips parted slightly and she breathed in a little sigh that sent heat sizzling through him.

His heart pounding, he crossed the last few inches between them, but before he could kiss her, the sharp, watchful part of his psyche that could never seem to go off alert heard footsteps on the wooden slats of the front porch. An instant later the melodious chime of the doorbell rang through the small house.

Allie swallowed hard as she watched firm control slip back over Gage's features. He quickly eased back into his chair and she swallowed again, not sure if that thick lump in her throat was shock or regret.

He had almost kissed her!

Somehow she managed to force a quick breath into lungs that suddenly seemed oxygen starved.

Still, when she spoke, her voice sounded thin, ragged, like she'd just hiked to the top of Soldier Summit. "That's probably Anna and Gaby back from the park. A…a neighbor girl took them. I told them to come here when they returned. I hope that's all right with you. I can send them over to my house with Jessica, though. She's the neighbor girl. She's sixteen and a really great baby-sitter. The girls already love her."

She snapped her jaws shut before she could spew out more inane chatter. How was she supposed to react, though? She had a perfect right to act a little disconcerted.

The man acted like a wounded grizzly bear most of the time who couldn't stand having her around. But in the last half hour he'd shown her more kindness and compassion than she had received in a long time and then had complicated everything by nearly kissing her.

And she regretted fiercely that he hadn't had the chance, she realized with chagrin.

"You don't need to send them home. I'm going back to my room." He didn't look at her as he started to wheel away from the table.

What must he think of her? Did he know that her body had craved his kiss, that it was still humming in reaction to something that hadn't even happened?

He probably figured she was some kind of desperate creature who made a habit of kissing anybody who showed her kindness.

She forced herself to swallow her embarrassment. "Did you want to lie down? After I answer the door, I can help you transfer from the wheelchair to the bed."

"No. I can handle it on my own."

His tone was so abrupt that she blinked at him. She didn't know what to say to him and was almost grateful when the doorbell rang through the house again.

"I'd better get that," she mumbled. Allie took her time heading for the door, desperate for a moment alone to absorb what had just happened.

Mr. Sexy FBI Man had nearly kissed her. Her insides shivered as she relived that stunning moment when he had lowered his mouth to within a heartbeat of hers.

Those long dark lashes had slid nearly closed, hiding the intensity of his gray eyes, and she could smell the leathery scent of his aftershave.

She paused in front of the door, one hand splayed across her still-racing heart.

What was worse? That Gage McKinnon had nearly kissed her? Or that she had wanted him to, with a hunger that terrified her?

She didn't want to be so attracted to him. Working here was complicated enough without her entertaining silly fantasies about what it would have been like if he'd followed through on his intent.

Now wasn't the time to think about this, though. Not with the girls back. Putting thoughts of that almost-kiss behind her, she pasted on a smile for her daughters' sake and swung open the door.

To her shock, it wasn't the girls after all. It was one of the men who had brought Gage home from the hospital. Agent Davis, she thought she remembered, and he was giving her a stunning smile that would have completely flustered her if her nerves weren't already churning like a hive full of wet bumblebees.

''Hello,'' he said cheerfully.

''I...come in. Gage didn't say anything about expecting you.''

''That's because he didn't know I was coming. I had another errand to run up this way. Since he asked me to drop by some paperwork when I had the chance, I figured this was the perfect opportunity to check up on him.''

''I'm sure he'll be thrilled to have a visitor,'' she said, not sure of any such thing. ''He was just heading to his room.''

Wet hair, sexy mouth and all.

''He's getting around okay, then?''

''Relatively. It's not easy for him to squeeze through doorways and around furniture, but he's beginning to manage.''

She led him back to the bedroom and knocked on the closed door. ''Gage? You have company.''

Silence met her statement, then she thought she heard him sigh. ''Yeah? Who is it.''

Agent Davis grinned at her. ''Doesn't sound like two weeks off work has softened his disposition any.''

She smiled back at him, then felt a trifle disloyal, for some strange reason. ''He's still in a lot of pain.''

''Oh, is that it?''

She didn't answer him, just opened the door. "Your friend Agent Davis is here. I'll be in the kitchen if you need me."

Before she walked down the hall, she heard Davis greet him. "I brought those files you asked for. Personally I think you're crazy. Why not take the six-week vacation the Bureau gave you instead of spending your sick leave working cold cases?"

"I can't stand just staring at the walls all day," Gage answered. "With a phone and Internet access I can at least pretend to stay busy."

They closed the door after that and Allie couldn't hear more. It was enough, though. What she *had* heard left her cold.

Internet access. She'd never even thought about that. She wasn't sure just how the FBI worked, but she thought they probably disseminated information across the Net. What if her case file was already out there somewhere? Her picture, pictures of the girls?

Gage could probably access it right now if he wanted to.

She blew out a shaky breath. She should leave. Just grab the girls from the park and drive out of town.

Oh, she didn't want to. She had two weeks' wages coming to her in just a few days that she would forfeit if she disappeared, and she hadn't yet paid off the balance on the car repair Ruth's son had performed for her.

Besides that, she hated the idea of fleeing again. Not yet. She just wasn't ready, mentally or physically, to uproot the girls and herself and head for a strange town where she knew no one.

Could she take the chance that even if the FBI had posted her picture somewhere on-line, Gage wouldn't have any reason to go looking for it? Even if he stumbled upon it, she had created an effective disguise. There was no reason why he should connect blond nurse Alicia DeBarillas with gawky, glasses-wearing Lisa Connors.

Surely she was safe for a few more weeks, just long enough to pay Ruth's son and to make plans for the future.

That wasn't too much to ask, was it?

Chapter 8

"Care to tell me why you have such an interest in these particular case files?" With all the appearance of a man who looked like he was taking up residence, Davis settled into the recliner Lisa had dragged in from the living room earlier in the week.

Gage was so preoccupied with that almost kiss his words didn't register at first.

Where the hell had he stored his brain during that little interlude? He certainly hadn't been thinking about the ramifications of starting something with her, that was for sure.

If he had possessed one ounce of common sense, he would have hurried back to his room the moment she finished washing his hair. He didn't need to know all that personal history about her, about her diabetes and her father's rejection and her worries of not being able to care for her daughters if her disease progressed.

That was the problem with getting to know someone.

Once you learned private details like that about people, it was almost impossible to treat them like polite strangers.

Now he was afraid he had lost any chance to be able to continue viewing Lisa Connors with the cool distance he had carefully maintained this past week.

"McKinnon? Hello?"

He blinked away thoughts of her and turned his attention to Davis. "What was that?"

"The files. What's your interest in these particular cases?"

He glanced at the small stack his partner had placed on the table next to his laptop. "Why not? What else do I have to do but sit here all day and track down cold cases?"

"These aren't just cold, they're in a deep-freeze, man. Six unsolved kidnappings of young girls that happened twenty to twenty-five years ago. Are you thinking they might be linked?"

Gage scanned the folders, copies of files he had been slowly earmarking as long as he'd been with the FBI. "I'm just playing a hunch. There are certain similarities between them."

But plenty of disparities, too, he had to admit.

"What connection did you see? I'll admit I didn't go through every single page, I just looked at the case summaries. The only thing that jumped out at me was that they all happened in a four-state region—Idaho, Montana, Utah and Nevada."

"They have a few other links. All were taken in the afternoon from either their own yards or from a park close to their homes. And all the girls were blond, between the ages of three and twelve."

He pictured Charley, blond curls gleaming in the sun and her dimples winking at everyone she met.

"That's a wide age span if you're looking to profile a pedophile. Usually they favor a more specific age range."

He hated even considering the idea that his sweet baby sister might have ended up in the hands of somebody sick and twisted like that, but he had long ago accepted the odds were good that was exactly the kind of person who had taken her.

"I'm not looking to do anything other than study some old case files and see if I can find any fresh leads."

"Why these particular cases?"

"Their families deserve to know what happened to them. It's never too late for justice."

Davis cocked his head, and Gage had a feeling the man wasn't fooled. He should have realized Davis wouldn't settle for some superficial explanation. The other agent was a brilliant investigator with a reputation that rivaled Gage's own for stubborn determination. They had been roommates at Quantico and Gage figured the other man probably knew him better than anyone else alive.

He had few friends, so he tended to treasure the ones he had. Cale Davis was among the best.

"Any relation?" the agent finally asked.

He couldn't pretend ignorance. Not with Davis. He should have known the other agent would pick up on the last name on the tab of one of the files and manage to connect the dots. It was right there in black marker. Charlotte McKinnon. All that he had left of her was this slim manila folder full of a motley, pitifully slim assortment of facts.

"My sister."

He hoped that would be the end of it, but Davis met his abrupt statement with a glare. "How long have we known each other?"

"I don't know. A dozen years, maybe."

"And not once in all that time have you ever bothered to mention you even *had* a sister or any of the rest of this." He gestured to the case files with a jerky movement, and to his surprise, Gage realized the other man wasn't merely annoyed, he was angry.

"What would be the point?"

"Well, for one thing, it explains a whole hell of a lot about you."

"Like what? Why I'm such a son of a bitch most of the time?"

Cale grinned. "That, too."

Just as quickly as it flashed over his features, the grin disappeared and he sobered. "Maybe it helps explain why you do what you do. The Crimes Against Children assignment you fought so hard to get and won't let anybody take away. Why you make sure you're assigned to all the cases involving missing kids. The whole 'bloodhound' nickname, why you work like a dog until your cases are put to bed."

Gage shifted, uncomfortable with the whole discussion. So he had become a crusader of sorts at finding missing and abused children. What difference did that make when he was no closer to finding the one child who meant the most to him?

"You should have told me, McKinnon."

"Why?"

"Maybe I could have helped somehow. I'm assuming you've been working the case on your own time. If I know anything about the bloodhound, you've probably been working it on the side as long as you've been with the Bureau, am I right?"

"Yeah." Gage thought about the fruitless leads he'd followed up over the years, the clues that always led him exactly nowhere. The idea of sharing the investigation seemed foreign. This was a burden he carried alone and it was tough to think about sharing it.

"Made any progress?"

He thought of the leads he'd accumulated, a pitifully slim collection despite years of digging. Davis was right. Charlotte's case was stuck in a deep, dark freeze.

"Not much. I've mostly been going back over what's in the file to see if anything was missed by the original task force. A couple months ago I followed up on a possible sighting reported in Texas a few months after Charlotte disappeared. I reinterviewed the eyewitness, a convenience store clerk who reported twenty years ago that she thought she saw a girl resembling Charley come into her store with a woman."

"She remember anything new?"

"She's pushing eighty now and barely remembers the names of her own grandkids. Says the little girl had the same curly blond hair as the kid on the milk carton she saw and she remembered a lisp and a broken front tooth, something she never told the original investigators."

"I'm assuming your sister lisped."

"Yeah. And she broke a tooth just the day before she was kidnapped when she was trying to ride my kid brother's bike."

"Did she remember anything new about the woman?"

"No. According to the original report, she says the woman was in her midthirties and acted like she was drunk or stoned. That's why she remembered them in the first place, because the woman tried to walk out of the store with a gallon of milk hidden under her shirt. Before the clerk could call the police, the woman ran out of the store, dragging the kid with her."

Cale settled back in the recliner. Gage had worked with him enough to know the wheels in his head were spinning as he tried to work out connections in the case. "So what are you thinking might link that and these other five kidnappings?"

"I don't know. Probably nothing. Like I said, I'm just trying to play all the possibilities. Study every angle." It would probably be fruitless, just like every other lead he tried to follow in Charley's disappearance. But at least he felt like he was doing *something*. He hated the paralyzing helplessness of inaction.

"I wish you'd told me," Davis said again. "But I suppose it's not much of a surprise that you preferred to keep it to yourself, knowing what I do about you."

They spent the next few moments discussing the case files and bouncing theories off each other. Gage had to admit he was grateful for Davis's sharp insight. The other agent made several good suggestions about the direction he could take his unofficial inquiries.

He was busy writing them down when a knock sounded at his bedroom door. A moment later Lisa stuck her head inside.

"Sorry to interrupt but I wondered if Agent Davis planned to stay for dinner. I can easily fix enough for two."

"No, ma'am."

Gage wasn't sure why the charming smile Davis gave her annoyed him so much.

"Thanks, anyway," he went on, "but I've got dinner plans."

"Hot date?" Gage asked, a bite to his voice.

"Oh, yeah. You know that receptionist for the law firm on the second floor?"

"No."

Cale rolled his eyes. "You're the only male with a heartbeat in the entire building who hasn't noticed her, then. Italian. Long, curly dark hair, lush lips, big, soulful brown eyes.''

''Sorry. Doesn't ring any bells.''

''And you call yourself an FBI agent.'' He grinned at Lisa again. ''It baffles me how the man can be such a genius at his job but still be completely oblivious to the rest of the world. Or the female half of it, anyway.''

Lisa's gaze flashed to his and he could see the memory of the kiss they had almost shared in her eyes.

He wondered what Davis would say if he told him he noticed plenty of things about at least one female in his life. That she nurtured everyone she came in contact with. That she smelled like spring. That her eyes made him think of walking through a mountain meadow full of wildflowers.

An appealing blush spread over her features. Something else he'd noticed about her before, that she certainly colored up easier than most brunettes he knew. But maybe Lisa Connors had unusually sensitive skin.

For all his astuteness, Cale seemed oblivious to the undercurrents ebbing and flowing through the room. He rose from the chair. ''Anyway, thanks again for the dinner invitation but I really should be heading back to the city. Wouldn't want to keep Teresa waiting.''

''Thank you for dropping off the files,'' Gage said.

''Not a problem.'' Davis turned serious again. ''Hey, let me know if you need somebody to run interviews out in the field on any of these cases until you're up to it again. I'd be willing to help any way I could. I hope you know that.''

Gage only nodded, touched by the sincerity of the offer. He never would have believed it, but he was actually glad the other man now knew about Charlotte.

Uncomfortable with the depth of his emotion, he was

relieved when Lisa offered to show Davis out. The two of them walked from the room, leaving him alone with the frozen remains of his sister's case.

Sometimes memory lane could be a dark and lonely road.

Allie leaned against the brass headboard of her bed and gazed at the pictures in the single photo album she had allowed herself to pack along that frenzied night when she and the girls fled their Philadelphia home. Forcing herself to choose only one to take with them had been agonizing but she had to hope whoever might eventually go through their things at the brownstone would save the pictures.

This was all she had left of Jaime. A few photographs, an old shirt she still liked to sleep in and her memories. And the girls. She couldn't forget her girls. They were a precious piece of him, a gift that reminded her daily of the loving marriage they had enjoyed so briefly.

She turned the page then smiled at the images there. On one side was a picture of Jaime sleeping with a tiny Anna curled up on his chest. The other showed a smiling Jaime during the trip they'd taken to Florida just a few weeks before his accident. He and Gaby were building a sandcastle, heads bent close together, and the sun gilded their dark hair.

She remembered that day vividly—the cry of the gulls overhead, the waves brushing the shore, the scent of sand and sea and sunscreen and her own fierce happiness.

She traced his dark, lean features. The pain and loss were still there but somehow tonight they didn't seem as intense as usual, more like a quiet, hollow sadness than the howling, raging anguish she had known right after he was killed. It was all part of the grieving process, she knew. Hearts eventually begin to heal, sorrow to fade.

She didn't want to heal, though. It seemed so much more safe to stay in the secure, isolated harbor of her pain.

Allie sighed and traced Jaime's features again. She supposed she didn't need a degree in psychology to figure out why she had pulled this photo album out of the drawer, tonight of all nights. If she had any question, all she had to do was look for the answer out the fluttering curtains at the window toward the house next door. She only had to remember those breathless moments when Gage McKinnon had nearly kissed her.

She was scared. Plain and simple. Terrified of the needs and wants beginning to stir to life within her like the colorful splash of crocuses breaking through snow.

She had thought herself frozen forever after Jaime's death, had believed that all her desires had been trapped for eternity on some barren, lonely tundra somewhere. That had been fine. She had wanted it that way. But now her unwilling attraction to Gage was forcing her back into warmth, like the sweet breath of spring blowing through all the corners of her life, thawing her frozen edges.

When she thought he would kiss her back in the kitchen earlier, her blood had churned through her, thick and slow, waking all those dormant needs. How could she possibly put them back to sleep now?

What other choice did she have, though? Gage McKinnon was *not* the man to help her feel alive again. He was surly and bad-tempered and aloof. Besides that, he was an FBI agent! The last man on the planet she should be thinking about in any kind of romantic way.

All the rationalizations in the world couldn't change the chemistry between them. He was attracted to her and she, heaven help her, shared that attraction.

So what was she supposed to do about it? Just go on ignoring that sizzle under her skin, pretend that her heartbeat didn't race whenever she was in the room with him, that her body didn't instinctively sway toward him whenever she was close to him?

She would have to. Either that or quit.

Before she could follow up on that line of thought, through the open window she heard a loud crash coming from next door.

She froze for a moment, then thrust the scrapbook away and rushed to the window. A light burned in Gage's room but she could see no movement through the blinds.

Had he fallen? He must have—what else would have made such a horrendous commotion?

For an instant she hovered at the window, torn about what to do. Her instincts snapped at her to get her butt in gear and go see what had happened. But she knew how ferociously proud and independent he was, how he hated needing her help.

"Gage?" she called softly. "Is everything okay?"

He didn't answer and she mentally consigned his pride to the devil. She couldn't stay here, not if he was hurt.

Her heart pounding, she rushed next door, heedless of the wet slap of grass against her bare feet, then the cool rough bricks of his sidewalk.

After unlocking his door, she paused inside. "Gage?" she called. "Where are you? Is everything okay?"

Silence met her call for several seconds, then he answered in an aggravated voice. "Go away. I'm fine."

Despite his cross tone, she thought she could hear pain threading through his voice. Ignoring his command, she headed through the living room toward the light she saw burning in the kitchen.

In the doorway she gasped to find him sprawled in front

of the open refrigerator, the wheelchair on its side next to him. The half gallon of milk she'd bought earlier in the day was on the floor beside him, now half-empty. The rest of it puddled on the floor and soaked his T-shirt.

She realized at a glance what must have happened. It looked as if he had wheeled himself into the kitchen for a snack and had reached too far into the refrigerator and lost his balance, tipping the chair and ending up on the floor.

She rushed to him and righted the wheelchair.

"Don't you have anything better to do with your time than lurk outside my door in the middle of the night waiting to barge in where you're not needed?"

"Apparently not," she murmured, biting back a sharper reply when she saw the lines of pain etched around his mouth.

"I can do this," he snapped when she reached down to help him back into the wheelchair.

He was likely frustrated and hurting, she thought, and forced herself to step back and hold the chair steady while he hefted himself with his arms back inside.

"I could have done it alone eventually. I just couldn't reach the brake to set it, and the damn chair kept slipping away from me."

"Did you reinjure anything?"

"I don't think so."

Just his colossal masculine pride, she would wager. She tried to keep that in mind while she unobtrusively did a visual check of his casts. She couldn't see anything out of the ordinary. "Be sure you tell me if you experience any unusual swelling or pain, okay?"

"Sure. Good night."

She sighed at the clear dismissal in his tone. He obviously wanted her gone, but she wasn't quite ready to leave him until she was sure he hadn't aggravated his injuries. "Is there something I can get for you out of the fridge while I'm here?"

Though he looked for a moment as if he would stubbornly refuse any further help, after a moment he answered. "I was reaching for a piece of that cherry pie you made the other day."

"Let me get you a dry shirt to change into and then I'll cut a slice for you."

In the laundry room off the kitchen, she found a pile of folded T-shirts neatly stacked on the dryer where she'd left them, since she hadn't wanted to bother Gage while the other FBI agent had been there by returning them to the drawers in his bedroom. The one on top was a soft navy-blue cotton shirt with FBI emblazoned on the front in white letters.

She grabbed it and returned to the kitchen, then had to stop in the doorway, swallowing hard. He had taken off the damp shirt and now sat with his chair pulled to the kitchen table, completely bare-chested.

Oh, mercy.

Hard, tight muscles rippled in every direction, without an ounce of fat in sight. How could his shoulders be so impossibly broad? They filled the wheelchair with no room to spare.

Her pulse fluttered and the blood seemed to rush from her head. Exasperated at herself—at the reaction she didn't want to feel but couldn't seem to control—she tossed the shirt at him.

"There you go. Clean and dry."

She picked up the wet shirt where he'd left it on the counter and carried it back into the laundry room. While there, she gave herself a stern lecture about keeping her hormones in check.

It almost worked. At least by the time she returned to the kitchen again—where all those delicious muscles were now safely covered up, she saw with relief—she was almost certain she could carry on a halfway coherent conversation.

"Would you like ice cream with your pie?"

"No. Pie is fine. Thanks."

She sliced a piece and heated it in the microwave for a few seconds then poured him a glass of milk. She set them in front of him, then took a seat next to him at the table.

"Looks like there's plenty for two if you'd like a piece."

"Better not. I've had more than my share of sweets today."

He took a sip of milk. "You must have built up incredible willpower over the years."

"Not really. It's all about learning how to stay away from things you know aren't good for you."

Or people. So what was she doing sitting alone in Gage McKinnon's kitchen with him when she knew perfectly well he was worse for her system than eating that entire pie by herself.

"Look, I'm sorry for snapping at you before," he said after a moment. "Believe it or not, I really do appreciate you coming over. If you hadn't, I probably would have been on the floor for a while before I managed to make it back up."

She knew the admission was hard for him so she didn't say anything.

"How did you know something was wrong, anyway?" he asked. "You don't have some secret baby monitor set up somewhere that I don't know about, do you?"

"No, but that's not a bad idea," she said with a laugh.

"Actually, my bedroom window was open. I was awake and heard the crash through the open windows over here. I'm glad you weren't seriously hurt."

He made a wry face. "Couldn't sleep, huh?"

She hoped he had no inkling why she had still been up at this hour, that she couldn't forget that moment when they had nearly kissed. She'd been too busy thinking about *him* to get any rest.

Heat soaked her cheeks and she prayed fervently that he wouldn't notice. "Um, no. Neither could you, I guess."

"It's tough to find a comfortable position flat on my back. I'm more of a side sleeper."

"Maybe we can talk to the physical therapist or your orthopedist. We might be able to rig something up with pillows or something so you can lie on your side."

Before he could answer, she noticed something she'd overlooked earlier. "Oh! Your hand is bleeding. Why didn't you tell me?"

His fingers curled over his palm. "It's no big deal. Just a scratch. I think I might have caught it on the fridge shelf on my way down."

"You should have said something. We need to clean that up and put some disinfectant on it."

"I can do it."

She made a face. "But *will* you? That's the question. It will only take a moment for me to get some first-aid supplies."

She hurried to the bathroom and found disinfectant, antibiotic cream and bandages in the medicine chest. Back in the kitchen, she pulled her chair close to him and took his hand in hers, trying not to notice the warm strength of his fingers in hers.

"It might hurt a little," she warned.

His laugh sounded gruff. ''With all my other aches and pains right now, I probably won't notice a thing.''

Still, he winced a little when she wiped the wound clean. ''Sorry,'' she murmured and slowly blew on it to ease the sting.

''I'll live.'' His voice had a rough, husky note she hadn't noticed earlier. She glanced up and found him watching her, his eyes a murky gray. Something about the expression in those gray depths sent her pulse racing, her stomach fluttering.

Heat sparked between them like dry lightning, and the room suddenly felt airless. His gaze fastened on her mouth and she hitched in a breath. He wanted to kiss her again and, oh, how she wanted to let him!

She wasn't consciously aware of leaning toward him, of tugging his hand to pull him closer, but she must have because she found herself nearly in his lap. He growled an oath and an instant later his mouth found hers.

A hint of cherries lingered on his lips, tart and sweet and delicious, and she craved it suddenly, wanted to relish every taste.

A part of her mind warned her this was a colossal mistake, but she ignored it, lost in the wonder of reawakened desire. Later she would have time for regrets but for now she simply wanted to *feel.*

Chapter 9

What was wrong with him?

He had spent a week telling himself he had no business being attracted to his lovely neighbor. Hell, more than that, he'd spent a *lifetime* keeping women like her at a safe distance. Women with soft, needy eyes and trunks full of emotional baggage and *children*.

And now here he was tangling tongues with the woman. Tasting the sweet minty traces of toothpaste in her mouth, inhaling the scent of violets that clung to her, basking in the warmth that surrounded her in a soft, hazy cloud.

One part of his brain knew it was a mistake kissing her like this—knew damn well that he would be swamped with regret just as soon as he could manage to wrench his mouth from hers—but the rest of him wanted nothing more than to tug her onto his lap and fill his hands with her softness and heat.

He couldn't remember the last time he had tasted anything as sweet as Lisa Connors. If he ever had.

With a soft, erotic moan, she kissed him back with an enthusiasm that took his breath away.

Had he imagined that first quick flash of panic he thought he had glimpsed in the depths of her blue eyes just before their mouths connected? He must have.

She didn't seem anything close to panicked now—her hands were wrapped around his neck, her small, unbound breasts pressed against him, and her mouth kissed him with a hunger that matched his own.

It was easy to lose track of time. He had no idea how long they stayed that way, tangled together in his kitchen while the night breeze fluttered the kitchen curtains through the open window and the only sound was their rapid breathing mingling together and the occasional erotic murmur she made against his mouth.

As long as he could continue to pretend he didn't hear the warning bells in his head, he would have been content to spend all night kissing her. But suddenly she shifted position—not much, but enough to softly bump against his left leg, the one with the compound fracture.

The quick, sharp stab of pain worked better than jumping into a cold, mountain lake to yank him back to his senses.

What in the hell is wrong with you?

This time the voice barked harsh and loud, and he knew he couldn't ignore it any longer. He drew back, wishing he could put more distance between them than merely to slide a few inches farther into the blasted wheelchair. He could taste her on his lips, still feel her heat surrounding him like seductive chains.

He wanted to run for the door, to jump into his Jeep and head as far and as fast as he could. Since he was stuck in the damn chair, he forced himself to face her with a studied casualness at strict odds with the torrent of emotions surging through him.

"You'd better hurry back next door before your girls wake up and find you gone."

He might as well have just picked her up and tossed her into that mountain lake he'd been thinking about earlier. At his casual tone, she stared at him, her blue eyes wide and her mouth still swollen from his kiss.

"Wh-what?"

"Your kids. You shouldn't leave them alone at night, even for the few minutes it takes to rescue your idiot of a neighbor who can't even manage to get a midnight snack for himself."

He forced himself to ignore the baffled shock in her eyes at his cool dismissal of their kiss, and the flash of hurt and dismay that followed it.

"You…you're right. I need to leave." She bounced up so forcefully the kitchen chair she'd been sitting in toppled backward with a crash that would have made him jump if he hadn't already been holding himself in such tight control.

With her color high, she righted it again, her gaze focused everywhere in the kitchen but him. "Um, your hand should be fine. Just try to keep it clean. I…good night."

Without another word, she rushed out of the kitchen. A few seconds later he heard the front door click shut, and he screwed his eyes shut, painfully aware of the tantalizing hint of violets lingering in the air and the hot craving in his gut.

He wanted her. Desire churned and bubbled through his blood, and he was hard and aching. He could have gone on kissing her forever. Worse, in a heartbeat, he would have taken things beyond kissing. If he could have figured out a way to work around the blasted casts, he could have shimmied her out of those shorts and had her on top of him, around him.

He groaned just thinking about it. He was damn lucky things hadn't progressed that far. If kissing her was a mistake, making love would have been utter disaster.

Lisa Connors was soft, tender, nurturing. And he was a complete son of a bitch.

He had wounded her by his casual dismissal of their kiss. He knew it, had seen the shadows of hurt in those expressive blue eyes. What else could he have done, though?

Things were better this way. If he had to pretend those heated moments had left no effect on him, he could fake with the best of them.

Maybe he had fooled her enough that she would forget the hunger in their kiss and think he hadn't been affected by it. He didn't want a repeat of those few incredible moments. He couldn't afford it. She was already sneaking her way under his defenses, softening him in a way that scared the hell out of him.

He would just have to make sure their mouths never tangled like this again. Even if the thought of never again sampling that sweetness left him restless and hungry and filled with a vast, empty ache.

"Mommy, why doesn't Mr. McDonalds like us?"

Gaby's question came out of the blue. One minute she was shaping a wad of play dough into something roughly the shape of a dinosaur, the next she was looking intently across the kitchen table at her mother and throwing something like that at her.

For a moment Allie didn't know what she was talking about. Who was Mr. McDonalds? An instant later, realization hit. She winced and sent a quick look down the hallway to make sure Gage's bedroom door was closed and he was safely out of earshot. ''Do you mean Mr. McKinnon?''

''Yeah. How come he doesn't like Anna and me?''

''I'm sure he does, sweetheart.''

Gaby shook her head hard enough that her thick, glossy braids swung in every direction, whapping her on the side of the face. ''Does not. I don't think he likes little girls very much.''

Or their mothers. Especially the ones who baby him and moon over him and kiss him in the quiet hush of a late-night kitchen.

She sighed. Since their kiss the night before, Gage hadn't exchanged more than a few words with her, just enough to inform her tensely that he didn't want breakfast. He had work to do in his room, he said, and didn't want to be disturbed.

It was now close to lunchtime and he had effectively ignored her most of the morning. This stalemate couldn't possibly go on all day. He needed to eat and he also needed her help with his home regimen of physical therapy exercises.

Eventually she would have to beard the cranky lion in his den but she had delayed as long as she could, especially when just being in the same room with him left her nerves raw and her thoughts scrambling.

She turned back to Gaby and forced a smile. Children could be remarkably perceptive to the subtle nuances flowing around them, far more intuitive than most people gave them credit for.

''I'm sure he likes you and Anna just fine, honey. You know how when you don't feel well it can sometimes put you in a bad mood? Mr. McKinnon's broken legs hurt him a lot.''

"So he's grumpy to me and Anna because his legs hurt?"

"And maybe because he's not used to being around little girls much. He's not lucky enough to have any of his own."

Gaby appeared to think this over, her hands busy with the play dough. "Maybe we could play some games with him, like you do with me when I'm sick. Do you think he would play Chutes and Ladders with us?"

Heaven forbid! "Maybe when he's feeling a little better, okay? In the meantime, you and Anna can help by doing just what you've done already—being the best girls you can be. Can you do that?"

Gaby nodded, then poked her sister until Anna looked up from the blue snake she was rolling out and nodded, too.

"Good. Now I'm going to go see what Mr. McKinnon wants for lunch, okay?"

"Okay," Gaby said cheerfully. "I hope it's S'ghettios 'cause me and Anna really, really want S'ghettios."

She smiled, imagining Gage McKinnon's face if she showed up at his door with canned pasta for lunch. "Even if he wants something different, I can still fix Spaghettios for the two of you if that's really what you want."

Both Gaby and Anna nodded vigorously and Allie couldn't resist tugging their shiny dark braids. "It's a deal, then."

If she had her way, she would stay right here in this sun-warmed kitchen and roll out play dough with her girls for the rest of the day. But she knew she couldn't hide out here like a scared little mouse. Avoiding Gage would only make matters worse, only delay the inevitable and make their eventual confrontation that much harder.

With a deep breath for courage, she rose from the table

and walked to his bedroom door. Inside she could hear the low murmur of CNN and the clicking of computer keys. Before she could talk herself out of it, she rapped on the door.

After an excruciatingly long pause while she wondered if her knock had been a shade too timid, he finally spoke, his voice gruff. ‘‘Yeah?’’

She eased open the door and found him in the recliner, his legs in their bulky casts outstretched and his laptop propped on a pillow across his lap. He met her gaze and her stomach started that darn trembling again. Really, this was ridiculous!

‘‘I'm sorry to interrupt but it's nearly lunchtime. I have some turkey cold cuts and can make you a sandwich or there are some chicken enchiladas left over from yesterday. Whatever sounds better.’’

‘‘I don't care. Anything is fine.’’

Despite the nerves fluttering through her like a flock of meadowlarks in the backyard, she couldn't help a teasing smile. ‘‘How about Spaghettios, then?’’

He raised an eyebrow. ‘‘A sandwich would do.’’ After a moment he added, ‘‘Thank you.’’

‘‘You're welcome.’’

She paused, gathering her thoughts and her courage while she tried to figure out how to face the topic they were both circling around as if it were a feral wolverine. Her silence dragged out long enough that he finally sent her an impatient look. ‘‘Was there something else?’’

This shouldn't be so hard. It was only a kiss, for heaven's sake. She should just let it rest—let the wild creature they had unleashed crawl back into his hole on its own—but she was afraid this awkwardness would continue between them if they didn't deal with what had happened the night before. How was she supposed to do her job if the man couldn't bear to be in the same room with her?

With a heavy sigh she settled onto the edge of the bed that he had somehow managed to make neatly, even from a wheelchair.

"Do you want me to quit?" she asked bluntly.

He stared at her. "What?"

"I like working here but I will go back to cleaning houses for Ruth if you don't want me around anymore."

A muscle in his jaw worked. "I don't want a keeper. It has nothing to do with you."

"What about last night?"

"What about it?" he asked with a wariness that would have made her smile under other circumstances.

"It's going to be a little tough to help you with your physical therapy exercises if you can't bear to be in the same room with me because of this…awkwardness between us."

"Is that what you call it?"

"We both made a mistake last night. Can't we just leave it at that and go back to the way things were before?"

Gage studied her sitting on his bed with her little wire-rimmed glasses perched on her nose and her long legs crossed at the ankle. A mistake. Yeah, he would definitely call their kiss a mistake. One that had haunted him and left him tossing and turning all night long—as much as he could toss and turn with two casts on his legs.

He wanted nothing more than to repeat the same damn mistake right this moment—to capture that soft mouth under his, to taste her sweetness again, to press her back on that bed until both of them were hot and sweaty and sated.

Her next words yanked him out of the fantasy. "I would like to think we could be friends," she murmured.

He gazed at her, surprised by the shade of vulnerability in her columbine eyes. She meant her words, he realized. All this talk wasn't just about keeping her job.

To a man who kept most people at arm's length by choice—who had only a few people he considered more than acquaintances—the idea of mourning a friendship that had never really begun seemed alien.

"Friendships are important to you, aren't they?"

Her smile was small and a little sad. "I haven't had the chance to make many of them since we've been in Utah. I would hate to lose one of the few I've found."

He wasn't sure he was capable of being friends with a woman who had the power to fire his blood. But if she was willing to try after he'd been such a bastard the night before, he didn't see how he could close the door to it. "There's no reason for you to quit over a kiss unless you're uncomfortable working for me."

"I'm not." Though she sounded confident enough, she managed to avoid his gaze.

"Good. That's settled, then. End of discussion. We don't need to bring it up again."

She opened her mouth as if she wanted to say something else but she closed it again just as the doorbell rang out front. She rose from the bed with her typical fluid grace and looked as relieved as he was that their awkward discussion was over. "That's probably Ruth. She talked about stopping by today to work on her flowers."

What ever happened to his nice, solitary life? Suddenly he found himself with a houseful of people, entertaining visitor after visitor and collecting friends he didn't know what to do with.

Lisa gave him a quick smile then hurried from the room to answer the doorbell before her girls could get to it.

A few moments later, just when he was trying to force himself to focus on the computer screen again, she reappeared at his bedroom door, an odd expression on her delicate features.

''Um, Gage. Sorry to disturb you again but it wasn't Ruth at the door.''

''Who was it?''

She stepped aside, and a tall, lanky man moved forward. For a moment Gage could only stare at his brother, Wyatt, the last person on earth he expected to show up at his house.

Just as they did every time he saw the brother who had become a stranger to him in the past twenty years, a torrent of emotions washed over him.

Love and regret and loss. Above all, a vast, overwhelming guilt.

He was helpless to keep them away and he hated it. That was one of the reasons he avoided these tense encounters whenever possible, why he had maintained a careful distance between them since their parents' divorce, a year after Charley's kidnapping, when he was thirteen and Wyatt was a gangly, awkward ten.

He had seen his brother on only a handful of occasions since then, the last time two years ago at their father's place in Las Vegas when one of his visits with the old man happened to coincide with a visit of Wyatt's, who had been in town researching another in his string of best-selling true-crime books. It had been an awkward and uncomfortable few days, and Gage had been grateful when a break in a case had called him away.

So why was Wyatt standing in the doorway to his bedroom looking like some kind of cowboy scholar in worn Tony Lamas and wire-rim glasses and ready to spit nails?

"If your legs weren't already broken, I'd be tempted to do it for you," Wyatt snapped.

Gage blinked at the unexpected attack. It didn't escape his attention that Lisa had tactfully slipped away, leaving him completely at his brother's mercy. "Good to see you too, bro."

"What the hell is wrong with you?"

"Too many things to count."

"So I make what I expect to be a routine stop at the FBI office in Salt Lake City, trying to track down some paperwork for the latest case I'm writing about. While I'm there minding my own business, somebody mentions the name Gage McKinnon. Imagine my surprise when not only do I find out that my only brother has been transferred to Utah and has been living just an hour away for the past two months but I also learn he suffered a major injury in the line of duty, all without saying a single word to the rest of his family."

"It's no big deal."

"Maybe not to you but it sure would be to Mom. You should have called her, at least to let her know you were living just over the mountains. She would have wanted to know. Hell, Gage. How many times do you have to break the woman's heart?"

He didn't need this. His relationship with their mother was even more complicated than the prickly one he had with Wyatt. He knew he hurt Lynn with the careful distance he maintained between them but he just couldn't bear being around her and seeing the soft hurt in her eyes.

"Back off, Wyatt."

"You should have called her," his brother repeated.

"Would it have been that tough? A simple phone call once in a while to let her know you're still alive?"

While talking to Wyatt might spark this storm of emotions, seeing his mother was like standing in the eye of a hurricane. If he thought she really wanted to see him, he would have made more of an effort over the years to stay in touch with her. But he'd long ago accepted that their brief, tense encounters were as painful for Lynn as for him. No, this self-imposed exile was best for everyone concerned.

"I'm doing fine."

Wyatt studied him for a moment then plopped onto the edge of the bed. "What happened to you, anyway? The guys at the Bureau weren't feeling exactly chatty."

Gage sighed, recognizing the signs of someone settling in for the long haul. "A stupid rookie mistake. I was an idiot and let myself get injured by a suspect trying to flee an arrest. But I'm just cruising right along now on the road to recovery. You can tell Lynn that."

"Why don't you pick up the phone and tell her yourself?"

"Fine. I'll call her." Though he dreaded the idea, he would be willing to do it just to get Wyatt off his back. "How is she doing, anyway?"

"Good. She misses teaching but seems to enjoy being the big, bad Liberty Elementary School principal."

"Small-town life still agrees with her, then?"

"She's happy in Liberty, with her old friends and family around her. Most of her family, anyway."

Gage ignored the jibe just as he tried to ignore the headache brewing at his temples. "I read your latest book. *Shadow of Fear.*"

"Yeah?"

For one painful instant something about the quick expression flitting across Wyatt's features reminded Gage of the skinny kid in the thick horn-rim glasses showing off a bug he'd identified or his newly acquired skill at riding a two-wheeler.

Before that August day when everything safe and secure in their life had sheared away like wet sandstone crumbling into the sea, Wyatt used to follow him everywhere. It had been a pain in the neck, really, for a twelve-year-old punk who considered himself too cool to have a nerdy kid brother for a constant shadow.

Wyatt didn't make friends as easily as Gage had in those days. He'd been gangly and bookish. A little shy, maybe.

When they moved to Vegas at the beginning of the summer so their father could open his own cabinet-making shop, Gage had no trouble hooking up with the neighborhood gang.

Wyatt hadn't been so lucky. Gage could remember his kid brother following him and his new buddies to the movies, to ball practice, to their hideout in Joey Scarletto's basement, where they spent most of their time sneaking Mrs. Scarletto's filtered cigarettes and talking about girls.

Maybe because he had treated Wyatt with such scorn back then, he wanted to atone a little for the smart-ass punk he'd been.

"I can see why it was on bestseller lists for so many weeks," he said now. "Why they all have been. Eight so far, right?"

Wyatt nodded, looking faintly embarrassed but pleased at the same time.

"You're good. I worked the fringes of the Highway Killer case in Sacramento. In your book, you managed to crawl inside Barry Sommers's head better than the profilers who helped catch him."

"It wasn't a very pleasant place to be."

"So why do it?"

"Why are you the FBI's bloodhound, always working crimes against children?" Wyatt countered.

He had no answer to that but he was fairly sure his brother wasn't really looking for one. To his relief he was spared from having to come up with one when Lisa showed up in the doorway again. Gage had to admit he didn't like the way his brother sat a little straighter and watched her with undeniable masculine interest in his eyes.

"Lunchtime," she said in her low, musical voice.

She had two plates, he saw with resignation, brimming high with sandwiches, pasta salad and chips, which meant he wouldn't be able to get rid of his brother anytime soon.

"Can I get you something to drink?" she asked, smiling at Wyatt. "There's cola, bottled water and I think there might be a few stray bottles of beer in the back of the refrigerator."

He returned her smile with an engaging one of his own that reminded Gage painfully of their mother. Apparently Wyatt had inherited all of Lynn's charm.

"A cola would be terrific," Wyatt said. "This all looks delicious. Thanks."

Lisa set the lunch tray on the table, then left again, leaving behind that sweet, alluring scent of violets.

"You've certainly become domesticated since the last time I saw you," Wyatt said after she had walked out. "Quite a cozy setup you've got here. Room service and everything."

Gage gave his brother what he hoped was a warning

frown. "She's my next-door neighbor and hired babysitter until I can get around a little better. That's it."

"You sure? I'm definitely picking up a vibe here."

Their kiss the night before whispered into his mind, lush and sensual and intense. Yeah, there was a vibe between him and Lisa Connors. He didn't want it and sure didn't like it but he couldn't deny it was there, simmering and percolating between them every time they were together.

He wanted her with a fierceness that scared the hell out of him, but he wasn't about to share any of that with the kid brother he barely knew.

"The only vibe you're picking up is the one warning you to leave it alone. She's a nice lady with a couple little kids who's been dealt a tough hand."

Wyatt looked as if he wanted to press him, but she returned with their drinks before he could. When she left again, Gage moved in quickly to distract him from the topic. "You said you stopped by the Bureau researching your next book. What are you working on?"

Though his brother obviously wasn't a naive nine-year-old anymore and didn't look fooled by the transparent ploy, he answered readily enough. "The Hunter Bradshaw case."

"The Salt Lake City cop who killed three people last summer?"

"Yeah. That's the one. I'm just doing the preliminary research right now. It's a fascinating case."

"I was in San Francisco at the time but even there it made headlines. It's not often a decorated police detective winds up on death row."

They spent the next half hour over lunch discussing the details of the Bradshaw case and other cases where the orbits of their respective careers had collided, however briefly. Gage was surprised to find himself actually relaxing in his brother's company, for the first time he could remember as an adult. He was almost sorry when Lisa came back in.

"Can I get you anything else? Another sandwich, maybe? There's still some cherry pie left and I've got chocolate chip cookies, too."

Wyatt glanced at his watch. "I've actually got to run. I have an appointment back in the city. But thanks. Everything tasted great."

"No problem." She smiled at him again, then started to collect their lunch dishes.

"Thanks for stopping by. It was good to see you," Gage said, a little surprised that he meant the words.

"You should call Mom."

Okay, maybe he spoke too soon. "Yeah, yeah."

Wyatt narrowed his eyes at him. "Would it be so damaging to your lone wolf image to let your mother know you're still alive once in a while? Not only alive but living just an hour from home."

"Liberty might be your home but it's not mine."

"You lived there for the first twelve years of your life. That's got to count for something."

Gage had a sudden memory of his grandfather's cattle ranch where he'd lived until that summer his folks had moved them all to Las Vegas. It had been a great life for a kid—horseback rides, floating on inner tubes in the irrigation canal, overnight fishing trips into the Uintas with Wyatt and their father and grandfather.

All before a jagged tear had been ripped through their world.

"You're going to be late for your appointment," he said with a pointed look.

"Right. I'm going. Thank you again for the lunch,

ma'am.'' He smiled at Lisa once more, all lanky cowboy charm, then walked from the room.

Gage told himself he was glad that awkward visit was over, but still he felt a little pang in his heart for the nine-year-old kid who used to look at him as if he was a hero.

Chapter 10

After Gage's brother left, Allie fought the urge to dump the lunch dishes all over her stubborn employer's lap.

What on earth was wrong with the man?

He had a family close by—a mother and a brother, anyway—and he hadn't even bothered to let them know he was injured and needed help. Allie couldn't even contemplate it. From what she had overheard, it sounded as if they didn't even know he'd taken an assignment in Utah.

It wasn't fair. In the past year she would have given anything to have a family to lean on during her custody battle with Jaime's parents. And here was blasted stubborn Gage McKinnon, who apparently had a family ready and willing—eager, even—to help him during his time of need and he just shoved them away.

She wanted to smack some sense into his big, stupid head.

It wasn't her business, she reminded herself. She was

just the hired help. If he wanted to keep the whole world at arm's length, he certainly had that right.

That didn't stop her from wanting to give him a good piece of her mind. With effort she chomped hard on her tongue to keep her words in check while she finished piling everything onto the tray, aware of Gage watching her brisk movements, his expression closed, as usual.

"I wanted to do some of my exercises," he said just as she headed for the kitchen with the dishes. "After you're done with those, do you think you might have a minute to help me?"

She drew in a breath and reined in her temper, knowing how much he hated to ask for anything. "Sure. The girls have finished their lunch and are going over to play at Jessica's house for a while."

By the time she loaded the lunch dishes into the dishwasher and returned to his room, some of her anger had faded. She couldn't know the dynamics of his family. Maybe he had good reason for keeping them in the dark about his life.

His brother had seemed a decent enough sort, though. Very nice, with a smile she had to admit had been charming and easygoing. Wyatt must have gotten all the charm in the family.

She glanced at Gage, who had transferred to the bed in preparation for their home therapy session and was now stretched out, his long body nearly hanging off the bed. Okay, maybe Wyatt had a smile that was something spectacular, but she had to admit he certainly didn't make her weak-kneed and jittery the way his brother did.

Whatever else might be amiss in the McKinnon family, they certainly had some fine genes to turn out two such very sexy male specimens.

She smiled a little at the thought and then felt the heat of Gage glaring at her. ''What?''

''You could at least pretend you don't enjoy these little torture sessions,'' he growled.

She couldn't help laughing at his disgruntled tone. ''What's not to enjoy? You're so cheerful to work with.''

He made a face and she took pity on him and told him the truth. ''Actually, I was thinking about something else. I'm sorry. Are you ready to start?''

He nodded and began with the range of motion exercises ordered by the physical therapist. Halfway through the first rep she stopped abruptly.

''Your brother is Wyatt McKinnon!'' she said suddenly, as all the pieces clicked together.

He grunted. ''So they tell me.''

''The author Wyatt McKinnon?''

''That's the one.''

''I've read several of his books. They're gripping! I'm not usually into true-crime books but a friend recommended *The Hunted* and after that I was completely hooked. Oh, I wish I'd had more of a chance to talk to him about his work.''

He had a strange expression on his face, one she couldn't quite identify. Pride was there, she thought, and maybe resignation. And even a little jealousy, though she thought she must be mistaken on that one. ''Yeah, the kid has done pretty well for himself.''

''And he lives here in Utah? I didn't realize.''

''About an hour away from here. Last I knew, he bought a place near our mother's family ranch in Ogden Valley. Little town named Liberty.''

''Why didn't he know about your injury?''

''I guess because I didn't tell him.''

''Or your mother. Why not?''

He was silent for so long she thought he wasn't going to answer. When he spoke, his voice was tight and distant. "We're not close. After our parents split up, I stayed in Las Vegas with our dad, and Wyatt moved back to Utah with our mother. We haven't seen much of each other in the years since."

"How old were you when your parents divorced?"

He didn't look thrilled at her nosy barrage of questions but he still answered her. "Thirteen. Wyatt would have been ten."

The year after their sister was kidnapped. The two events—his sister's disappearance and his parents' divorce—had to be connected.

Compassion for the boy he had been washed through her. He had lost not only his sister in a terrible, hideous way, but his younger brother when their family broke up.

And from what she could gather, his mother, too.

All the more reason why he should welcome the chance to reconcile with them while they were living so close.

Stay out of it, common sense warned inside her head. *Mind your own business.* She listened to it for a moment but finally discarded the advice. How could she heed it when she had sensed the tension in him while Wyatt had been here, when she had seen the tangle of emotions in his eyes as he looked at his younger brother.

"Why don't you get along with your mother and brother? Besides the fact that you apparently don't get along with anybody?" she added with a teasing smile.

A muscle flexed in his jaw. "I get along with them fine. We just live separate lives."

"Why is that?" she persisted. "I didn't mean to eavesdrop, but from the way Wyatt spoke, it sounded as if your mother will be heartbroken when she finds out you were hurt and didn't let her know you needed help."

"Wyatt doesn't know what he's talking about. And neither do you." He spoke through gritted teeth, but she wasn't sure if that was because of the topic of conversation or because of the exercises.

"Maybe not," she said after a moment. "But I'm a mother and I know that if one of my girls needed me, I would crawl across a thousand miles of broken glass, bloodthirsty wild animals and enemy sniper fire to reach them, no matter what it took."

"This is different. I'm a grown man, not some drippy-nosed little kid."

"Do you think age matters? There are times in our lives when we all need our mothers." She paused, then added quietly, "I only wish I still had mine to lean on sometimes."

His expression briefly softened into one of compassion, but something about the implacable set of his jaw told her he wouldn't budge. "This is different," he repeated. "I don't need my mother."

Even though everything from the tight set of his features to his stiff body language warned her to leave the subject alone, she couldn't let it rest. "Maybe she would like to see you. To make sure you're really all right. Don't you think you should call her and give her the chance?"

"Back off," he finally snapped, wrenching his leg away. "I had enough nagging on this from Wyatt. I don't need it from you, too."

When would she ever learn to control this busybody streak? A fine nurturer she was. The man couldn't have made it more clear he didn't want to talk about his family, that it was a painful subject, but she had thoughtlessly, selfishly insisted on pushing and prodding until he snapped.

"I'm sorry," she murmured. "You don't have to say

it, I'll say it for you. I need to learn to mind my own business.''

He blew out a breath. ''Whatever Wyatt says, I know the truth. My mother isn't any more comfortable spending time with me than I am with her. We live separate lives because we both prefer it that way.''

One more thing and then she would shut up, she promised herself. ''I'm sure you're wrong,'' she said gently. ''You're her son.''

''Yeah. And I'm also the one responsible for the disappearance of her daughter.''

His harsh words were spoken so low it took her a moment just to register and even longer to absorb them. He blamed himself for his sister's kidnapping? Why? And what a terrible burden for a boy of twelve to carry!

Shock and sympathy squeezed her heart and she couldn't think how to answer him for several long moments. He didn't look as if he wanted her to say anything—his mobile mouth was a tight, hard line and his eyes were cool, distant.

To her surprise, instead of changing the subject, he went on in that same low voice. ''When we're together, neither of us can seem to banish the ghost of my sister. She's always there, hovering between us. An image I can barely remember, with blond curls and freckles on her nose, riding a little pink tricycle with tassels hanging from the handlebars and a white daisy basket clipped to the front.''

His voice trailed off, and the pain in his eyes sent an answering ache through her bones. She wanted to pull his dark head to her chest and hold him close until the hurt faded away.

Knowing this was unstable ground, that one wrong turn could be disastrous, she chose her words with care. ''Why do you think your mother holds you responsible for your sister's disappearance?'' she asked quietly.

''Because I was!''

''How can that be? You were only a child yourself.''

''I was tending her. Or supposed to be, anyway. My mother had to run some errands and she asked me to watch Charlotte and Wyatt for an hour. I agreed—I gave her my word. Then I proceeded to completely ignore them, just so I could talk to some friends. Paul Kaiser's dad had just bought him a new dirt bike and he wanted me to come over to check it out. Of course I had to go, to hell with what I'd promised my mother about watching Charley and Wyatt.''

He appeared lost in thought, once more stuck in a purgatory she could only imagine. ''I left them playing in the front yard while I went around the corner to Paul's house. I was only over there for ten, maybe fifteen minutes. But when I came back, Charley was gone.''

''Oh, Gage,'' she whispered, wishing she had never brought up such an agonizing subject. She didn't have a whole world of experience with twelve-year-old boys—or the men they grew into, when it came to that—but she could well imagine how one could convince himself he was responsible for such a devastating event.

''Wyatt was hysterical,'' Gage went on. ''Just a few moments after I left for Paul's, he had fallen off his bike and broken his glasses for about the hundredth time that summer. He was sitting on the dried-up grass of our front yard trying to find all the pieces and jam them together when a car pulled up and someone grabbed Charlotte and shoved her inside. He couldn't describe anything about it other than the color of the car because he was blind as a bat without his glasses. Didn't even know if it was a man or woman. That's the last any of us saw her.''

How devastating for everyone involved. Gage, Wyatt, his mother and father. And how tragic, that one single August afternoon could forge a man's entire life.

She had no doubt that Gage had become an FBI agent in order to pay penance somehow for the blame he placed on himself over his sister's disappearance. Maybe by helping other families find their own missing children—or at least helping them attain some kind of closure, if that was possible—Gage was unconsciously seeking atonement for the thoughtless actions of a twelve-year-old boy.

"I'm sorry," she murmured, shamed by the complete inadequacy of the words.

"You can't imagine what it was like to face my mother when she returned home to find the police already swarming the neighborhood. She trusted me to take care of Wyatt and Charley and instead I ran off and ignored them. I'll never forget the look in her eyes."

She wanted to take his hand, to wrap her arms around him and give solace, but she had to content herself with touching his leg in a gesture of comfort. "I'm sure your mother doesn't blame you, Gage. You were just a foolish boy. None of it was your fault."

"If I had stuck around where I was supposed to be, I could have protected Charley. I don't know, maybe if I had been there, I might have somehow kept her out of that car."

"You don't know that. Maybe the abductor would have taken you along with your sister."

He didn't look as if he even heard her. "I should have been there to protect her. I was her older brother. She was my responsibility."

Allie was suddenly positive he had never willingly shirked a responsibility since that terrible day. "Your mother probably feels exactly the same about the choices *she* made. If she hadn't gone shopping on just that afternoon, maybe it wouldn't have happened. I'm sure she doesn't blame you, Gage. No mother could."

"Maybe not consciously. But I can see it in her eyes every time we're together. Like I said, it's easier on everyone if we just go on the way we have been, each busy with our own separate lives."

Though she wanted to argue the point, she knew she couldn't, not when talking about his sister was far more painful than any physical therapy exercises.

They finished the exercises in a stilted silence, each lost in thought. Allie couldn't bring herself to make inane conversation, not now, when she was beginning to suspect her feelings for Gage McKinnon were undergoing a monumental shift.

Somehow in the course of the last few days, she had gone from being attracted to him—a woefully mild word for the heat that sizzled under her skin when she was around him—to feeling something more. Something deeper. A terrifying storm surge of emotions lurked inside her, just waiting until she could find a moment of peace to sort them all out.

This was *not* that moment, though. Not when his skin was warm under her hands, and tension still seethed and coiled between them and he watched her out of those veiled gray eyes that saw entirely too much.

After they finished the exercises and Lisa left, Gage transferred to the wheelchair and maneuvered as close to the bedroom window as he could manage. Here he could look out on the backyard, at the masses of flowers his landlady tended so assiduously and the leaves of the big maple fluttering in the breeze and the sunshine gleaming on the grass.

The door had been left ajar, and he could hear Lisa moving around in the kitchen, no doubt busy with preparations for his dinner. He wanted to tell her he wasn't at all hungry, to order her just to pack up her girls and her pretty little face and the compassion in her blue eyes and leave him the hell alone for a while.

He couldn't wait for her to be gone, to be alone for the evening. He craved solitude, needed it like a man who was starving to death yearned for a mouthful of bread.

Why had he spilled his guts to her like that?

He hadn't intended to. One minute they'd been arguing about his mother, the next all that terrible wash of guilt and shame had gushed out of him like blood from a gaping wound.

He shouldn't have said anything. He couldn't quite figure out why he hadn't just told her to mind her own damn business about his family, to let the whole subject drop. He didn't owe Lisa Connors any explanations. None whatsoever. She wasn't his pal or his therapist or, heaven knows, his girlfriend, despite their charged kiss of the day before.

She was only his nosy neighbor, his hired baby-sitter. Nothing more.

Yet once again she had somehow managed to wring out of him words he had no intention of revealing to anyone.

Yeah, the unexpectedness of Wyatt's visit had left him off balance and disconcerted, but that wasn't explanation enough for why he had shared his most private thoughts with Lisa.

What was it about her that inspired such confidences? He didn't know, but whatever it was, he'd sure like to be able to bottle it and whip it out the next time he was interrogating a suspect in a case.

Maybe it was some combination of those unfeigned emotions she made no effort to hide. When he had told her the whole grisly story about that August afternoon, he had seen compassion and empathy and a heartfelt sorrow in those blue eyes.

She was genuine. Lisa Connors had a softness about her, a sincerity that he hadn't encountered in too many people. Unlike a lot of women he knew, she didn't play games or try to hide what was going through her head. When she looked at him, everything she was thinking was right there out in the open for the world to see.

And she didn't hold much back. Whether she was chasing her daughters across the grass in that backyard out there or talking to that home-care nurse, Estelle, or trying her best to comfort a cranky lawman with two bum legs, she threw her whole heart and soul into the task at hand.

He had to admit, she had taken good care of him during the time she'd worked for him. To a man used to eating out and bachelor fare, the meals she cooked were manna. He hadn't eaten this well since before his parents split up. Beyond that, she was always careful to make sure he had everything he needed within reach.

Lisa Connors was a nurturer, clear to her bones. It was obvious in everything she did, from the frequent affectionate hugs and kisses he saw her give her daughters to the fresh flowers she cut for his room each day, to the care she took to inflict as little pain as possible whenever she had to fuss with his injured legs.

He wasn't sure why that aspect of her personality appealed to him so much but it drew him to her. Maybe because he had lived so long in a hard, unforgiving world that being around her soft gentleness was like sitting for a few moments somewhere peaceful and quiet like that garden out there.

It would be far too easy to develop feelings for her.

The thought scared the living hell out of him. He couldn't afford to have feelings for her. He had nothing to offer someone like Lisa, absolutely nothing soft or gentle inside of him to give back to a woman who had already lost so much.

As soon as he could get around again on his own, he would return to work and they would go their separate ways. She'd get a job at some hospital or nursing home or doctor's office somewhere, and they probably wouldn't even see each other again, except maybe for the occasional encounter on the way to the mailbox.

She and her sunny smile and her spring-like scent and her daughters would be out of his life, and he could go back to normal.

That's the way he wanted it, the way things had to be. So why did he find the prospect so depressing?

Chapter 11

Her arms aching, Allie hurried through her house to the laundry room off the kitchen, then set down the heavy plastic basket full of soaking-wet bedding.

It was just her luck that Gage's dryer decided to blitz out on her when she still had three loads of his laundry left to do that day. Until Mrs. Jensen had a chance to send her son over to take a look at the blasted thing, Allie would just have to cart everything over to her own place to use her dryer—either that or she could hang it all up to snap and blow in the June sunshine.

As if she needed one more thing to worry about. Her blood glucose levels were being wacky, she hadn't slept well the night before and she'd nearly had a heart attack earlier that morning on the way back from the grocery store when a police officer had followed her for six blocks.

The squad car had eventually pulled off onto a side street, but her pulse still hadn't settled down. If she couldn't manage to somehow develop a tougher skin and stop panicking at every little thing, she would never survive life on the run.

And if she didn't hurry here, she would never get through the laundry, she chided herself. Sighing at her own paranoia, she removed the load of towels she had thrown in the dryer the night before then quickly transferred Gage's linens inside.

She had left Anna and Gaby playing in his backyard and she didn't want to be away from them for too long. Still, she decided she had time to fold that batch of towels rather than leave them on top of the dryer. That would be one less thing she had to do later that night when she and the girls returned back to their own house.

Except for that day's near encounter with the Park City police officer, things were going quite well, she reminded herself. She had nothing to complain about.

Working for Gage really was a perfect situation in nearly every way, almost like working from home, since she was close enough to run over here if she needed anything—if the girls ran out of toys or she needed to run a test strip or, like now, she just needed to run over and toss a load of clothes into the dryer.

Gaby and Anna had settled into a routine where they played together outside or watched a video in the morning, then went to the park with Jessica Farmer and her younger siblings for a few hours in the afternoon.

They loved those times with friends but also seemed to be basking in the extra time and attention Allie was able to give them in the mornings. It would be hard on them all when this little idyll ended.

Not exactly an idyll, she corrected herself. Maybe it would be if not for Gage and her tangle of feelings for him. But she was coming to care for him far too much, and it scared her worse than any Park City police officer tailing her in a squad car.

Their conversation the day before hadn't helped matters. She thought of his reluctantly shared revelations about his sister's kidnapping and the guilt he still carried inside him, more than twenty years later. Sadness flooded through her again just remembering it. No child should have to cope with that burden of shame and culpability.

Why hadn't his parents sensed what he was feeling? They should have insisted on counseling of some sort for both Gage and his brother to help them cope with the tragedy and their own loss.

Did his mother truly look at him with blame in her eyes when they were together, as he said? She couldn't imagine it. What loving mother could encumber her son with such a millstone?

She didn't even know his parents, probably never would, but for a moment she wanted to find them and give them both a good, hard shake. They should have done more to reach out to their son so he wouldn't still be carrying this heavy load into adulthood.

Of course, it was easy from the outside to pass judgment on what had happened more than two decades ago. How could she presume to know the hell his parents had gone through?

Gage said they had divorced and gone their separate ways shortly after his sister disappeared. Obviously, the stress and grief of losing their youngest child had been more than their fractured family unit could survive. Somehow his complicated feelings about his sister's disappearance had slipped through the cracks of their broken home.

What he had told her did much to explain his prickly exterior. Of course he would be impatient and frustrated by his injuries and the inaction that had been forced upon him.

For a man so passionate, so dedicated to his career—and to atoning for the mistakes he believed he had made—finding himself at loose ends must chafe terribly.

She wasn't sure if she liked being able to see past his thorniness to the man inside. Knowing and understanding what drove him only showed her what a good, decent, caring man he was.

Oh, she was in trouble. She cared about him far too deeply already. Allie folded the last towel and blew out a breath. She was afraid to use a word like *love*—how could she love a man she had only known for a few weeks? It seemed impossible, wholly inconceivable.

But she couldn't deny the burgeoning strength of her own emotions. How could she, when they seemed so wonderfully familiar?

She and Jaime had shared a deep, satisfying love for five years. When he died, she thought she would never know those feelings again. It terrified her to find them fluttering to fledgling life inside her again—and for a hard, callous man like Gage McKinnon, someone so very different from her gentle, lighthearted Jaime.

When the time came to move on with the girls, how would she be able to avoid having to nurse a broken heart along the way? She didn't see any way around it. A broken heart was all she would receive from Gage McKinnon. All she *could* receive.

She could see no good outcome. How could there be anything but heartache and pain? Any way their time together ended, it would end badly. Either she would be forced to run again, leaving him without a word, or Gage would discover she was a fugitive.

He would hate her for deceiving him these past few weeks!

She sensed he was a man who didn't give his trust easily. It had taken a huge measure of trust for him to confide in her the day before about his sister, something she sensed he didn't tell many people. If he found out how unworthy she was of that trust, he would be livid.

She had lied about her identity, about her past, about *everything*. She had no doubt that Gage was not the sort who would be quick to forgive such a betrayal.

On the other hand, if—when?—she was forced to flee with the girls, her abrupt disappearance would likely make him confused and angry.

What a tangled mess. She supposed one of the first rules of life on the run was not to allow herself to form any attachments to anyone. Far better to stay aloof and isolated than to have to deal with these kinds of painful complications.

Too bad there wasn't some sort of fugitive handbook that spelled such things out, but she supposed she would have to make her own stumbling way. In the future she would just have to forsake any close ties, no matter how foreign that might be to her personality.

The trick now was how to unravel herself from the mess, to safeguard what was left of her heart so she wouldn't be left completely devastated. Surely she was strong enough, smart enough, to protect herself. She just had to be as tough and remote as Gage.

With firm resolve to avoid further emotional encounters with him, Allie picked up the empty laundry basket and headed back toward his house. On the way, she decided to make a quick detour to his backyard so she could check on Gaby and Anna.

Her mind was still on her jumbled emotions when she

opened the latched gate and slipped through, into the fragrant, beautiful garden Ruth Jensen had created. Her gaze scanned the garden, the towering spires of the irises and the smaller, delicate alyssum and the bright, cheerful clumps of daisies.

Nothing moved but the old wooden swing the girls loved to play in swaying a little in the breeze and a magpie on a tree branch screeching at the neighbor's cat, which had decided one of Gage's windowsills made the perfect spot to stretch out in the sun.

Where were the girls? For one terrible moment, all she could think of was Gage's sister, disappearing from his life in one foolish instant of inattention. Her breathing quickened, and raw fear clutched her stomach as she scanned the garden again with wild eyes.

Settle down, she chided herself. No need to panic. Gaby and Anna probably just went inside for a drink of water or a bathroom break. Still, her heart pounded as she rushed up his back steps.

She heard them before she saw them—high-pitched giggles and then a lower rumble, like an oboe base line set against a duo of flutes.

Relief flooded her, sweet and pure, and she pushed open the door separating the utility room from Gage's kitchen. The greeting she started to give them jammed in her throat at the sight that met her gaze and her jaw sagged.

"Oh, my," she whispered, unable to say anything else.

Anna and Gaby giggled again. "Look, Mommy," Gaby exclaimed with glee. "We're playing beauty shop."

"Don't say a word," Gage warned on a growl. "Not one single word."

She blinked several times, but the same image reappeared each time—the three of them at the kitchen table, the girls grinning at Gage in his wheelchair, masculine and commanding and brusque.

And currently decorated with what looked like a hundred pastel barrettes stuck in his short dark hair, tufting it out in every direction.

"Oh, my," she said again. How on earth had this happened? She couldn't have been gone longer than ten minutes. Leave it to Hurricane Gaby and her little sidekick to wreak havoc in their mother's absence.

"Me and Anna wanted to try out the new barrettes you bought us at the store today and Mr. McDonalds said it was okay."

"McKinnon. Remember, I told you his name was Mr. McKinnon. Not McDonalds."

"Gage is probably easier to say," he said, his voice gruff.

"Gage," Anna said suddenly. "Gage, Gage, Gage."

Allie didn't know what to do about the warmth flooding through her. So much for her determination to protect the intact remnants of her heart. Oh, heavens, it would be far too easy to tumble hard and fast, completely, for this man!

"Doesn't Gage look nice?" Gaby asked.

"Yes. Very." Despite her sudden fear that any barriers she tried to build between them now would go up far too late, she couldn't hide her grin. "I especially like the row of ducklings there in the front."

"I did those," Gaby said proudly.

A ruddy color accented his cheekbones like the russet feathers of a mallard drake and he looked as if he would rather be anywhere else on earth than here in this warm kitchen with her two little budding hairstylists. Allie couldn't help but take pity on him.

"As nice as Mr. McKinnon looks, I think we need to

take out the barrettes so they'll be ready for the two of you to wear another day."

Both girls opened their mouths to protest but she forestalled them. "Why don't you each get one of those Popsicles we bought at the store? You can take them out in the backyard and eat them."

As usual, the promise of sugar provided an alluring enough distraction. Gaby hurried to the freezer and pulled out two frozen treats. After handing one to her younger sister, she led the way outside, leaving Allie and Gage alone in the kitchen.

"You do look very nice," she teased after the back door slammed shut behind her two little beauticians in training. "Are you sure you wouldn't like to leave them in for the rest of the day?"

"That's not funny." He glared at her, in the midst of pulling out one of the barrettes along with several strands of hair.

She couldn't help laughing again. "You might think differently if you could see what you look like. Wait," she said suddenly. "Don't take any more out for a second."

It only took her a moment to rush to the front room where she left her purse and find a mirrored compact inside. She returned to the kitchen and held it out for Gage.

She might have been offering him an anaconda for all the enthusiasm he showed as he took the compact from her, but as he studied his reflection, a wry smile lifted the corners of that sensual mouth.

"Smashing. Who knows? I might start a new fashion trend at the Bureau."

She laughed and took the compact from him, slipping it in the back pocket of her shorts. "Don't hold your breath, Agent McKinnon."

He tugged another barrette out and she winced at the strands of hair he yanked out along with it.

''Keep that up and you're going to lose half your hair by the time you're done. I promise, they come out easier if you just unclip them.''

''Sorry. I haven't exactly had a whole lot of experience with hair thingies.''

''Hold still.'' Though she knew it probably wasn't a good idea, she moved behind him and started unfastening the barrettes, trying not to pay attention to the way the thick silk of his hair caressed her fingers or the heat that emanated from him or her own unruly desire to smooth down the strands and press her mouth just there, on that strong neck.

All she could focus on was the kiss they shared two nights earlier in this very spot. How his mouth had been firm and strong and tasted of cherry pie, how their breaths had mingled, how her body had ached and yearned for more than just a kiss....

She jerked her mind from that dangerous road. ''It was very sweet of you to put yourself through all this,'' she said after a moment, then prayed he didn't notice the breathiness of her voice.

He snorted. ''Yeah, well, that oldest girl of yours doesn't give a man much choice once she sets her mind to something.''

''Oh, dear. I'm sorry. Gaby can be...a little overwhelming sometimes.''

''Right. That's like saying Park City sees a little bit of snow every winter. Face it, Lisa. Your kid's a steamroller.''

''She's just opinionated and not shy about sharing those opinions with anybody who will listen.''

''Hmm. I wonder where she gets that?''

Allie laughed at his dry-as-dust tone. ''Not from me, certainly. Must have been her father's side.''

''Right. Well, I have to admit, the whole hair thing wasn't really a conscious decision on my part. All I did was make the mistake of coming into the kitchen for some bottled water. I was just pulling it out of the fridge when the two of them burst in from the backyard chattering and giggling about the idea of fixing somebody's hair. I was unlucky enough to be the one they found first. Next thing I knew, they were sticking all those little do-dads in my hair before I could get a word in.''

She had to smile at the idea of Gage pretending helplessness against a five-year-old and a three-year-old. ''I'm sorry I wasn't here to keep an eye on them. Or at least to watch the show. I was only next door taking care of some laundry and thought they would be fine in the backyard for a few moments. Next time I'll take them with me.''

''You don't have to do that. They're fine over here.'' He said the words with his characteristic gruffness, but to her surprise he sounded as if he meant them.

''I know you don't want to be bothered with them,'' she said after a moment. ''I completely understand, Gage. I've done my best to keep them out of your way, but I'll try harder from now on.''

''You don't have to do that,'' he repeated. ''They don't bother me. Not really.''

Though she wasn't completely convinced, she decided to take him at his word. ''Well, I promise I won't let them jump all over you. And no more beauty shop.''

His oath of gratitude was heartfelt and unfeigned, and she laughed again as she plucked the last barrette from his hair. ''There. All done.''

The hair accessories had left his hair sticking out in several directions so she ran her fingers through the thick strands in a vain effort to smooth it down. "I think you're going to need a comb to fix this all completely," she said, then flushed at the hoarse note in her voice. Could he guess how he affected her? Oh, she hoped not.

Still, she was aware of a sudden tension humming between them, a charged anticipation in the air.

Her gaze met his and she was stunned by the banked desire she saw there. The breath caught in her throat and she swallowed.

Time seemed to freeze and all her senses seemed more sharp, more intense suddenly.

She was almost painfully aware of the softness of his hair under her fingers, of the slow rhythm of his breathing, of the clean, male scent of him drifting toward her.

Her body swayed toward him again, but she caught herself just in time before she would have melted against him like one of the girls' favorite candy bars left in the back window of the car.

She swallowed and pulled her hand from his hair. "There you go. No harm done."

"I wouldn't say that." His low voice vibrated in the kitchen. Before she could summon any kind of coherent thought about backing away toward safety and sanity, his hand fastened on her wrist and he tugged her toward him.

Because of his height—and her lack of it—they were nearly the same level even when he was sitting in the wheelchair.

She didn't have to angle her head too much for his mouth to find hers with unerring heat, then she forgot anything as silly and inconsequential as trying to escape. Why would she want to, when this was exactly where she wanted to be?

Her arms twined around his neck and she nestled against him, aware of his heart pounding through the cotton of his shirt, of the swell and ache of her breasts where they brushed against his hard chest.

Even as she reveled in their embrace, some corner of her mind still whispered a warning note. This was dangerously foolish. How could she expect to keep the tattered remnants of her heart intact if she engaged in this kind of crazy, risky behavior?

She disregarded the warning and settled against him with a sigh.

"I can't think about anything else but this," he murmured against her mouth. "All day long, all I can think about is kissing you again. Touching you. I would give anything to be out of this damn chair so I could show you how much I want you."

His words were as arousing as the hand that had somehow pulled her T-shirt free of her shorts and was caressing the skin at her waist.

"I've thought of it, too," she confessed, then flushed at her boldness.

She was embarrassed suddenly about the insulin pump and the catheter that fed into her skin, but Gage barely paid attention to it. He kissed her again, his tongue slipping inside as his hand explored higher under her shirt.

She wasn't aware she held her breath until his fingers found the underslope of her breast and she exhaled in a long, aroused sigh. Oh, this was what she wanted. His hands on her skin, on her body, his mouth warm and alive against hers, this tenderness gushing up inside her like water from a broken sprinkler head.

No, she wanted more. She wanted to be stretched out beside him with no barriers between them, to feel the urgent press of his body cover her, the hard strength of him inside of her.

Her cheeks flamed at the thought even as her breath

caught in her throat and she closed her eyes against the mental picture conjured up by her entirely too-vivid imagination.

She opened them when a sound reached in and yanked her back to reality, ringing through her consciousness like a fire alarm—the sound of two little girls laughing outside the kitchen window.

She stiffened. Oh, heavens. She'd forgotten all about her daughters, playing alone out back. How could she have been so irresponsible to tangle tongues—and dream about more—with Gage while her children played just a few feet away?

She scrambled up, yanking down her T-shirt. "I...I need to check on the girls."

His hair was still mussed, his breathing ragged, but he had never looked so gorgeous to her. "Yeah," he said after a moment. "That's probably a good idea."

She should say something more, take some kind of firm stand that they simply had to stop this lunacy, no matter what kind of chemistry bubbled and frothed between them, but she couldn't manage to string two thoughts together. Not with him watching her out of those hooded gray eyes. So she just sent him a distressed look and hurried out the back door toward her daughters.

Gage watched her go, too paralyzed by what had just happened to move from the kitchen.

He couldn't believe he had kissed her again, after all his noble intentions to leave her alone. All his adult life, he had prided himself on his self-control, his restraint. He never drank to excess, he worked out religiously, he tried to eat healthy foods, for the most part.

But he didn't know himself around Lisa. He had suddenly become a stranger who gave in to his cravings, who grabbed an innocent woman in his kitchen and kissed her like she was a cool flask of water and he'd been crawling through the desert for decades.

This had to stop. He didn't know how, but he somehow had to find the strength and self-discipline to ignore his body's hunger for her.

If only he could figure out how to ease the yearning in his heart.

Chapter 12

His mother arrived just after lunch.

When the girls had finished devouring their second-favorite meal of macaroni and cheese, Allie sent them off for their daily trip to the park with Jessica then returned to her house to throw the last load of Gage's laundry into the dryer.

She wasn't avoiding him, she assured herself, even though she had to admit she was grateful for the opportunity to be on her own for a moment, to try to regain some desperately needed equilibrium.

The laundry room sweltered from the dryer and from the hot sun blazing through the windows—not the most pleasant place to spend a June afternoon, but at least she had a little solitude here.

While she folded linens amid the torpid heat and the sweet, clean scent of laundry detergent, the dazzling intensity of that kiss looped through her mind over and over.

His strong hands on her skin, his mouth hard and urgent on hers. Her own eager response.

She didn't know she could catch fire so quickly, so completely. She had been totally lost to everything but Gage and to the sheer wonder of being in his arms.

What a tangled mess. So much for her plans to keep a careful distance between them until she could leave Park City. That resolution had lasted all of a half hour, only until she had walked into the kitchen and seen him acting so sweetly around her daughters.

How foolish she had been to think she could pluck out her growing feelings for him like Ruth going after weeds in her flower garden. Already he was rooted so deeply in her heart that she didn't know how she would ever be able to break free.

With a snap, she shook out the last of his pillowcases and folded it neatly, smoothing her fingers over the cotton to straighten the fold. Wouldn't it be nice if she could get rid of the rest of the wrinkles in her life so easily? Just flip her wrist and make them all disappear?

Much as she'd like to, she couldn't hide out here in her laundry room all afternoon. She was made of sterner stuff, anyway. She kept telling herself that as she loaded the clean and folded linens into the basket and walked back to Gage's house.

As she reached his porch steps, the low throb of an engine purred through the quiet summer afternoon. She turned to see a small late-model Toyota SUV parked at the curb in front of Gage's house.

Curious, she paused on the steps and watched as a trim woman in her midfifties wearing navy capris and a cheerful yellow shirt hopped from the sporty vehicle. Bright sunlight glimmered off artfully streaked blond hair and classically applied makeup.

This was a woman with confidence and grace, one of those timelessly beautiful women who had always left her envious.

With her own shorts and T-shirt, choppy haircut and unattractive dye job, Allie felt as sweaty and grubby as one of the girls after a day spent at the zoo.

For some reason she didn't quite understand, something about the woman's smile as she approached sent sharp foreboding prickling through her. *Don't be silly,* she chided herself. *She's probably just a lost tourist looking for directions.*

"Hello," Allie said with a polite smile. "May I help you?"

"You must be Lisa. My son Wyatt told me about you. I'm Lynn McKinnon, Gage's mother. Please, let me help you with your basket."

Gage's mother. Oh, no! He would *not* be happy about having his mother show up suddenly at his doorstep, not after his revelations the day before about the tense, awkward relationship the two of them shared and the reasons for it.

"Thanks, but I've got it." For all the heat of the afternoon, she felt frozen on the steps, unsure what to do, what to say.

"Um, come in," she finally managed to squeak out. "I'll just let Gage know you're here."

"Wait. To be honest, I would really like to speak with you first before I see Gage."

She stared blankly at the other woman, baffled and nervous. "Oh?"

"I know my son, Ms.…Connors, isn't it?"

Allie nodded, hating the alias. She wanted to be Alicia DeBarillas again not the stranger named Lisa Connors.

She hated this deceit and the reasons for it.

"I'm afraid Gage won't be very thrilled to see me," Lynn said bluntly. "I'm also afraid he won't want to tell me the truth about his injury. Before I face him and hear all his macho lies about how he's fine and has barely a scratch, I wanted to ask you as his nurse how he's really doing."

She wasn't sure how Gage would want her to answer that. She couldn't claim total insight into the man who employed her, but she thought she knew him well enough to guess he wouldn't want her sharing his complete medical history with his estranged mother.

On the other hand, this smiling woman seemed to genuinely care about her son's welfare. Allie couldn't bring herself to lie to the woman. "He's in pain but he tries hard to pretend he's not."

"That sounds very much like Gage."

"I can only tell you what the doctor said when I drove him there a few days ago. His right leg is healing quickly. Because of the angle at which he was hit, it sustained only a simple fracture. A few more weeks and the doctor thinks he'll be able to start weight bearing."

"And the left leg?"

"It still has a ways to go. He's probably looking at another month or two in the cast, then rehab after that."

"I see."

"He still has a long road of recovery ahead of him, but he's able to get around better every day."

The other woman nodded and touched her arm with cool fingers. "Thank you for being honest. You must think I'm a nosy, interfering old woman but I knew Gage wouldn't tell me the truth. He's my son and I love him but I'm the first one to admit he can be a little stubborn sometimes, as I'm sure you have discovered."

Again, Allie didn't know how to answer. She *did* know

she had a hard time believing this warm, friendly woman could possibly blame her son for something that had happened when he was only a child.

"Come in and I'll let him know you're here."

"Thank you."

Allie led the way up the porch steps and into the house, then left Lynn McKinnon waiting in the living room. At Gage's closed bedroom door, she paused, her nerves scrambling.

He wasn't going to be happy to see his mother. She only hoped he wouldn't stomp all over Lynn's maternal concern.

No. As gruff and taciturn as he could be sometimes, Allie knew he was also capable of great gentleness. Only look at that morning, how he had tolerated her girls and their mischievousness.

She had a feeling that despite his own discomfort around his mother, he would treat her with only respect.

She knocked, then swung open the door after he bade her to enter. He was on the bed working through some of the physical therapy exercises that didn't require her help. His features were strained as he extended his leg, and sweat beaded his forehead.

"Sorry to interrupt but you have another visitor."

Irritation flashed through his gray eyes and he muttered an oath. "Can't a guy get a moment's peace around here?"

"Sorry." She paused, loath to tell him the rest of it. "Um, Gage, it's your mother."

She expected him to show some reaction to her announcement but he only continued his stretching. All she could see was a hint of resignation in the set of his mouth.

"You don't look surprised."

"I expected her last night. The only surprise is that she could stand to wait until today to show up."

"Can I send her in?"

"Give me a minute, will you?"

She studied him, trying to figure out what was going through his mind, then she shrugged. "Sure. I'll stall her."

She returned to the living room and found Lynn tracing her finger along Gage's CD collection. Trying to find some clues into the son she didn't know? Allie wondered.

She cleared her throat and Lynn looked up quickly, flushing a little.

"He'll just be a moment," Allie said. "Would you like something to drink while you wait?"

"No. I'm fine. Thank you."

They stood awkwardly for a moment. "Gage tells me you live about an hour away."

"Yes. I grew up in the little town of Liberty and I've lived there most of my life. And what about you? What brings you to Park City?"

A nightmarish custody battle and raw terror at the idea of losing her girls. She couldn't say that, of course, so she offered only the bare bones of her story. "My husband was killed in a car accident a few years ago and I decided my girls and I could use a fresh start. We were heading to California when we had engine trouble and ended up staying."

"I'm so glad you did, for Gage's sake. Wyatt assured me you're taking very good care of him."

"I don't know about that. He would much rather do everything by himself."

Lynn smiled suddenly. "This was an awful thing to happen to anyone, and I wish with all my heart my son didn't have to go through such an ordeal. But sometimes it's not necessarily a bad thing for certain people to learn they can lean on someone else once in a while.''

She was quite sure Gage would strongly disagree, but she smiled politely.

''Let me ask you something else,'' Lynn went on. ''Do you think I would be in the way if I stayed around town for a few days? I'm in the middle of summer vacation from school and, like you, could use a change of scenery. I was thinking about renting a condominium somewhere nearby for a week or so. It would give Gage and me a wonderful chance to catch up. What do you think?''

He had a spare bedroom going unused, but she knew it wasn't her place to offer it to Lynn. ''I think you should talk to your son about it.''

''I'll do that.''

They lapsed into silence, and after a moment Allie decided to see if Gage was ready yet.

''Excuse me for a moment and I'll check on Gage,'' she murmured to the other woman.

When she returned to his room, she found he not only had changed into a clean shirt and a pair of nylon sweats that snapped up the sides and over his casts but he had also transferred from the bed to the recliner.

''Can I bring your mother back?'' she asked.

He nodded, and Allie returned for Lynn. She showed his mother to the bedroom then hovered in the doorway, though she wasn't sure why.

In just one brief moment when Lynn walked into the room, Allie saw a myriad of emotions pass between the two of them. Lynn's gaze brimmed over with a sort of anguished love as she looked at her son and Gage wore a look of mingled stoicism and yearning.

Allie closed the door behind Lynn, then touched a hand

to her chest, to her heart. She could almost feel it break apart as she realized what she would have to do.

How could one small woman leave him so totally exhausted?

By the time his mother left two hours later—after pressing a smooth cheek that smelled of lavender and sage to his and promising she would return the next day—Gage felt as if he had just run twenty miles through blinding rain, broken legs and all.

As much as he loved his mother, she somehow managed to leave him weary and drained, maybe because he had to navigate so carefully through the minefield of emotions between them. Two hours listening to his mother's cheerful chatter was more grueling than spending two hours interrogating the worst of criminals.

He was tempted to indulge in a little nap for a while but he had a feeling if he did, he would only end up spending a restless night tossing and turning in his bed. He didn't want to risk it, not when he knew he would already have a tough time sleeping because of that kiss he and Lisa had shared earlier, the one he couldn't stop thinking about.

Lynn had left his door ajar and he could hear Lisa laughing quietly in the kitchen, then the higher-pitched music of her daughters joining in. He could picture them together, sharing smiles and stories and affectionate touches.

She was a toucher, he had noticed, with her daughters and with everyone else. A comforting hand here, a gentle squeeze there. He'd never been one who liked casual physical contact—he was usually uncomfortable with it, even—but for some reason he didn't mind it from her.

As it had done all too often that afternoon, even when

he'd been talking to his mother, the memory of their kiss earlier in the morning played through his mind again, of the incredible *rightness* of having her in his arms. He had never experienced anything like it, that wild jumble of tenderness and sweetness and raw desire.

If not for her girls, he would have pulled her onto him, buried himself inside of her, lost himself in her.

Even hours later, his body still ached for her. Not just his body, he admitted. As crazy as it seemed, his whole soul yearned and burned for Lisa Connors.

He wanted to be near her. To talk to her and listen to the low murmur of her voice and watch her face soften and glow with her smile.

He heard her and her daughters laugh again and suddenly wanted desperately to be in that kitchen with them, not trapped here in this damn bedroom by his physical and emotional limitations.

Even as he told himself how foolish it was—how, if he had any kind of a brain in his head, he would keep his butt planted right where it was—Gage transferred with painstaking care from the recliner to the wheelchair.

When he wheeled to the kitchen, he paused in the doorway. None of them noticed him at first so he settled in to watch, drawing a strange peace from the domesticity of the scene.

Lisa stood at the kitchen counter wearing the same apron she had worn on that first day when he'd come home from the hospital. The girls stood on chairs set at either side of her, watching their mother's actions with their cute little faces bright with glee and anticipation.

He loved watching her, too, he had to admit. Everything about her seemed so fluid and graceful, like watching some rare, exquisite bird floating on air currents. She made even an action as mundane as mixing some kind of batter in a bowl look elegant and smooth.

The littlest one, Anna, saw him first. She gave him a small, painfully sweet smile and a bashful little wave, then ducked her head. He lifted his fingers to wave back just as the other one caught sight of him.

"Hi, Mr. Gage!" she exclaimed. "We're makin' brownies. Me and Anna love, love, *love* brownies."

"Who doesn't?" he asked wryly.

She frowned, giving his off-the-cuff remark far more consideration than it deserved. "Mommy doesn't. She doesn't eat them, anyway. She says these will be just for me and Anna and you."

He glanced at Lisa, who shrugged and returned his gaze with a rueful look. "Okay. You caught me. The truth is, I love, love, *love* brownies, too, but I can't afford to eat them very often. They and my diabetes don't get along very well."

He found it poignant and heartrending that she would make treats for her daughters she couldn't enjoy herself. What a good mother she was, so very different from a lot of the women he came in contact with on the job. The ones who were too high or drunk to notice when their boyfriends spent an inordinate amount of time alone with their children or the bruises or the frequent trips to the emergency room.

"There's that superstrength willpower again."

She studied him for a moment then looked away, her cheeks dusted with color. "Not really. I just know the consequences of overindulging better than most."

"Do you want to help us make the brownies, Mr. Gage?" Gaby asked.

"How about if I just watch?"

"Okay," she said cheerfully. "Once we made a cake

with Grandma Irena and she let us lick the spoon but Mommy says we can't 'cause we'll get worms in our tummies. That's gross, huh?''

''Gabriella!'' Lisa exclaimed. The spoon clattered against the metal of the mixing bowl with a discordant sound.

What had the little girl said to put such raw panic in her eyes, such sternness in her voice? Gage wondered.

Gaby looked confused, too. ''Well, it is gross. Who wants worms in their tummies?''

''We don't need to talk about this right now,'' Lisa said sternly. ''I think we're done mixing now and ready to pour the mix into the pan. Hold it steady for me, okay?''

He couldn't help thinking she was changing the subject and he racked his mind trying to figure out what in such an innocuous statement had set her off.

Finally he gave up trying to puzzle out her strange reaction and just enjoyed the sight of them working together. Both girls held tight to the pan on either side, as if it were a wriggly puppy trying to escape. Their tongues were thrust tight between their teeth in concentration while Lisa poured the batter and scraped the remainder out.

''I want to set the buzzer,'' Gaby begged when she finished.

''Okay.'' Lisa handed her the small kitchen timer. ''Thirty minutes. Do you remember how to do that?''

Gaby nodded and twisted the dial, that solemn look on her little face again, then held it out for her mother's inspection. ''Three zero. Thirty minutes.''

''Good job. Now you two need to wash your hands, then go out in the backyard and start gathering up your toys to put into the basket. As soon as the brownies are done, we need to go back to our house for the night.''

The girls jumped down from their chairs obediently and dragged them to the sink.

''Bye, Mr. Gage,'' Gaby said when they finished washing up and were on their way out the door. ''Don't eat all the brownies without us.''

''I won't, I swear.''

Her sister gifted him with another shy wave and smile before following at her loquacious sibling's heels, leaving him alone with Lisa.

He shifted in the wheelchair, uncomfortably aware this was the first time he had been alone with her since their kiss that morning. Tension seethed through the kitchen, taut and cumbrous, and suddenly Lisa seemed to have an inordinate preoccupation with wiping down the counter.

''So how was your visit with your mother?'' she finally asked.

He shrugged. ''We both survived.''

Somehow the look she sent him was both reprimanding and sympathetic. ''I thought she was very nice. And it's obvious she's concerned about you.''

''Right. So concerned she's decided to rent a condo in town for a few weeks so she can keep an eye on me.''

''She told me she was thinking about it. I hope you told her how silly that was. Did you tell her you have a spare bedroom and she could stay here with you?''

''No.''

She frowned. ''Why not?''

Guilt pinched at him but he staunchly ignored it. ''Because I don't want her here.''

She set down the cloth she'd been using on the counter and faced him, a militant light in her eyes that made him more than a little edgy. ''Gage, she's your mother.''

''I believe I'm aware of that fact, thanks.''

''So you should welcome this chance to spend some

time with her! I know things are awkward between you, but they don't have to be that way. You could use this time together to heal the rift between you."

He ground his back teeth. "There is no rift between us. We just prefer to go our separate ways."

"You might prefer things that way, but your mother doesn't sound as if she agrees. Otherwise, she wouldn't feel compelled to stick around for the next few weeks, would she?"

He couldn't answer because he'd wondered the same thing, just what his mother was after by deciding to take up temporary residence in Park City. Surely she didn't want to try to build a relationship with him after all these years. It didn't make any kind of sense. But what other explanation could there be?

All these years he thought she preferred things the way they were, that she needed that distance between them as much as he did, but now he was beginning to wonder if he had been wrong.

Even if he had been, he couldn't imagine having her stay here. Hell, just a few hours with her left him wrung out. Limp as a worn-out fiddle string, as his grandpa would have said. Having her here on even a semiperma-nent basis would be more than he could survive.

If she was here, Wyatt would probably turn up, too. Before he knew it, he would have more family than he knew what to do with.

"Just leave it alone," he growled to Lisa. "I don't remember asking your opinion about how to run my life."

As soon as the words skulked out, he regretted them. Her eyes darkened to a wounded midnight blue, and that soft mouth that had tasted so delicious earlier in the day thinned and straightened.

"You're right," she said after a moment. Her voice

sounded small, flat. He had hurt her, he realized, and hated himself for it. He wanted to apologize but he couldn't find the words.

"I'm only the hired help," she went on. "It's none of my business if you want to throw away a chance to make your peace with a mother who loves you."

"Lisa..."

She shook her head. "Excuse me, but I need to put fresh sheets on your bed before I go home for the day."

She walked out, leaving him alone in the kitchen with his guilt.

Chapter 13

"What do you mean, you're quitting? You can't quit!"

Allie faced an irate and baffled Gage, trying not to flinch beneath the weight of his shocked anger.

"Sure I can." Her calm tone belied both the pounding of her heart and the sleepless night she'd spent, agonizing about what to do. "I believe I just did."

"Why? Just tell me that."

She didn't know how to answer him since none of her reasons for quitting were things she could share with him.

Because I'm in love with you and will already walk away with my heart bruised and bleeding.

That might be the biggest contributing factor to her decision to quit, but of course she couldn't tell him that. Nor could she tell him she had decided it would be less painful when she left town in a few weeks—after her car repair bill to Ruth's son was paid—if she did all she could to put as much distance as possible between them now.

He also probably wouldn't appreciate knowing she was

willing to sacrifice her last few weeks with him in the hopes that he could reestablish a relationship with his mother.

She couldn't give him any of those reasons, so she settled on the one palatable excuse she had come up with during her sleepless night. It was true, though not anywhere close to the whole truth.

"I told you. I think we'd both be more comfortable with me working somewhere else, in light of the… tension…between us."

"What tension?"

Despite her off-the-charts stress level, she couldn't help the disbelieving laugh that gurgled out. Could he really be that oblivious?

What tension? Right.

Only the constant simmering strain of trying to pretend they didn't notice the attraction sparking and humming between them like a glowing-red live wire downed in a storm. Or maybe she was the only one with that problem, the one who couldn't seem to be in the same room without going weak in the knees.

No. He felt it, too. She remembered the heat of his kiss and the words he had whispered against her mouth, words she hadn't been able to forget, no matter how hard she tried.

All day long, all I can think about is kissing you again. Touching you.

He was every bit as attracted to her. He was probably just better at controlling it.

"I think I would be more comfortable working somewhere else," she repeated.

"So just like that, you're going to walk out?"

"It's not as if I'm completely abandoning you to fend for yourself. Your mother will be around."

His gray eyes narrowed and he frowned. ''That's what this is about, isn't it? You think if you quit, I'll have no choice but to spend more time with my mother.''

''Do you really think I would be that devious?'' she asked, trying desperately to sound innocent. ''Besides, you were right about what you said yesterday. Your relationship with your family—or any lack thereof—is certainly not my concern. If you don't want your mother to help, talk to Ruth about hiring someone else. Like you said, it's not any of my business what you do.''

''I was a jerk yesterday. I'm sorry. Okay? Is that any reason to quit a situation that has worked out pretty well for everybody?''

''I'm not quitting because of anything you said yesterday, Gage. I've thought long and hard about this and I think it's the best thing for me to do right now.''

In truth, his vehement opposition to her resignation surprised her a little. She hadn't expected him to object to her quitting so strenuously, not after he hadn't exactly acted thrilled about the whole setup from the beginning. If anything, she would have thought he would be relieved to be rid of her, with her nosiness and interfering ways and her two rambunctious young daughters always underfoot, her girls who were so very adept at destroying his peace.

But he was acting as if her announcement was a personal betrayal. ''I don't think it's the right thing at all,'' he snapped.

It would be so tempting to weaken, to tell him she had changed her mind and would continue working for him—to the devil with all the rationalizations she had come up with during her sleepless night. That would be utter disaster, though, she reminded herself sternly. She had to be tough, resolute.

She straightened her spine. ''I'm sorry. I've already taken my old job back with Ruth and arranged for Jessica Farmer to help me with the girls. She's the girl who has been taking them in the afternoons and they adore her. I start cleaning houses again tomorrow.''

''You would rather scrub toilets and make beds than work here?''

''Gage, face it. You really don't need as much help as you did a few weeks ago, after you first came home from the hospital. You're getting around much better now, and in a few weeks you can start putting your weight on at least your right leg and getting around on crutches. Really, I'm more in the way these days than anything else. I feel like I spend half the day hovering around looking for something to do.''

''That's not true.''

''It is. Anyway, your mother will be here this afternoon and she's ready to take over.''

Suspicion flitted across his features. ''You've talked to my mother already? Before talking to me?''

She hadn't exactly meant to let that slip. She flushed. ''Yes. I got her number from information and called this morning. I wanted to make sure of her plans before I talked to Ruth about resuming my old job.''

''You've thought of everything, haven't you?''

Except how she would survive not being with him every day. She hadn't figured that one out yet. Or how she would go on without seeing his gentleness with the girls or his strong determination to overcome his injuries or even their battles of will.

''Yes,'' she lied. ''I think so.''

He should be relieved, Gage told himself. No more chirpy little girls sticking do-dads in his hair, no more listening to Lisa nag about his medication, no more physical therapy sessions that left him hard and hungry to kiss that lush mouth of hers.

Yeah, his life would be much simpler without Lisa Connors and her daughters around. But the thought of her leaving left him dispirited. Bereft, even.

It shouldn't bother him. The logical side of his brain knew that. But somehow in the past few weeks Lisa and her girls had slipped beneath his skin. He liked being with her. Simple as that. She was sunshine on a summer afternoon and just-picked raspberries melting on his tongue and brownies, warm from the oven.

He frowned, suddenly depressed at the idea of returning to the life of solitude he had cultivated so carefully as an adult.

He never thought he would admit it but he was tired of being the lone wolf. A part of him had relished being part of a family, a pack, during these few weeks, even a makeshift one like Lisa Connors and her two cute, giggly little girls.

With her gentle hands and her nurturing spirit, Lisa had made the ordeal of his recovery far more bearable than he might have expected.

He thought about the tension she was talking about between them, the attraction that prowled between them like a living creature. Yeah, it made things uncomfortable. But it also lent an edge of anticipation, excitement, to days that could have quickly become dreary and mundane.

The idea of never kissing her, never again tasting the sweetness of her mouth or feeling her body soften against his was just too terrible to even contemplate.

"I'm sorry, Gage," she said quietly. "Whether you believe it or not, I *have* enjoyed these weeks working here. Please believe me when I say that I truly wish you all the best with your recovery."

She turned away and walked out of his bedroom door, leaving him gazing after her, feeling more alone than he ever had in his life.

The late-afternoon sun sent stretchy shadows over everything as Allie pulled her Honda into the driveway of her house ten days later.

Oh, she was tired. Though she was as eager as always to see Gaby and Anna at the end of the day, she just wanted to stay here in the cool air-conditioned solitude of her car for now, lean her head against the steering wheel and just sleep for a while.

Cleaning a half-dozen vacation units a day was hard labor, physically taxing even if it wasn't any particular mental challenge. She wanted to think she could have handled the work without complaint if she wasn't subsisting on a few hours of sleep a night—and if she could keep her blood glucose levels from going haywire.

Though she was diligent about checking her levels throughout the day and adjusting her pump accordingly, she was having a tough time gaining control.

Just stress, she assured herself. That and fatigue. It was all interrelated. She wasn't sleeping or eating well, which made her more tired during the day, which taxed her body unnecessarily.

Whatever the reason, she would have to snap out of it in order to take the girls later. She'd promised them a special outing and it was important that she stick to her word.

Over breakfast while they had been debating ideas, Allie had given them the choice of taking a walk down Park City's steep historic Main Street then stopping to enjoy an ice cream or popping some popcorn and taking a blanket to the city park for the free open-air bluegrass concert.

She had a feeling that as much as she would prefer the concert option, the girls would go for the ice cream.

She supposed she couldn't complain since either option seemed like a pleasant way to spend a warm Sunday evening, especially if she was spending that evening with her daughters.

Though she wasn't exactly refreshed by her brief respite, Allie decided she couldn't linger out here in the car any longer, not when she was eager to see her daughters.

She picked up her purse and the nice, crisp envelope with her two-weeks' pay and slid out of the car. As of this payday, her debt to Ruth Jensen's son for the extensive repairs he did to the Honda was paid. What a huge relief. It felt wonderful to be out of debt.

Maybe it was time she started thinking about pulling up stakes, now that she had nothing really keeping her in Park City—nothing but a deep, profound yearning to stay.

Next door she could see Gage's Jeep Cherokee and his mother's sporty little Toyota SUV still parked behind it in the driveway.

In the ten days since she quit working for him, she had only seen him twice. Once when she'd been heading for work, he and Lynn had been leaving for physical therapy and the three of them had spoken briefly.

The second time had been the night before. After the girls had drifted off to sleep, she had been sitting on the steps of her front porch in the cool, sweet evening air, arms wrapped around her knees as she gazed up at the dark silhouette of the mountains in the moonlight.

She'd been out only a few moments when she heard the squeak of a door opening next door, and a few moments later Gage had wheeled himself out onto his twin of a porch.

By the suddenly tight expression on his face, she could

tell the instant he noticed her. For a moment she thought he would thrust open the door again and wheel back inside. Before he could, she jumped up on impulse and crossed the strip of grass to him.

She closed her eyes now, remembering their brief, stilted conversation. They had only spoken for a moment. She had asked about his injuries and he told her they were healing well. He had asked about work and about the girls and she had told him both were fine.

The whole time they had talked, she had been painfully aware of him—the strong line of his jaw moving when he spoke, his broad shoulders filling the chair, the silver-gray of his eyes flashing in the moonlight.

Finally, after ten minutes of enduring their agonizingly polite conversation, she had made some excuse about going back inside to check on Gaby and Anna and left him sitting on his porch.

There was no one there now. The porch was empty, the curtains drawn. Just as well. She was simply too tired to face him again so soon.

Luck conspired against her, though. When she opened the door to her house, she realized it was as empty as Gage's porch. In the kitchen, she found a note from Jessica on the table. She read it quickly then groaned.

> Lisa—My little brother cut his finger and my mom needed me to watch the other kids while she took him to get stitches. I was going to take the girls to our house but Mrs. McKinnon offered to watch them for a half hour, until you got home. They should be next door. Sorry! I'll call you later.

So much for being too tired to face him. Apparently, she wasn't going to have a choice in the matter. But maybe he would be working in his room and she wouldn't even have to see him. A girl could only hope.

With a deep breath for fortitude, she marched next door and rang the bell, praying Lynn or one of the girls would respond. But just like so many of her other prayers, this one was doomed to go unanswered. After a few moments, Gage himself swung open the door. He looked gorgeous and strong, and for one crazy moment she wanted to sink onto his lap and just sleep there with his arms around her.

He gazed at her expectantly and she suddenly remembered her purpose. "The sitter left me a note that Gaby and Anna are over here," she said.

"In the backyard. They're, uh, having a tea party with my mother."

"I should have thought to look there before I bothered you. Sorry. I'll just grab them and get out of your way."

Even as she said the words, she couldn't manage to make her feet cooperate. She stood there on the porch, savoring the warmth of being near him. This might be the last time. With painful surety, she suddenly knew she couldn't keep avoiding the inevitable, that she was going to have to leave soon. It would already be so hard, but the longer she stayed, the more difficult leaving would finally be.

Wouldn't it be heavenly to forget all of that and just lean against him for a while? Let his hard strength absorb all her worries?

"You look tired," he observed quietly.

She blinked back to the hard, cold reality of her life. "It's been a long day. I...haven't been sleeping well."

"You look like you're going to fall over. How's your blood sugar?"

The concern in his voice and in his eyes touched a cold, lonely place inside her, made her realize how long it had been since anyone had worried about her. "It's been a little crazy," she admitted. "But I'm working on it."

"Why don't you sit down and I'll wheel out and get Gaby and Anna for you?"

"You can't maneuver that thing through the laundry room to the backyard. I'm fine, anyway. I just need to put my feet up for a while, which I'll do as soon as I get the girls."

He opened his mouth to argue but she held up a hand. "I'm fine, Gage. Honestly."

"Maybe you need to adjust your medication. Have you seen a doctor lately?"

Her painfully tight budget didn't allow the luxury of doctor visits just now. "I'm fine," she repeated. "Don't worry about me, Gage."

"Not so easy when you're the one being fussed over, is it?"

A small laugh escaped her. "Revenge is sweet, isn't it? Okay, you've made your point. Really, I appreciate your concern but all I need is to rest for a while, which I'll do as soon as I get the girls and head home. Thanks for lending your mom to Gabriella and Anna for a while."

"I think she was thrilled for the chance to spend some time with them. Mom loves kids. That's why she's an elementary school principal."

Before she could answer, Allie heard the back door open. A few seconds later the girls rushed through the house and into the front room, followed closely by Lynn, who looked trim and fit and together in a coral cotton shirt and denim jumper.

Gaby and Anna caught sight of her and immediately rushed over.

"Mommy! You're home!" Gaby exclaimed, flinging her arms around Allie's legs just as Anna jumped into her arms. She buried her face in Anna's hair that smelled of sand and sunshine and baby shampoo and hugged Gaby close with her other arm.

Like magic, her fatigue slipped away, along with the blues that had dogged her since the night before. Oh, how she loved her daughters. As long as she had these two precious girls with her, she could handle anything—a broken heart, life as a fugitive, menial jobs that sapped her brain and taxed her body.

For them she would face the worst life could throw at her.

She lifted her face and found Gage and his mother both watching her. Gage had a strange, intense expression on his face that left her insides trembling. He looked… hungry. It was the only word that came to her.

For a moment she was hypnotized by his expression, spellbound. An answering ache spread through her like the pitcher of orange juice Gaby had spilled on the kitchen floor that morning. Shaken by the depth of her yearning and praying she wasn't as transparent as she felt, she forced herself to turn away from him and face Lynn.

"Thank you for watching them. I'm sorry if it was an imposition."

"No imposition whatsoever. They're a joy."

The other woman smiled and Allie couldn't help returning it. "I think so, too," she murmured, hugging both girls tighter to her.

Lynn tilted her head, her eyes thoughtful as her gaze shifted between Allie and Gage. "Actually," she said after a moment, "how would you feel if I borrowed them tonight?"

"Borrowed them?"

"Only for a few hours. There's a new Disney animated

movie premiering tonight and I would love to take the girls to it."

The invitation took her by surprise. "I don't know...."

"You would be doing me a favor." Lynn smiled, but Allie sensed determination behind it. "I've been wanting to see this movie since I first saw the trailer for it, but I've never been comfortable sitting in a movie theater alone. Since neither of my sons has seen fit to give me any grandchildren of my own, I would dearly love a chance to spoil your daughters for a while. Believe me, I would enjoy the movie so much more if Gaby and Anna came with me."

Gaby squeezed her legs so tightly Allie feared she would lose her balance. "Please, Mommy? Oh, please, oh, please?"

She didn't know how to respond. The girls had chattered on and on about seeing the movie, too, and she had thought about taking them to the cheap matinee on her next day off. But if they were going to be leaving and trying to settle in a new town somewhere, she wasn't sure when she would get the chance.

Even Anna decided to get in on the action. She turned her huge dark eyes to her mother and Allie couldn't miss the plea in them. "I want to see the movie," she whispered.

How could she say no to that? An evening of solitude stretched out ahead of her, long and depressing. Maybe she could use the time to start packing their belongings, tying up loose ends before they all ran away again.

"Of course," she murmured. "It's very sweet of you to invite them. Let me just run them home to get cleaned up and round up some dinner."

"Oh, no," Lynn said quickly. "I'm also in the mood

for some McDonald's fries. How about we make that our first stop?''

''Yeah!'' Gaby let go of Allie's legs and rushed over to give a startled Lynn a hug. ''Mr. Gage,'' she confided. ''I like your mommy.''

Gage gave a startled laugh, though he looked a little uncomfortable. ''I, uh, like her, too.''

''Oh, no,'' Lynn said suddenly. ''I forgot about your dinner, Gage. I've got some chicken breasts marinating in lemon-herb sauce, and I planned to grill them out back tonight, but now I'm afraid I won't have time.''

He shrugged. ''I'll figure something out. I can always order a pizza.''

''No, no. I should have thought of this.''

She looked so distressed that Allie instinctively stepped forward. ''I can fix his dinner, Mrs. McKinnon. It's the least I can do.''

''I'm not helpless,'' Gage muttered.

His mother ignored him. ''Can you, dear?'' she said with a satisfied smile. ''That would be wonderful. Everything is all ready except the chicken and that shouldn't take you long. And there's plenty for two so make sure you stay and eat with him.''

Now why did she have the funny feeling that she had just been conned? Allie wondered. Surely a woman as gracious and thoughtful as Lynn wouldn't be up to anything devious.

Still, she suddenly suspected that Gage's mother had some kind of hidden agenda with all this maneuvering.

Don't be ridiculous, she chided herself. What possible ulterior motive could the woman have? Lynn had just offered to take her daughters out on the town for the evening, and it would be ungrateful and suspicious to question her motivation.

She should just take the invitation at face value and be happy someone enjoyed spending time with her girls as much as she did.

"I'll just run them home to get washed up and changed into clean clothes."

"Will a half hour give you enough time?"

"I think so."

"Wonderful," Lynn exclaimed. "Oh, this will be such fun."

As Allie herded her excited daughters out the door, she still couldn't shake the niggling sensation that she'd just been duped.

Chapter 14

His mother was up to something.

A half hour later, Gage sat on the patio in the blasted wheelchair he was so tired of, a book in one hand and the barbecue tongs in the other. Between flipping the chicken breasts, he was trying to concentrate on one of the mysteries Wyatt had dropped off on his last visit.

He wasn't having much luck. Though the book's plot was intriguing and imaginative, the dialogue sharp and witty and the characters vividly painted, he couldn't seem to focus, too busy trying to figure out the motives behind his mother's manipulations.

Gage hadn't missed the calculating gleam in Lynn's devious eyes before she left with Lisa's kids. Trouble was, he still couldn't figure out what, exactly, she might be calculating.

Maybe she had been telling the truth, that she just planned to go to the movie and wanted some company. Anna and Gaby were cute enough kids and he supposed it wasn't so unusual that Lynn might like to take them on an outing.

Still, the whole thing left him with an itch between his shoulderblades, like the time he and a partner walked into a drug deal gone bad.

Despite his suspicions, he had to admit this wasn't a bad way to spend an evening—in the middle of a flower garden that smelled sweet and rich and alive, underlaid by the mouthwatering scent of grilling meat.

The day had been warm earlier but clouds were gathering overhead, cooling everything off. The hot July sun had set behind the mountains enough that the backyard was now shady, with a comfortable breeze blowing down out of the Wasatch range to rustle the leaves of the trees and make the wind chimes sing softly.

He should have been out here every evening, Gage thought, instead of using his injuries as an excuse to stay cooped up inside.

After trying in vain for a few more moments to concentrate on the page, he finally set the book aside on the picnic table and returned to the grill. He found it a little tricky lifting the lid at the angle required by the wheelchair, but he managed.

The chicken breasts were cooking up nicely. Another fifteen minutes or so and they would be done.

Just as he started to close the lid again, Lisa rounded the corner of the house. She had changed her clothes after work, he noted, into a pastel-flowered sundress that drifted enticingly around her legs. Her ever-present insulin pump was clipped to a pocket on the dress and her brown hair was pulled back with a snowy headband.

She looked cool and sweet and delicious and he wanted to savor every bite.

"Hey, I'm supposed to be doing this," she protested.

"Contrary to popular belief, I'm not completely helpless," he said. "I told you that. I think I can manage to toss a couple of chicken breasts on the grill."

"How did you get down the back steps?"

"I didn't. I went down the ramp out front and just rolled around the house."

It had been a little tricky since the path was gravel and barely wide enough for the wheelchair, but he wasn't about to tell her that. If he had learned anything during his temporary stint in this damn chair, it was a deep appreciation for the myriad challenges encountered by those who used these things on a permanent basis. Things he had always taken for granted now seemed like insurmountable tasks without the use of his legs.

"Would you like me to take over now?" she asked.

"No. I want you to sit down and relax."

"I promised your mother I would fix your dinner."

"There's nothing to do now. Sit."

She looked a little astonished by the idea, as if she didn't quite know how to relax, and he wondered how long it had been since she had taken a moment for herself.

After a pause she finally obeyed, sitting on the edge of one of the cushioned patio chairs. For a moment she sat tensely, her shoulders stiff, then gradually, accompanied by the birdsong and the wind chimes and the soft breeze, she began to settle into the chair. She leaned her head back against the cushion and closed her eyes.

"Nice, isn't it?" he murmured.

A tiny smile played around the edges of her mouth. "Mmm. Very."

The tension in her shoulders began to ease inch by inch, and after only a few moments she drifted off to a light sleep, her breathing slow and even.

He was struck by the picture she made in the golden

twilight. She was so beautiful, with those long eyelashes and delicate features and that lush, kissable mouth.

He could sit here watching her sleep for hours. The depth of the contentment easing through his insides scared the hell out of him. He was a tough-guy FBI agent. How could he be content sitting out on a quiet patio on a summer evening, watching his next-door neighbor sleep?

The truth was, he had missed having her around these past few weeks since his mother had come. He hadn't realized just how much until right this moment.

He left her sleeping for several minutes, until a quick check of his watch told him it was past time to turn the chicken breasts again. Though he tried to be as quiet as possible, he couldn't avoid making some noise as he lifted the lid of the gas grill.

It wasn't exactly a huge commotion, but she startled awake as quickly as a soldier on patrol.

"Oh." She blinked several times. "Did I fall asleep?"

"Looks like."

She flushed, her eyes mortified. "I'm so sorry."

"Don't apologize," he said gruffly. "You needed the rest. I'm only sorry you didn't get more. After we eat, you ought to just go catch an hour or so of sleep before your girls get home from the movie."

She ignored the advice. "How long on the chicken?"

"Just a few more moments."

"I suppose I'd better go in and take care of the rest of the meal then." She rose and her dress fluttered around her legs.

"If you wouldn't mind bringing everything outside, we could eat back here."

"That would be nice. I'll be right out."

Though he knew it was a lost cause, he tried to focus on the hapless mystery novel again until she came out the back door carrying a wicker basket and wearing a strange expression.

"What's the matter?" he asked.

"I think we've been set up."

"What do you mean?"

"I don't suppose you happened to notice the dining room before you came out, did you?"

"No. Why?"

"It looks like something out of a fancy restaurant. White tablecloth, crystal glasses, wine chilling on the table. The whole works. Your mother went to a lot of trouble on our account."

Ah. Now it all was starting to make sense. He grimaced. The blasted woman was matchmaking! He thought of the strange looks his mother had split between him and Lisa and hoped like hell he'd been successful at concealing his complicated feelings for her.

Embarrassed at Lynn's anything-but-subtle maneuverings, he growled an oath.

Lisa's laugh chimed through the backyard. "Oh, it's not that bad. I think it's rather sweet of her, actually. I haven't been set up on a date since my freshman year of college."

"It's not a date," he growled.

"Right. Well, whatever it is, I was sure you wouldn't want all your mother's hard work on our behalf to go in vain so I brought out the wine and the glasses."

"As dark as it's getting with those clouds, we might need the candles too."

"Good point. I'll bring them out on the next trip."

With a flick of her wrists she spread out a crisp white cloth on the picnic table, then began setting out dishes and flatware.

Despite his lingering chagrin and annoyance at his

mother, he enjoyed watching Lisa bustle around. She had such unconscious grace. It was there in everything she did, from the way she rolled the cloth napkins and set them by the plates to the efficient manner she lit the slim candle tapers to the small, bright handful of flowers she carefully picked from the garden and set in a vase from the kitchen.

Just as he turned off the propane to the grill and prepared to remove the chicken, Allie came out of the kitchen with the rest of the meal Lynn had prepared—a tossed salad and two huge russet potatoes smothered in butter and sour cream.

"Remind me to thank your mother," Lisa said after a few moments of small talk while they began to eat. "This is lovely. I can't remember the last time I had a grown-up meal, with wine and everything. Usually it's Kool-Aid at my house."

Some wild impulse prompted him to speak the thought that had been rolling around his mind ever since she had walked into the backyard—longer even than that, if he were honest about it.

"We should do this for real sometime," he said. "Go somewhere nice, just the two of us. My mom could watch Anna and Gaby for you, or maybe that neighbor girl who tends them for you."

For a moment she looked shocked by his invitation—awkward and out of practice though it was—then her eyes softened. A corner of her mouth lifted, then she quickly looked back down at her plate, but not before he saw what he thought might be regret in her eyes.

"I'd like that, Gage. I really would."

"We'll do it then. How about next weekend?"

Her gaze met his and once more he thought he saw

sadness in those blue depths. "I think I'll have to see how next week goes, okay? Can I...let you know?"

"Sure. We could call it a celebration dinner."

She took a sip of wine, then set her glass down carefully. "Oh? What would we be celebrating?"

"I have a doctor's appointment in the morning. At the last visit he said he was just about ready to take off the casts and thought he might do it at my next appointment. I'll probably still be stuck in this chair for a week or so while I work on the weight bearing, then it's on to crutches."

"That's wonderful, Gage! I know how anxious you are to have the casts taken off."

"Right. Mostly I'm eager to get back to work again."

To his surprise, the joy on her features gave way to wariness. "Oh? When are you planning on going back?"

"Tomorrow, for starters. I've made plans to go in for a few hours in the afternoon. I'll have to see how much Potter, the agent in charge of the Salt Lake field office, will let me handle."

"I'm sure you can't wait." He couldn't figure out why her voice sounded wooden, stilted.

"It's been tough having to stay on the sidelines. I had to leave several open investigations, and I'd like to be updated on them."

Allie tried to show proper interest as Gage talked about returning to work, but all the while she wanted to stand in the middle of this beautiful flowery space and weep.

Here it was, then. The inevitable had finally caught up with her. If he planned to return to work in the afternoon, she knew she and the girls would have to be gone by morning. The risks of staying were simply too great—she couldn't afford to take a chance, not with her daughters at stake.

This would be the last moments they would share together before she and her girls disappeared from his life.

She sincerely hoped he couldn't hear the sound of her heart crumbling apart.

If this was their last time together, she didn't want to spend it moping and dreary, dreading the morning. She wanted to savor every moment, store it up in her memory for all the dark and lonely days ahead.

She wanted to seduce him.

The thought whispered into her mind, and even the evening breeze couldn't cool the heat that leaped to her cheeks.

Oh, my. She fought the urge to press her hands to her face. She couldn't possibly! What did she know about seduction? Okay, Jaime had always seemed to enjoy it when she made the first moves toward intimacy but that was vastly different. He had been her husband. They had a relationship built on love and devotion. He adored her, and anything she did had been with the blissful confidence that he would never dream of rejecting her.

Gage, on the other hand. How would she ever dare have the courage to seduce him?

This would be her only chance, though. She was leaving in the morning and would never see him again. Her heart ached as she realized she could either gather her courage and make the first move or she could spend the rest of her life with cold, lonely regret.

Whatever she decided, she didn't have to do it right this second. They had a few hours before Lynn would be back with the girls. She jumped to her feet so abruptly her chair teetered backward then settled on four legs once more.

''Your mother said something about peaches and vanilla ice cream for dessert. Would you like some?''

He looked baffled by her behavior but nodded. ''Sure. That sounds great.''

Grateful for the temporary reprieve, she hurried into the kitchen and found the fresh sliced peaches in the refrigerator. While she dished the ice cream, she watched him out the window. With the breeze ruffling his hair and a slight smile on his beautiful, hard features, he looked more relaxed than she had ever seen him.

A low, insistent ache began in her stomach and spread out in rippling waves. She felt weak, trembly, but she knew she didn't need to check her glucose level. The reason for her jitters sat outside the window, oblivious to her turmoil.

She wanted to be with him more than she wanted her next breath. She took several deep breaths to try to center herself, then carried the bowls outside again.

''No ice cream for you?'' he asked after she handed him his dessert.

''I'm happy with just peaches.'' She would be even happier with just *him* but she couldn't tell him that so she contented herself with savoring the sweet, summery fruit.

When her bowl was nearly empty, she looked up after taking a bite and found him watching her, glittery desire in his eyes.

She swallowed the mouthful, her nerves fluttering. So she wasn't the only one who felt the low tension simmering between them. The realization gave her the courage to lean forward.

''You have a little ice cream right there.'' With her thumb, she slowly dabbed at the corner of his mouth. His lips were cool from the ice cream, a sensual contrast against the heat of her skin.

"Is it gone?" His voice sounded almost harsh in the soft quiet of the evening.

"Not quite." She leaned in and pressed her lips with aching gentleness to the spot then she drew back slightly, sweetness on her lips.

"There," she said breathlessly. "Now it's gone."

He exhaled a low, heartfelt oath. "If you want to start something, let's start something," he growled and reached for her.

His mouth devoured hers with a hunger that matched her own, and she wanted to laugh for joy. Maybe she was better at this whole seduction thing than she thought. One tiny kiss later, here they were.

She lost track of everything—the approaching darkness, the girls, her inevitable departure. For this moment there was only Gage and his mouth against hers.

And a rainstorm.

At first she was too wrapped up in the kiss to register the cool drops on her skin as anything more than something odd that didn't quite belong. A moment later those first few tentative drops gave way to one of the rapid summer deluges that could spring up so suddenly in the Rockies.

"Oh!" she gasped, wrenching her mouth away. "We need to get you inside or your casts will be a soggy mess! Even if they are coming off tomorrow, you don't want to get them drenched or you'll have to spend a miserable, itchy night."

"That would be nothing new." His words were gruff but for once the meaning in his eyes was clear—*she* was more to blame for any of his nocturnal misery than his casts.

"Hurry inside!" she said, even though it took every bit

of self-restraint she had not to kiss him again. "I'll take care of the rest of this."

He looked as if he wanted to argue, but after a moment he complied, wheeling quickly toward the front of the house. Wondering if she would have to start all over now, she quickly began gathering the remains of their meal, stowing it all in the same wicker basket she had found in the house earlier to haul everything out.

She rushed into the kitchen with the intention of hurrying through the house to help Gage up the steeply angled ramp to the porch but to her surprise she found him inside ahead of her.

"That was fast!"

"I'm sorry the rain ruined your grown-up dinner."

"I'm not. I love a good summer rainstorm." She smiled, wiping sodden strands of hair out of her eyes, amazed at how fast they had been drenched by the quick storm. She probably looked like a drowned rat, but she couldn't worry about it. Nothing as minor as a little rain would ruin her last moments with him.

"We're dripping all over the floor," Gage murmured.

"It will wipe up." In the hallway linen closet, she found a neat stack of clean, fresh-smelling towels and pulled several out. When she returned to the kitchen, she bent to clean up the small puddle dripping from his wheelchair then started carefully wiping down his casts.

"You don't have to do that."

She glanced up to find him watching her with that same glittery look he'd worn earlier. "I know. I want to, though. Is that okay?"

His laugh sounded ragged. "I think anything you wanted to do right about now would be just fine with me, unless it involved you walking out the door."

She couldn't contain her smile. "Then you won't mind

if I do this.'' Leaning over the arm of the chair, she pressed her mouth to his softly. He pulled her across his lap and deepened the kiss. For several long moments, they were tangled together, lost to everything but each other.

''Why do we always seem to end up doing this in the kitchen?'' she murmured.

His eyes held laughter and unbridled desire. ''Where else would you like to be doing it?''

Words hovered on her tongue but she was too chicken to tell him. What kind of wanton would he think her if she dared utter them? On the other hand, she reminded herself again, this was her one and only chance to be with him. Ever. She couldn't let a silly thing like nervousness ruin it.

''The bedroom,'' she whispered, meeting his gaze with what she hoped was an expression of confidence.

He froze and stared at her, his gray eyes intense and aroused. ''Are you sure?''

''Absolutely positive.''

He kissed her fiercely, then groaned. ''I'd give anything to be able to carry you into my bed like some conquering hero. A few more weeks, maybe.''

In a few weeks she would be long gone, just a memory. She touched his face. ''I don't need that. I only need you.''

''How about a ride, then?''

She gasped as he started to wheel toward the bedroom. It was a tight fit through the doorway but she curled her legs up and they managed to make it through. Inside his bedroom, he closed and locked the door behind them, then captured her mouth with his again.

''It just occurred to me that the logistics of this might be a little tricky,'' he murmured, his breath tasting of wine and peaches and vanilla ice cream. "I'm not good for much with these damn casts on my legs."

"Don't sell yourself short, Agent McKinnon. I think you're good for plenty," she said on a gasp as his wandering hands found the curve of one breast through the wet cotton of her sundress. Fiery need shot through her, rich and exhilarating.

"A few things, maybe." He dipped his head and suckled her through the damp material. "Still, you're going to have to do a lot of the work here, I'm afraid."

"Poor little old me," she teased and shifted enough that she could pull off his damp shirt, revealing all those wonderful sleek muscles she had admired for so long. Her hands explored his skin, but the tight space in the wheelchair limited movement.

By unspoken agreement she rose so that he could transfer to the bed, then she followed him, taking care not to jostle his casts.

"I bet you're wishing now you and Ruth hadn't been so quick to move my nice big king-size mattress out of here."

A quick laugh escaped her. "Are you still sulking about that?"

"Hey, I love that bed."

"But do you really think we need acres of room?" She leaned across his bare chest and brushed her lips across his. "I don't think cozy is necessarily a bad thing."

His smile was dangerous. "Good point."

His hands worked the front buttons of her sundress and he pulled it down over one shoulder. As he bared her to his gaze, she was glad she wore a pretty, lacy bra—one of her favorites—instead of a plain, old everyday cotton one. A small corner of her mind wondered if she might have subconsciously planned something like this even before she had come over and found the intimate dinner Lynn had arranged for them.

Then Gage lightly drew his thumb across her skin just above the cup of the bra and she forgot to think. She shivered and closed her eyes, absorbing every sensation. When he dipped a thumb under the lace of her bra and touched bare skin, she gasped and shifted to give his exploring hand better access.

Her nipples were swollen, achy for his touch. A moment later he worked the front clasp of her bra and found the hard, taut peaks.

"Oh, my," she murmured.

His low laugh scored across her sensitive nerve endings. As he touched her, caressed her, his mouth found hers again. She drowned in his kiss—in the taste of him and his clean male scent and the warmth of his tongue tangling with hers.

His hand shifted from her breasts and moved down her skin. An instant later she felt his hand near her infusion site and she suddenly panicked and scrambled up.

"What's the matter?"

"I forgot about this." Embarrassed, she covered the spot to the lower left of her navel where the insulin pump fed into her. If she'd been thinking earlier, she would have tried to unobtrusively pull out the catheter before they got to this point so that he wouldn't be confronted with such a stark reminder of her condition.

"I'm sorry. It can be kind of a mood breaker."

"Lisa, it would take a whole lot more than that to break the mood for me."

He pulled her back to him and kissed her again. She could still feel the heat of his arousal jutting against her insistently.

"I can remove the pump. It will just take a minute."

"Whatever you're most comfortable with. I don't care."

He didn't, she realized, and tumbled into love with him all over again. Oh, how she would hate walking away from this man. With a strange mix of sorrow and sweet joy tumbling around inside her, she scooted to the edge of the bed and turned off the pump then pulled the catheter from the infusion site and set them both on the bedside table.

"Is it safe to turn it off?" Gage asked.

"I can do without it safely for an hour or so at a time. I should be fine. I'm afraid we don't have any more time than that since your mother and the girls will be back by then."

"It really doesn't bother me."

She smiled and traced the curve of his jaw with tenderness. "I know. I can't tell you what that means to me."

Since she was already standing, she used the chance to shimmy the rest of the way out of her sundress and bra. His eyes darkened like the stormclouds still flinging raindrops against the window.

Clad only in lacy panties that matched the bra, she returned to the bed and reached to help him out of his sweats.

"You think your insulin pump is a mood breaker, try having two miserable casts on your legs," he said ruefully.

"We're quite a pair, aren't we?"

He gazed at her with one of those unreadable expressions on his face. "I'm beginning to think so."

No. They weren't a pair at all. The only thing they would have together was just this one incredible night. A tiny slice of time for her to show him how much she loved him.

Her breath seemed to catch in her throat, but she pushed away the sorrow and regret. Later she could focus on her broken heart. For now she wanted to savor every moment of this.

Not wanting to waste any time, she kissed him with all the passion inside her. For a long time they explored each other, learning pleasure spots and secret hollows. As they touched and tasted, tension coiled within her, needy and demanding.

She wanted him inside her, wanted his strength and his heat. With a boldness born from the desperate urgency of knowing their time together was running out, she reached for him, cradling his hardness in her fingers.

He groaned an oath and shifted his hips. ''I think I've got condoms in the drawer,'' he murmured.

In seconds she found one and covered him, teasing and touching as she went. By the time she finished, he was breathing hard.

''I'm not so sure I like being at your mercy here.''

Her laugh was rough and aroused. There was something incredibly erotic about being the one making all the moves. ''Too bad. You're completely under my control. Face it, you're helpless against me, Agent McKinnon. I can do whatever I want with you, and there's not a single thing you can do about it.''

With her hands clasped in his, she straddled him then sheathed him inside her. A gasp of sheer pleasure escaped her lips, and she moved her hips again.

''And all this time I thought you were so sweet and innocent. Truth is, you're a wicked woman, Lisa Connors,'' he murmured, his features taut and his stormy gaze filled with laughter and desire. ''Just don't forget this is a temporary situation. In a few weeks I'll be back to normal with full use of both legs. We'll see how you like payback.''

''I'll just have to take full advantage of you while I have the chance, then.''

It was tricky, but after a moment she developed a rhythm of sorts. With each movement, he seemed to stretch deeper inside her. Soon both of them were trembling, their breathing harsh. The tension spiraled unbearably and she gave him a hard kiss, her mouth urgent on his. She was hungry for release. Burning for it.

Finally his fingers reached between their bodies. Just as she lowered herself onto him again, he touched the aching center of her desire, and the world exploded in a burst of bright, vivid colors. With a ragged moan, he joined in her pleasure.

Her body spent, she collapsed against him, careful to keep her weight off his legs. He pulled her to his side and held her, his hands gentle as he pushed damp strands of hair from her face. ''You can take advantage of me like that anytime you want.''

She smiled weakly even as she felt tears burn against her eyes. No, she couldn't. She wouldn't be around. ''Same goes, Agent McKinnon.''

Even though she knew Lynn and the girls would be back soon, they stayed in a tight, bittersweet embrace for a long time, just touching and caressing each other softly while she worked to choke back the heartache she hoped he couldn't see.

She should never have let things go so far, she realized grimly. Yes, she would have this one precious, incredible memory to take with her when she left him.

But she knew now with desolating clarity that one memory would never be enough.

Chapter 15

The sun was still hours away from cresting the mountains to the east of Park City when Allie loaded the last suitcase into the trunk of her Honda.

Though it was a tight squeeze, she had somehow managed to pry, cram and stuff their belongings into every available space of the car, leaving just enough room for the girls in their booster seats.

She closed the trunk and stepped away from the car. She supposed she should carry the girls out so they could leave. With luck, Gaby and Anna would stay asleep on the road for a few hours, until they were well on their way.

She wasn't sure she was up to coping with Gaby's inevitable barrage of questions for a while.

Though she knew she had no excuse for lingering out here, really, she stood in the driveway, gazing at the dark silhouette of the mountains around her. An owl hooted softly in a tree down the street. His call was answered from somewhere nearby, and in the distance she could hear the sharp bark of a dog then silence once more.

Oh, she didn't want to run away. She and the girls had been safe here, had made good friends like Ruth Jensen, Estelle Montgomery, Jessica Farmer. At the thought of never seeing any of them again, a lump rose in her throat, and hot tears burned behind her eyelids.

How she hated this life—this constant looking over her shoulder, the subtle tension always simmering beneath her skin. The knowledge that she would likely never again have the chance to sink down roots like the bright blossoms Ruth planted.

Right now, with the town asleep and peaceful and the cool mountain air fresh and clean in her lungs, she couldn't bear the thought of leaving this place. The future loomed ahead of her, dark and scary and unknown, and she wanted to run back inside her snug little cottage, jump into her warm bed and yank the covers over her head so she didn't have to face it all.

She had to admit, the main reason she couldn't bear to leave this comfortable little nest was just a dozen yards away, most likely asleep in the bed where they had shared such tenderness.

She shifted her gaze to Gage's darkened house. The tears threatened to break free but she quickly blinked them back.

She didn't want to remember him with heartbreak. When she thought of Gage from here on, she wanted it to be with joy and laughter, to remember those heavenly moments they had spent entwined together the evening before. Not with regret and loss.

How cruel life could be. For the last two years, she thought she would remain locked forever in her grief over Jaime. She never would have dreamed a gruff, wounded soldier like Gage McKinnon could help her realize she could one day find love again in a most unexpected place—or that she would find that love with the one man she couldn't have.

What would Gage think when he discovered she and her girls had cleared out without a word? Would he be angry or hurt or both?

Maybe neither. Though she knew he was attracted to her and she sensed he might have deeper feelings than just the physical heat they generated together, he was so hard to read. Most of the time she couldn't tell what was happening inside his head or in his heart.

She had a crazy wish that she could see him one more time, just to see him again and to tell him goodbye. It was impossible, though. She had left things too long already, had allowed herself to be lulled into a false sense of peace and security. She should have packed up her girls and fled weeks ago, before Gage McKinnon and his gray eyes and his strong shoulders could creep into her heart and threaten her future.

That afternoon he would be returning to work at the FBI, to a world of mug shots and forensics and all-points bulletins.

She could be one of those bulletins. Maybe no one was looking for her and the girls—maybe Irena and Joaquin had never reported her missing—but she couldn't take that chance. Too much was at stake.

Headlights suddenly sliced through the predawn darkness and she watched as a delivery truck lumbered down the quiet road. The milkman, she realized, charmed all over again by the contrast of Park City—cosmopolitan resort destination one moment, sleepy small town the next.

Allie rubbed at the one dratted tear that escaped before

she could stop it. Enough. She couldn't stand here all day mourning what she would be leaving behind. It would accomplish nothing.

Even though she might long to see Gage again, she knew she couldn't. She needed to be on the road without having to face him or his mother or anyone else. It would be far easier to make a clean break without having to come up with some convenient lie to explain why she and the girls were skulking away in the middle of the night.

With one last, regretful look toward the cottage next to hers, she went inside to gather her sleeping daughters.

''Are you sure you're comfortable, dear? I can bring out more pillows before we leave.''

With a mental groan, Gage settled deeper into the passenger seat of his mother's sporty little Toyota SUV. ''I'm fine.''

Lynn frowned at him, her soft features twisted into a suspicious look. ''Are you sure? You're just so tall and I'm afraid I don't have much leg room in this thing. Your brother is always complaining about it.''

''I'm fine. Really,'' he repeated, working hard to keep the bite out of his voice. He had swallowed so much of his irritation these past few weeks it was a wonder he didn't have a raging case of bleeding ulcers.

Lynn wasn't to blame. She was only trying to help, he knew that—that's why he worked so hard not to take his frustrations out on her. He just wasn't any good at being mollycoddled, and he still hated the circumstances that had made it necessary.

His mother studied him for a moment longer as if trying to gauge the truth of his words. Finally she gave a little sigh and shifted into reverse. ''If you're sure.''

''I am. The doctor's office is only ten minutes away.''

Before she drove away, Lynn nodded in the direction of the house next door. "It looks like Lisa went somewhere early this morning," she said. "Her car is gone, anyway."

He didn't want to look, but as Lynn drove off, he couldn't help himself from gazing in the rearview mirror at her empty driveway, with no sign of her little Honda.

Maybe she had gone into work early, though he hoped not. She needed sleep more than she needed a little overtime.

He thought of how deeply she had fallen asleep in his arms after the heat and wonder they had shared. He would have given anything he owned if she could have been able to stay right there with him all night and slept in his arms, soft and warm and at peace. He had loved holding her, listening to her breathe, watching the worry that always seemed to shadow her eyes disappear for a while.

All too soon, though, he had been forced to wake her so they could be dressed before Lynn returned with the girls and discovered how very well her sneaky plan had worked.

How badly would Lisa rip into him if he called Ruth Jensen and told her she needed the day off so she could recharge her batteries? He pictured her reaction and couldn't help wincing a little. She would skin him alive if he dared.

Though she had a soft vulnerability inside her, it was covered by a hard, crackly layer of fierce independence. He found it ironic that for all the care she took to nurture everyone around her, she didn't take well to finding herself on the receiving end of some of that concern.

His own need to take care of her, to do a little nurturing of his own, was as terrifying as the tenderness that settled in his chest whenever he thought about her. He didn't have the first idea what the hell he was going to do about it.

"I like her," Lynn said quietly.

He blinked at his mother, unnerved by the way she sometimes seemed to see right through his skull into the workings of his brain. "Who?"

"You know. Lisa. I sense great courage in her. A strength of character you don't find in many people today. And those daughters of hers! They're just the sweetest things. They make me want to just grab them both close and hug them tight. I haven't had so much fun at the movies in years."

Just for one sublime instant, he allowed himself to remember what he and Lisa had been doing while his mother watched animated characters on the screen with Lisa's kids. Heat rushed through him and he couldn't contain his smile.

"Being with Gaby and Anna last night sure made me wish for a couple of granddaughters of my own," Lynn said slyly.

"Oh?" He pretended to ignore her extremely broad hint. "Is Wyatt seeing someone?"

Lynn gave a snort of laughter that she still somehow managed to make sound ladylike. "That one dates more women than I have lipstick colors. I've just about given up on him ever settling down."

"Don't look at me for grandchildren," he said gruffly.

"And why not?"

He was about to say he would stink at being a father, but the words seemed to sputter to a dead stop in his throat. Suddenly the idea of helping to raise a couple of beautiful little girls didn't seem so very terrible. A quick mental collage formed in his mind of a series of firsts—first day of school, first piano recital, first driving lesson.

Each image featured a smiling dark-haired girl and her mother. And him, looking on with pride and love.

Whoa. Slow down. One incredible evening together did not automatically translate to happily-ever-after.

So why did a future with Lisa seem to fit so well?

If he was stunned by the depth of his tenderness before, this turn of thought was absolutely staggering. A future with her? As in wedding rings and a house in suburbia and joint checking accounts? Impossible!

He drew in a shaky breath, grateful he wasn't driving or he probably would have run right off the road. No. As appealing as that pretty little picture might be, he didn't belong there.

"I've always thought I wasn't cut out to be a family man."

"Oh, that's nonsense. Wyatt says the same thing."

"Does he?" he asked, surprised that he and his brother might have even that much in common.

"There's no reason you both wouldn't make wonderful fathers. Just look at the example you had in Sam."

He stared at her, so astonished by her mention of his father—her ex-husband—that for a moment he couldn't think what to say.

In the entire ten days she had stayed at his house, she had never once mentioned Sam McKinnon. He assumed the enmity between the two of them ran so deeply that his father was too awkward a subject, though now that he thought about it, their divorce had always seemed painfully civil.

"Why do you look so surprised? Sam has always been a terrific father."

He thought of overnight campouts and heart-to-heart talks at their favorite fishing hole and baseball games where his dad never missed a chance to sit in the stands and cheer him on.

Fast on the heels of those childhood memories was his father the last time he had seen him, quietly asking questions about Gage's work at the FBI as they worked in Sam's cabinet shop with the smell of fresh-cut pine in the air and sawdust motes flashing golden in the sunlight that streamed in through dusty windows.

"Yeah, he is a good father," he said gruffly.

"That's why I agreed you should live with him after the divorce, Gage," Lynn said after a moment. "I hope you can understand that. Wyatt was still a child who needed his mother. But you were on the verge of becoming a man. Your father and I both thought it would be best for you to stay with him in Las Vegas until you went off to college."

He supposed he could see the reasoning to it now. At the time, though, it had sure felt like an abandonment.

He remembered the grief and loss he had struggled with after Lynn took Wyatt back to Utah. In his heart, he had known the reason she didn't take him, too—because she had counted on him and he had failed her and she couldn't bear to be reminded of it.

"Even boys on the verge of becoming men sometimes need their mothers," he murmured.

To his dismay, tears filled her eyes and her hands tightened on the steering wheel. "Oh, Gage."

He instantly regretted his words and wanted to beg her not to cry. He couldn't bear the sight of his mother's tears. "It doesn't matter. It was a long time ago."

"It *does* matter. Things were such a mess after…after Charlotte disappeared. *I* was a mess."

"It was a crazy time."

"I regret so many things about those first weeks and

months as we all tried to find our way without her—to live with the horrible, devastating loss of her.''

She blew out a ragged breath. ''But what I regret the most was that I really lost two children that day. One was taken from me by force, and that was a terrible, traumatic thing for any mother to endure. But the other one—my strong, wonderful oldest child—I gave up completely on my own.''

''You didn't. Not really.''

''Yes, I did. Maybe not exactly the day Charley disappeared, but that was the beginning. It doesn't matter that we thought it was the best option, you living with your father. It doesn't matter that I knew you were better with him, that you had a life there in Las Vegas that I didn't want to tear you away from. I still let you grow away from me.''

He didn't know how to answer her so he remained quiet, aware of his fist clenching and unclenching in his lap.

''I don't know,'' Lynn went on after a moment. ''Maybe I could have tried harder to keep us all together. But I did nothing, just stood by without even a whimper while time and distance took you from me, and I'm so sorry for that.''

All these years he had no idea she thought these things. Had he misinterpreted everything?

They had arrived at his doctor's office, Gage saw. Lynn parked out front, but neither of them made a move to start the complicated process of transferring him from the vehicle to the wheelchair. Lynn turned off the engine and faced him.

''I love you, Gage. I'm so proud of the man you've become. I can't tell you how much I have enjoyed these past weeks, getting to know you again. I'd like to try to build a relationship with you now, if it's not too late. Do you...do you believe you could ever find it in that tough heart of yours to forgive me?"

This time his fingers stayed clenched. Forgive her? She had it all backward. "There's nothing to forgive."

"There is," she insisted. "You and Wyatt needed me to be strong and I wasn't. I let my grief over losing Charlotte cloud everything."

"We both know who holds the most blame for Charley."

"What do you mean?"

She looked genuinely confused. Suddenly Gage abhorred the way they tiptoed around the subject as if it didn't exist. He wanted it out in the open, wanted to rip off the polite plaster cast that concealed the wound festering between them and let air into it.

"I was supposed to be watching her. Instead, I was screwing around with my friends. Because of that, some bastard took her. How can I blame you for not wanting me around afterward?"

Lynn gasped, her features going white. "Is that what you thought? That I blamed you for Charlotte's disappearance?"

He said nothing—what was left to say?—and her skin paled another shade. "Dear heavens. You do! That's ridiculous. Completely ridiculous! I *never* blamed you!"

"You should."

Before he realized what she was doing, she reached out and covered his fist with her smaller hand. Tears seeped from her eyes and trickled down her cheeks.

"No. Oh, son. I never dreamed you felt this way. I should have realized." Her voice caught and her fingers tightened over his. "It's not your fault your sister was kidnapped. If anyone shoulders any blame, it should be me! I should have just taken her to the store with me."

"You couldn't have known someone was out there watching."

"And you could? You were a child! I've long ago accepted I couldn't have prevented it from happening. Someone could have snatched her out of a shopping cart or taken her from the car when my back was turned. If I couldn't have stopped it, how could you?"

"If I had been tending her and Wyatt as you asked me to, she might still be here."

Lynn was quiet, her gaze out the windshield. When she looked back, the vast, aching sorrow in her eyes whipped through him like a blade, just about more than he could bear.

Even harder to handle was the realization that her pain wasn't for Charlotte or for her own loss of her daughter but for *him.*

"Do you tell the parents of all those missing children whose cases you work so diligently that it's their fault their child was taken?"

He frowned. "No. Of course not."

"Then how can you blame a twelve-year-old boy for something out of his control, something that happened more than twenty years ago?"

He stared at her, stunned. The truth of her words hit him like ten thousand watts of power rushing through every cell of his body. Damn it, she was right. If this had been a case he worked, he would have done his best to assure the family it wasn't healthy and would accomplish nothing worthwhile to spend their time assigning culpability.

But hadn't he done exactly that? He had spent twenty-three years blaming himself for his sister's disappearance.

Had he been wrong all this time? Just thinking about it made him shaky, numb.

''It was a terrible thing to happen to any family,'' she said quietly. ''But the only one truly responsible is whoever took her. Please don't punish yourself for someone else's sins.''

Lynn watched him for a moment then offered a watery smile and opened her door to begin setting up the wheelchair.

Lisa's car still wasn't in the driveway when Gage returned from the doctor's office, feeling about a hundred pounds lighter, figuratively and literally.

The doctor had removed both casts. The right leg, the one with the simple fracture, was mending cleanly and he'd been given the green light to start a little weight bearing on it and eventually transition to crutches. The left leg, with the pins and rods, would require more time to heal but the doctor had agreed to trade the cast for a brace.

Liberation beckoned him with tantalizing allure. Without the bulky casts, he could have far more mobility. Once he regained the full use of his right leg, he could drive himself places, could return to work, could regain the independence he had taken for granted but had missed so bitterly.

Even as he thought it, he had to admit he hadn't minded so much having his mother around these last few weeks. And before that, there had been Lisa with her sweet scent and her ready smile and her unfailing compassion.

He wanted to celebrate his newfound freedom with her. As he had suggested to her the day before, now that he would be able to get around easier, he wanted to take her out to one of the many fine restaurants in Park City.

She hadn't exactly bubbled over with enthusiasm for the idea, he remembered, but maybe she didn't like leaving her daughters more than she had to. He would figure out a way to convince her. If not, he could always make plans for some outing that included Gaby and Anna.

But first she had to come home so he could talk to her about it. With one last look at her driveway, he transferred from his mother's SUV to the wheelchair.

"Don't think just because your doctor took those casts off that you can start acting crazy. If you're not careful, you'll end up right back in casts."

He was feeling so good that he even managed to smile at Lynn's fussing. "Yes, Mother."

"It shouldn't take me long to change for work," he said once inside. "I appreciate you being willing to drive me in for a few hours. But really, like I told you before, there's no reason for you to stick around to bring me home. I can catch a ride with one of the guys."

"I don't mind at all," Lynn assured him. "I've been wanting to do some shopping in the city. This will give me the perfect excuse to check out some of the new stores until you're done at work."

"Thanks. I, uh, appreciate it."

Lynn smiled, and Gage was once more reminded of their conversation earlier and the air they had somehow managed to clear between them.

He liked this new ease between them, unexpected though it might be. The tension and guilt that always used to simmer under his skin whenever he saw his mother seemed to have disappeared. In its place was a relaxed, comfortable peace.

"I'll be out in a minute," he said again, then wheeled to his room where he quickly changed out of the loose side-snap sweats he'd come to detest into one of his familiar suits. Putting it on again was like climbing back into his own skin after far too long away. Even with the brace that had to fit over his left pant leg and the wheelchair he would have to use for a while yet, the suit felt *right.*

Once dressed, he wheeled out of his room and found Lynn in the kitchen washing the breakfast dishes.

She turned around as he rolled through the doorway and gave him an approving smile. "You're always handsome, but there's just something that's so appealing about a man in a business suit and crisp white shirt. Your father rarely wore one, but when he did, my-oh-my. He always could make my heart race a little faster."

Her face took on a dreamy expression and Gage couldn't help squirming. He didn't even want to *picture* his parents together.

Funny, he thought, but Sam always wore the same expression on his face whenever he talked about Lynn. Why had neither of his parents ever remarried? he wondered. Both of them were still young, really, only in their mid-fifties.

He didn't know about Lynn but Sam never even dated. Was it possible they still had feelings for each other? If so, why had they spent all these years apart?

He wondered briefly what would happen if the two of them ever had reason to meet up with each other again. As soon as the thought entered his head, he quickly discarded it. Was he crazy? Didn't he have enough trouble with his own love life? Why would he possibly want to start messing in his parents'?

"I'm ready when you are," he said quickly.

"Just one more pan to scrub and then I'll be finished here."

"I think I'll just head outside, then, while I wait."

He refused to admit that he secretly hoped he might see Lisa and her girls pulling up while he was outside. The need to see her again—to reassure himself those incredible moments they had spent together hadn't been just a dream—was intense, almost violent.

But no little green Honda had appeared while he was inside. He tried not to let himself be too disappointed as he wheeled to the passenger side of Lynn's SUV. He had almost reached it when he heard an engine approaching in the still, warm afternoon.

With an eagerness that dismayed him, he wheeled away from the car so he could see who was coming. Disappointment whipped through him as he recognized the small utility truck his landlady drove.

Ruth Jensen looked more dour than usual as she jumped down from the truck, hauling a toolbox in one hand and a caddy full of what looked like cleaning supplies in the other.

She marched up the steps of Lisa's porch, then used a key to unlock the door, something that struck him as odd. Granted, she was the landlady but should she really just be walking in like that?

''Mrs. Jensen,'' he called before she could disappear inside.

She turned and the glum look on her features lightened a little when she spotted him. ''Agent McKinnon. Good to see you up and around.''

''I'm trying,'' he said. ''Listen, is everything okay over there?''

''Don't know. Haven't been inside yet. But Lisa Connors and her girls were clean tenants. I don't expect they left much of a mess.''

''What do you mean?'' Sudden unease rippled through

him like the wind tossing the heads of the columbines in the backyard.

''Thought you knew,'' Ruth said, her voice abrupt. ''She and her girls cleared out this morning. Dropped a note round the office before we opened saying thanks for the help but she needed to be moving on.''

Chapter 16

Gage stared at his landlady, certain he must have misheard her.

"Moving on? What do you mean?"

Ruth shrugged. "Just what I said. Moving on means moving on. Clearing out. Heading out of Dodge."

"She's gone?"

"Guess so, since she left her last month's rent and told me in the note to keep the security deposit."

He was frozen suddenly. An ice sculpture carved by some artist's chainsaw. He couldn't think, couldn't feel, was only conscious of the vast, yawning emptiness in his stomach.

Gone. She had left his arms warm and contented and happy—he *knew* she had, dammit—then returned home to pack up her girls and drive out of his life without leaving a single word about where she was going.

The ice began to melt, leaving red-hot emotion. Betrayal and loss and shock vied for violent control inside him. Why did he feel as if he had just been hit by Lyle Juber's damn pickup truck all over again? Only, this time his legs weren't the only thing crushed—every square inch of him felt bruised, shattered.

He was in love with her, he realized. In love with a smart-mouthed little caregiver with a sweet smile and gentle hands. He had spent his whole adult life protecting his heart, but somehow she and her beautiful daughters had sneaked inside and nested there, made a home.

Then ripped it all out by walking away from him.

What the hell was he supposed to do now?

The raging flood of emotions threatened to drag him under. He wanted to crawl somewhere—well, wheel, anyway—and try to cope with his feelings and her betrayal, but before he could move, Lynn opened his front door and trotted down the steps.

"Hello, Ruth," his mother said cheerfully. "Isn't it a lovely day? That rain yesterday was just the perfect amount to green everything up and make the garden look fresh and clean."

"Won't last," Ruth muttered. "Heat will dry out the grass."

"I know. But in the meantime we can enjoy it. We'll all be remembering glorious summer days just like this in a few months when we've been snowed in for weeks."

Ruth said nothing, and after a moment Lynn continued in the same friendly tone. "I've been meaning to tell you how much I have enjoyed your flowers these few weeks I've been staying with Gage. At night, I like to sit on the back patio and just inhale all the delicious fragrances. It's been such fun trying to see if I can identify the different smells. You're a gardening genius. I'd like to know your secret."

"Cow manure."

Lynn laughed, then looked to Gage as if urging him to join in. He stared back stonily, and his mother's smile slipped away, concern darkening her eyes. ''Gage, dear. Is everything all right?''

Nothing was right anymore. *Nothing.* But he knew he couldn't express the turmoil boiling through him. Not to his mother and definitely not in front of Ruth.

''Fine. Everything's fine,'' he lied. ''Are you ready to go?''

Lynn raised an eyebrow at his clipped tone but only nodded. ''Sorry to keep you waiting. Let's be on our way, then.''

He spent the forty-minute drive into the city trying to conceal the depth of his shock and hurt from his mother's all-too-perceptive gaze. He had a feeling he wasn't very successful at it, especially after they entered the parking garage near the gleaming office building that housed the FBI's Salt Lake City field office.

His mother pulled into a parking stall and shut off the engine, then turned to him, her usually soft features set into definite battle lines. ''Okay, I've let you get away with it long enough. Are you finally ready to tell me why you're acting like a bull raised on sour milk?''

The expression took him aback. Lynn was usually so cultured and refined it was sometimes easy to forget she was the daughter of a rough-and-tumble Utah cattle rancher.

He didn't want to tell her the truth but he couldn't come up with a convenient lie. ''Lisa took off,'' he finally said. ''Moved out.''

Lynn gaped at him. ''When? Why?''

''I guess this morning. That's what Ruth Jensen was telling me back at the house. As to the why, I couldn't tell you.''

Her reason for running away had to somehow be connected to the intimacies they had shared the night before. Wouldn't she have told him she was leaving otherwise? She would have had plenty of opportunities over dinner and afterward.

Had he come on too strong with her? Scared her away, somehow? No, he remembered. Not that he had been an unwilling participant, but she had definitely been the one who initiated their kisses and who had pushed for more.

So she seduced him and then just disappeared. What the hell was going on?

"Where did they go?" Lynn asked helplessly. "I don't understand. Why would she just pack up and leave without a word?"

"I don't know. She left a note for Ruth but didn't tell her where they were heading."

"You're an FBI agent. Can't you do something to find her?"

He swallowed the bitter laugh scouring his throat. "It's not that easy, Mom. I can't file a missing persons report on an adult woman simply because she decided to move away."

"It's more than that," Lynn said, with an urgency that took him by surprise. "I know it is. She's in trouble, Gage. I sensed it several times when I was talking to her. She has problems. I don't know what they are but somehow her leaving must be connected to whatever has been bothering her. I should have done more to find out what that was, to help her with it. You've got to find her!"

"There's nothing I can do, unless she's committed a crime."

Just for a moment he wondered if that could somehow be the reason for her sudden, precipitous flight, if she might be running from justice. No. He couldn't believe it.

The Lisa Connors he knew was too innocent, too artless, to be involved in anything illegal.

''You can't just let her disappear like this!''

He wanted to ask his mother how he was supposed to find Lisa when he couldn't seem to unearth a single trace of the sister he had spent the last two decades seeking. But of course he couldn't. Lisa was gone from his life just as surely as Charlotte.

''I don't think we have a choice. She's a grown woman.''

Lynn opened her mouth to argue but he forestalled her by reaching behind his seat for the wheelchair in the back. He pulled it out and set it on the ground, then unfolded it.

''Thanks again for the ride. I can catch a ride home with Davis or Thom Lovell.''

''No. You'll do no such thing. I told you I'd be back in a few hours and I will.'' She still looked dazed, but to his relief she didn't press him about Lisa. Instead, she hurried out of the SUV and came around to help him transfer into the chair.

Once he was settled, she touched his arm and he was startled to see soft compassion in her eyes. Did she have some inkling of his feelings for Lisa? He sincerely hoped not.

''Gage. Honey, I'm so sorry.''

He didn't know how to answer her. Besides that, he wasn't exactly sure he was comfortable being on the receiving end of this kind of empathy from his mother. In the end, he decided he would be best just to ignore it.

''I'll see you around five,'' he muttered and wheeled toward the elevator.

Gage shifted in his chair, trying to find a more comfortable position behind his desk at the FBI's Salt Lake

City field office. With this blasted brace on his left leg it was definitely a challenge, but he would bite his tongue off before he would complain.

He was keeping mum about a lot of things these days. He refused to complain about missing out on all the action in the field or about having to pore over old case files or even about having to catch up on a month's worth of Cale's paperwork.

As much as he despised desk work and being planted in this office instead of out in the field where he belonged, it sure beat hell out of the alternative. He would gladly take a few more months of riding a desk just as long as he didn't have to spend another minute staring at the four walls of his bedroom in Park City.

He had been back at work a week now, since the day the doctor removed his casts. After the first day back, he decided if he ever broke a limb again, he would just beg the doctors to shoot him and put him out of his misery. He refused to take another day of sick leave.

The FBI was where he belonged. Here he had a purpose, a mission. He wanted nothing more than to slip back into the persona he was comfortable with, the man he had been before the accident—a hard-nosed FBI agent completely dedicated to his career, to closing cases, to finding justice.

A man who never had to deal with distractions like a mother who had suddenly barged into his life and seemed to have no intention of allowing herself to be pried out again or a brother who seemed determined to have a relationship again after twenty years.

Or a beautiful blue-eyed neighbor and her sweet little girls and her problems, who disappeared without a word and left this damn gaping hole in his heart.

He missed Lisa so much he thought he would go crazy with it. He couldn't go ten minutes without thinking about her, without worrying about her blood sugar levels and whether she was sleeping enough and how she was keeping up with the girls.

He hated it. Part of him even thought he might hate her a little bit for putting him through this. He wanted to forget her, but no matter how much he tried to remind himself that she had made the choice to walk away—that she had turned her back on whatever they might have been just on the verge of discovering together—he couldn't seem to shake her from his mind or his memories.

Gage turned back to the field notes from one of the cases Davis had worked during his time away. He was trying to see if his partner had missed anything during the interrogation of a suspect in a child prostitution ring when Davis rapped on the open door and peeked his head inside.

"That the Bamburger file?" Davis asked.

Gage nodded. "Nasty piece of work there. I would have had a tough time not breaking the bastard's neck during the interview."

"Yeah, I have to admit it was a struggle to keep my hands off him. I had to play nice, though, since Potter was watching."

As Davis continued standing in the doorway, Gage began to pick up on the tension radiating from him. "Something wrong?" he asked.

"Yeah. Maybe." Finally Davis walked into the office. "I think you need to see this fax that just came over. It took me a few minutes to put the pieces together but you might be quicker than me."

He tossed a paper on the desk. Gage picked it up, registering that it was a watch bulletin sent out by the Philadelphia field office at the request of a private investigator.

The picture on the fax was blurred, but showed a solemn woman with long, straight, light-colored hair above the name Alicia Connelly DeBarillas. He narrowed his gaze, trying to place why something about the woman's features seemed familiar, but came up empty.

"We can play twenty questions here or you can fill me in."

"Check out the data sheet Philly sent along with it." Davis handed him another fax. After only a few lines, Gage's gut contracted as if he'd been slugged.

He gazed back at the picture, his insides suddenly numb. It was still grainy and indistinct, but now he could see the resemblance in the eyes and the bow-shaped mouth. Chop that light hair off, dye it brown and take away ten pounds or so and this Alicia Connelly DeBarillas was a dead ringer for Lisa Connors.

Even without having the picture to compare her to, he would have known it was her, just by reading the data sheet. DeBarillas was an emergency room nurse with diabetes from the Philadelphia area involved in a custody dispute over her daughters, Gabriella and Anna, ages five and three. She had been missing approximately two months, he read, right around the time he gained a new neighbor.

Gage swore long and low, a hot rush of betrayal sweeping through him. This was far worse than thinking she had just run off after their night together. She had played him for a fool. A helpless, invalid fool too stupid and too trusting to ever suspect a sweet-faced woman like her had been lying through her teeth.

What reason did he have to even think for a minute that Lisa Connors was anything but what she appeared to be? A single mother trying to get by on her own. He never would have suspected she was a fugitive, running from a custody battle over her daughters.

With whom? He wondered. The bulletin didn't say. Maybe her husband hadn't really been killed by a drunk driver. Maybe that was another tale she had spun. Maybe the guy was somewhere back east searching as diligently for his daughters as Gage's parents had looked for Charlotte.

He felt sick thinking of it. How much of what she had told him was truth and how much was a lie? What could he believe?

Had the passion between them been real or feigned? Betrayal coated his throat in thick, greasy layers.

Now he understood why she left. While he had been stuck at home recovering from his injuries, she probably figured he hadn't posed much of a threat to her. But when he had told her he was returning to work, she must have known there was a good chance he would eventually connect the dots between Lisa Connors and this Alicia DeBarillas.

"I think we had better go pay a little visit to your lovely neighbor," Davis said.

A whole spate of emotions thrashed through him, and he wanted to throw something. The urge to topple this whole damn desk—computer, paperwork and all—was almost overwhelming.

"She's not there," he growled. "She packed up her girls and took off a week ago."

"Any idea where?"

Gage shook his head. "None whatsoever."

"Well, she's not facing federal charges, apparently. Pennsylvania only gave us the heads-up as a courtesy so we can be on the lookout for her. I guess that means she's not our problem."

Gage shoved away from the desk and grabbed the crutches he was still growing accustomed to. "She's *my* problem. I'm going to look for her."

He wasn't about to let her get away with kidnapping those little girls and disappearing like the bastard who took his sister.

Hell was a decaying two-room apartment in North Las Vegas in the middle of a July heat wave.

Though it was after ten o'clock at night, the temperature outside hovered around a hundred degrees and it wasn't much cooler than that inside Allie's apartment. A tiny air-conditioning unit rattled and coughed in the window but was about as effective against the heat as a pea shooter against a Sherman tank.

She didn't know when she'd ever been so miserable.

Allie sagged onto the lumpy couch that came with the apartment. It wasn't only the heat that bothered her, though, that weighed her down, left her limp and exhausted.

She could have coped with living in an oven, if her life here had any other redeeming qualities. But she hated this apartment with its grimy windows and ugly seventies furniture, she hated working as a maid at the dismal Four-Leaf Clover Hotel and Casino, she hated having to leave her daughters with a woman she barely knew.

More than that, she was scared.

She supposed she could finally admit it here in the solitude of her living room with the girls asleep in the bedroom, their bed an air mattress on the floor where it was a little cooler.

No, she wasn't scared. She was petrified. Since leaving

Park City three weeks ago, her diabetes had flared out of control. She hadn't had such wildly fluctuating levels since those awful months after Jaime died. Nothing she did seemed to rein it in.

She had adjusted her diet, she had monkeyed with her insulin, she had done everything she could think of to control it, but nothing seemed to be working.

Just that afternoon she had finally gathered her nerve and gone to see a doctor. It cost her nearly two hundred dollars cash for him to warn her in a smug, condescending tone that if she didn't take better care of herself, she would find herself in the hospital within the week.

What would happen to her girls if she ended up being hospitalized in this strange city where she knew no one? Just thinking about it left her shaky and weak.

Maybe Irena and Joaquin had been right. Maybe all this time she had been fooling herself to insist that she could care for them by herself, given the uncertainties she lived with daily as a diabetic.

At least with their grandparents they wouldn't have to live this crummy, hand-to-mouth existence, living in this kind of hole-in-the-wall apartment building.

They would be safe, secure, would never want for anything, even if Irena and Joaquin ended up taking off with them to Venezuela and she never saw them again.

She couldn't bear this. She *couldn't.* What was she supposed to do? She gazed out the window at the dismal urban landscape, all strip malls and crumbling apartment complexes and concrete, with hardly anything green in sight except for a few stunted cacti and a palm tree or two.

She should never have left Park City. There they had friends and a backyard to play in and a comfortable bedroom, where cool mountain breezes blew in at night.

But though she might wish with all her heart to be back in that little cottage, she knew it had been impossible to stay. Gage would have found out the truth, and she still would have lost the girls.

Gage. Oh, how she missed him. She pictured him the last time she had seen him, sleepy and naked and gorgeous, and had to press a hand to her heart at the physical ache there.

How could she have come to this? In love with the one man with the power to destroy her world? If only she had met and fallen in love with someone safe, someone she could have confided in. Someone who would understand why she'd made the choices she had.

But she had been destined to love a hard, dedicated FBI agent who would not look with a shred of kindness on a woman who had virtually kidnapped her own children. Not with his own family history.

"Mama?" Gaby whimpered suddenly, poking her head out of the bedroom. "Can I get a drink of water?"

To her horror, Allie suddenly realized silent tears were coursing down her cheeks. How long had she been crying? She wiped at them with a surreptitious hand, hoping Gaby wouldn't notice.

"I thought you were asleep, honey."

"I was but I woked up. It's too hot."

"I know. I'm sorry."

Gaby studied her for a moment, that sweet little face cocked to one side and her big dark eyes concerned. "Mama, why are you crying?"

She didn't know how to answer. To her shame, she wanted to gather Gaby against her and weep into her hair, but she knew she couldn't impose the burden of comforting her on a child.

"Do you have an owie?" Gaby asked. "I can kiss it better."

Only my spirit, honey, she thought. *And my heart. My heart has been shattered into a million pieces and I don't have the first idea how to put it back together.*

With fierce effort, she choked back the sob welling in her throat. "No owie. I'm fine. I'm hot and I'm tired, that's all. Let's both get a drink of water and then we'll go to bed."

Together they walked to the refrigerator where Allie found the pitcher she kept full there. She poured a glass for Gaby, who chugged it as if she'd been stuck in the vast Nevada desert for months.

"Mama, I don't like this place very much," Gaby suddenly said, her voice small and forlorn, as if she were confessing a terrible secret. "It always smells funny."

Allie had to agree. If hopelessness and despair had an aroma, it would probably be the sad scent of the Joshua Tree Apartments.

"It's just different than you're used to."

"I liked our other house. With Gage and Ruth and Jessica and Gage's nice mommy. Why can't we go back there?"

How was she supposed to answer that? She knew there were no words a five-year-old would understand so she didn't even try. "We'll like it here after we've been here a while. Now back to bed or you'll be too tired to play with Anna tomorrow."

To her relief, Gaby didn't argue. With one last hug, she went back into the bedroom. After Allie tucked her in again, she returned to the other room. On that lumpy couch again, she hugged her knees, wishing with all her heart that she could avoid the inevitable. She couldn't see any way around it, though, and the knowledge pierced through her like a thousand nails.

She had to turn herself in.

It would mean losing the girls to Jaime's parents and how would she ever survive that? She wouldn't, she knew. She would shrivel up and die without them.

But she had to. Keeping them in these conditions, with her medical condition so precarious, was cruel and selfish.

She had to think about what would be in their best interest. She finally knew she could no longer avoid the grim realization that the answer to that question wasn't to live constantly on the run with someone who might end up hospitalized—or worse—at any moment.

Just how did she go about turning herself in? She had no idea but she knew she would have to do it tonight or she feared she would lose her resolve. Should she just phone the nearest police department and say, *Hey, come get me?*

Here was another chapter she would have added to the imaginary fugitive handbook she'd been writing since leaving Philadelphia—when you realize the game is up, how do you fold your cards and get up from the table?

She could call Gage, she supposed. He would probably be able to alert Las Vegas authorities to pick her up. She shivered, imagining his reaction to that kind of late-night phone call. He would hate her for deceiving him. He would be livid. No, she couldn't face him.

What about Twila Langston? As much as she respected the woman who had represented her in the custody dispute with the DeBarillas, she doubted her attorney would be able to help her out of her predicament. No one could. But at least Twila might be able to tell her the legal steps she needed to take to turn herself in.

It was past 1:00 a.m. in Philadelphia, but she knew

Twila would take her call. Throughout the custody proceedings, they had become friends as well as having a good attorney-client relationship. Twila was probably sick with worry about where she had gone.

With her heart beating an uneven rhythm and her insides quivering, she crossed to the phone. She had no trouble remembering the attorney's home number and she dialed the digits with shaking fingers.

She paused before hitting the last number. This was it. With this phone call, her life would change irrevocably. She would lose everything she held most dear in the world. Did she have the courage to go through with it?

She had to, for her daughters' sake. Almost defiantly she started to lift her finger to finish poking in the number just as the sound of the doorbell rang through the small apartment like a funeral knell.

Chapter 17

Allie stared at the closed door, then back at the phone. Indecision wrangled within her. Should she complete the call to her attorney or answer the door? Maybe this was an omen that she wasn't supposed to turn herself in yet.

No, she couldn't take the easy way out, tempting though it might seem. She knew exactly what she had to do, and no late-night visitor could deter her from it now that she had found the courage to go through with it.

The doorbell rang again, followed by a heavy, insistent knock. She frowned and gazed back at the phone. At this rate, whoever was out there would wake up the girls and she would have to spend several more hours trying to settle them down again in the heat and misery of this dismal apartment.

Who could possibly be banging on her door at this hour? She knew no one in Las Vegas but Carla Galvez, the downstairs neighbor who watched the girls, and she would have no reason to come over this late.

With a sigh, Allie carefully hung up the phone, with a promise to herself that she would just see who might be here so late at night. Then she would call Twila and set the wheels in motion for her surrender.

She moved to the door and craned to look through the tiny peephole. At first, all she could see was what looked like a broad male chest covered in a maroon T-shirt, then she thought she glimpsed the silver gleam of aluminum crutches to the side.

Her breath rushed from her lungs in a whoosh. Impossible! It couldn't be. Of course Gage wasn't the only person in the western United States on crutches—but who else would be knocking on her door?

With hands that trembled, she worked the dead bolt and yanked open the door, forgetting about the security chain. Through the narrow gap, she spied two men, both large, both intimidating.

And both very familiar.

Gage and his partner, Cale Davis, stood on the walkway outside her door. In utter shock, barely able to think straight, she fumbled with the security chain but eventually managed to work it free so she could thrust open the door.

"G-Gage!"

For several seconds she could do nothing but stare at him, fighting a wild urge to leap into his arms.

"Mrs. DeBarillas." His voice was hard, like shards of glass from a broken window spilling onto a city sidewalk. Hard enough that Allie checked her body's instinctive sway toward the safety of his arms.

This man didn't offer safety. Far from it. He was tough and dangerous and bitterly angry.

And he knew her real name, which meant he likely knew everything.

"I…what are you doing here?"

"May we come in, Mrs. DeBarillas?"

With effort, she wrenched her gaze from the heat of Gage's expression to his partner, who was studying her with far more compassion in his eyes. "Yes. Of course, Agent Davis. Come in."

She swung the door open wider and stepped aside to let them enter. The apartment immediately seemed to shrink to closet size with two large males taking up so much space.

"Please. Sit down," she murmured, unable to quell the burn of humiliation at this tiny apartment, the outdated furnishings, the ugly wallpaper.

"We'll stand," Gage said.

The coldness of his voice made her wince. How stupid of her to be worried about an unattractive couch when her entire future—and that of her children—was at stake.

"I suppose you've come to arrest me."

A muscle worked in his jaw. "We're here to escort you and your daughters back to Philadelphia."

"I see." So he *must* know everything. Did that mean she was under arrest? Wasn't this where they were supposed to read her her rights or something?

If only he wasn't so very hard to read. She wanted to ask him to explain what would happen to her now, but she couldn't find either the words or the courage.

"Can we… Do I have time to gather our things?" she asked. "We don't have much."

"Our flight leaves at midnight. As things stand, we're going to be pushing it to make it through security. Just grab what you and the girls need right away, and I'll have someone pack up the rest for you."

She nodded but couldn't seem to make her muscles cooperate. "Can I ask how you found me?"

Cale Davis answered. ''Gage has been monitoring pharmaceutical transactions. He was notified right away when Lisa Connors filled a prescription for insulin today at a North Las Vegas pharmacy not far from here. It wasn't difficult to find your address from that.''

She should have realized that would be an obvious way for someone who knew she had insulin-dependent diabetes to trace her. Gage would have thought of it immediately. If she'd been thinking at all, she would have used a different name to fill her prescription when she ran out and used a disguise to pick it up.

Of course, she hadn't been thinking straight for weeks now. Not since leaving Park City.

At least she didn't have to figure out how to turn herself in. The choice had been taken out of her hands the moment she picked up the insulin she needed to stay alive.

''It should only take me fifteen minutes or so to pack a few things and wake and dress Anna and Gabriella.''

''Make it ten,'' Gage ordered in a stony voice, devoid of any trace of the man who had let her daughters fix his hair and who had shared his secrets with her and held her with such tenderness.

His left leg ached like a son of a bitch, worse than it had done in weeks.

He supposed it had something to do with the cramped airplane seats and the lack of leg room. Or it could have had something to do with being crammed into a rental car or standing in line for way too long at airport security or being awake for nearly twenty-two hours straight.

Whatever the reason, there wasn't much he could do about it but endure.

He gazed over Gaby's head at Lisa—or Alicia, he supposed he should remember to call her—who sat sandwiched between her girls. Cale was on the other side of Anna.

Cale and Lisa/Alicia were talking quietly over a sleeping Anna, and Gage strained to hear what they were saying. Something about her job cleaning hotel rooms at some armpit of a casino, he thought.

It was good of his partner to come along and help him escort her back to Philadelphia. He hadn't trusted himself alone with her, not with the anger still burning through him like an oil well on fire.

"I've never been on a plane before," a bright-eyed Gaby said suddenly. "It's super fun."

Now *that* was a matter of opinion. Try being six foot two in a seat made for munchkins. She looked perfectly comfortable, though, bouncing in her seat and swinging her legs and playing with the seat-back tray.

He tried to ignore his own discomfort. "It's more fun in the daytime when you can see the clouds outside the window. Sometimes you can see really tiny cars and people."

"Will we still be on the airplane when it's light outside?"

He quickly calculated the time difference and the flight length. Their arrival in Philadelphia would be sometime around 7:00 a.m. local time. "Just barely," he said. "Maybe when we land you'll be able to see a little out the window."

She seemed content with that answer. To his shock, a moment later she slipped her little hand in his. "I'm glad you came to get us, Mr. Gage. I didn't like that place."

Though he had only spent fifteen minutes in that miserable hole of an apartment, he hadn't been crazy about it, either.

What had Lisa—Alicia, he corrected bitterly—been

thinking to force her daughters to live in those conditions? He hadn't seen a playground—or even a strip of grass—anywhere in sight.

He glanced at Alicia DeBarillas. She looked completely worn-out, with dark circles under her eyes and exhaustion filling them. She wasn't exactly what he would call a glowing picture of health, either. Her skin was pale, and in the three weeks since she left, she had dropped another five pounds she could ill afford to lose.

Despite his anger at her, he was astonished at the powerful urge sneaking through him to pull her onto his lap, press her head against his chest and just hold her while she slept.

He was such a fool. Despite everything, he still wanted to take care of her. To protect her and cherish her and help ease the shadows from her eyes. Tenderness and anger made a strange mix.

He wanted to hold her, but he figured if he did, he'd just end up shaking her to try to put some sense in that stubborn little head. She should have told him what was going on. She should have trusted him.

The fact that she hadn't told him anything—and that she still didn't trust him—grated like metal gears grinding together.

Gabriella was still carrying on a one-sided conversation that didn't appear to require any response from him, he realized, jerking his attention back to her with unexpected amusement. Something about missing her friend Jessica and his mother, of all people, and about how she didn't get to go to the park like she used to.

He let her jabber on, strangely calmed by this adorable little chatterbox. In midsentence she suddenly gave a huge, jaw-popping yawn, then gazed at Gage with a wide-eyed, where-did-*that*-come-from? kind of look.

He swallowed his grin. "Here. If we raise the armrest, you can lean against me for a while."

The little heartbreaker gave him a sleepy smile, then nestled willingly under his arm. He pulled her close, astonished at the sweet peace he found holding this small, warm weight against him.

It might not be Lisa—Alicia—cuddled against him, but it wasn't bad, either.

She had been wrong before. Hell wasn't that hot, miserable apartment in North Las Vegas. It was spending four hours on a plane with the man she loved, the man who had tenderly held her sleeping child through nearly the entire flight.

The man who refused to even look at her.

They were in a rental car now, one that had been waiting for them at the airport. She sat in the back with the girls while Gage's partner drove. Cale seemed to know exactly where he was going, which was certainly more than she did.

The low drumbeat of fear seemed to grow louder inside her. During the long flight she had been able to ignore it, but now all she could focus on was the terrifying future.

She should have asked the FBI agents on the plane where they would be taking her but she hadn't, probably because she had been too afraid of how they might answer. Now, as they drove through heavy morning traffic, she was angry at herself for being so willing to bury her head in the sand, all for the sake of a few hours of peace.

The fear drummed louder, until she could hardly think past it. Finally she couldn't stand it any longer. She leaned forward and poked Gage's shoulder to get his attention.

''Can you tell me what's going to happen now?'' she asked after he turned around, in an undertone so the girls couldn't overhear. ''What will happen to Anna and Gaby when I go to jail?''

He narrowed his gaze at her. ''Maybe you should have thought of that before you decided to drag them off on this little half-cocked adventure of yours.''

''Is that what you call it?''

''What would you call it?''

''A nightmare.''

The last three weeks, anyway. The time they had spent in Park City seemed like a wonderful, rosy dream now, full of flower gardens and cool mountain breezes and Gage.

''Will they go with their grandparents?'' she persisted.

''I'm just the delivery man. I don't know all the details.''

''Can you at least tell me where you're taking us?'' she asked, frustrated by his reticence.

''I would think things were starting to look familiar.''

She gazed out the window and was astonished to see familiar landmarks roll past. *Very* familiar landmarks.

''This is our neighborhood,'' she exclaimed. There was the supermarket where she shopped and the preschool Gaby and Anna attended and the church where the girls had been christened.

A few moments later, Cale Davis drove into a residential area and pulled up in front of her own brownstone, the one she and Jaime had bought just after they married and had restored together.

She gazed blankly at the brownstone, then at Gage, who watched her with another of those blasted impassive looks.

''Look, Mama,'' Gabriella exclaimed. ''There's our

swing and our playhouse and Mrs. Wong's cute little dog. Anna, look!"

The girls pressed their noses against the window with glee. The joy on their features at the familiar surroundings cut through her with biting pain. She had been so terribly unfair to yank them away from this into a world of uncertainty and constant change.

"I don't understand. Why are we coming here."

"This is your house, isn't it?"

"Yes. But I thought..."

"That we were going to haul you straight off to prison?" Gage asked. "Sorry, Mrs. DeBarillas. Not today."

Before she could press him to tell her what was going on, he opened the rental door, grabbed his crutches then hobbled out.

The girls bounded out right after them, clearly delighted to be back on familiar ground as they raced across the lawn to touch the wrought-iron gate, the huge sycamore tree out front, Mrs. Wong's little wiener dog, who had come over to investigate the new arrivals.

Allie followed more slowly, trying to process this strange development. Did she even have a key to the house? She was pawing through her purse to find it when the door opened. Yet another shock wave rippled through her at the sight of her attorney standing in the doorway in one of her black power suits, her peppery hair pulled back in her customary knot and her smooth features set in a welcoming smile.

"Twila! What are you doing here?"

"Agent McKinnon called me from McCarron before your plane took off to let me know your arrival time. I told him I would meet you here. Didn't he tell you?"

Anna and Gabriella rushed past her and into the house.

Allie followed them blindly, only vaguely aware of Gage and Agent Davis right behind her. "No. I…I didn't realize you knew him."

"He's been working for me the past two weeks to help find you. I've been worried sick about you and the girls, Allie."

She gazed from Gage to Twila, trying to make sense of it all. "What do you mean, working for you? You mean he didn't bring me back here to face charges for violating the custody order?"

Twila turned to Gage, her eyes wide. "You didn't tell her?"

He only shrugged and said nothing, as apparently he had been doing since he showed up at her apartment in Las Vegas.

"Tell me what?"

Twila grabbed her hands. "You're not violating any custody order, Allie. You never really were. If you had stayed in town just a few more days you would have known. The appeals court immediately threw out the ruling that awarded joint custody to Jaime's parents. Their decision came down in record time—the speed of it stunned even me. They gave Joaquin and Irena supervised visitation with the girls, but that's all."

She stared at the attorney, not sure if her system could endure any more jolts. "But I ran away with the girls, took them across state lines. I'm a fugitive."

"No you're not. You have every right to move wherever you want. It's a free country, Allie."

Oh, how she wished she'd had a little more sleep in the past twenty-four hours. Or in the past three weeks, for that matter. Her brain felt fuzzy, drained, and she couldn't seem to process any of this.

"What about Gage? The FBI? Why did they come after me, then?"

The lawyer frowned at the agents. "Agent McKinnon wasn't acting in an official capacity. Frankly, I'm surprised he didn't explain that to you. As soon as you disappeared, I sent a private investigator looking for you. At one point in his investigation, word trickled into the FBI's Salt Lake City field office and Agent McKinnon contacted me with information about your whereabouts. I gather the two of you were acquainted in Utah."

Allie shot a quick look at Gage, remembering the heat and tenderness of being in his arms, of being wrapped around that strong body. "Yes," she said, her voice subdued.

"He offered to assist my private investigator. Let me stress again, this was not an official investigation of the Federal Bureau of Investigation. Agent McKinnon was helping on his own time. It was his idea to contact pharmacies."

"So I'm not under arrest?"

"Absolutely not," Twila said.

Allie looked at Gage for confirmation. After a moment he shook his head.

Dear heavens. Her knees wobbled and she had to sink down onto the couch. For two months she had lived with the constant specter of fear and uncertainty hovering over her, always looking over her shoulder for fear she would be caught, that she would lose her girls.

All for nothing.

What a terrible waste of energy, of emotion. All this time she and her girls could have been safe and sound here in the home she and Jaime had created together for their family. Her own job, her own bed, her own little backyard.

But if she hadn't left, she never would have ended up in Park City. She wouldn't have met Ruth or Lynn.

Or Gage.

She gazed at the three people in the room, all watching her with different expressions on their faces. She blinked several times, wondering vaguely why their faces were starting to blur together.

Her last coherent thought was that she hadn't checked her blood glucose levels since dinnertime the night before.

Chapter 18

She awoke sputtering and coughing and realized somebody was trying to squeeze the contents of a juice box into her mouth.

Gage, she realized. She was stretched out on the couch and he knelt beside her, his braced leg extended as he supported her head and tried to get her to drink. She swallowed a mouthful, mortified that her blood glucose levels must have dipped so low that she passed out.

"The girls?" she mumbled.

"Shh. Don't worry about them right now. Drink this. It's warm but it's all we could find in the house. Twila went to the diner down the street for some breakfast."

Allie tried to sit up. "I need to find the girls."

"Relax. Cale took them out back to play. They seem thrilled to be home."

Relieved that her daughters were in good hands, she quickly programmed the pump at her waist to deliver a bolus of insulin. That done, she leaned back against the pillow on the couch and tried to swallow a few more mouthfuls of warm juice.

"Feel better?"

"I'm getting there. Thanks. Where did you find the juice box?"

"In the pantry." He paused. "You ought to be skinned for not taking better care of yourself."

She sighed, knowing he was right. "It's been a wild couple of weeks. The last twelve hours haven't exactly been a breeze, thinking I was on my way to jail."

"I never said that's where you were going."

"But you didn't say I *wasn't* when I asked you what would happen to the girls."

With the help of one of his crutches, he rose and took the wing chair next to the couch. "I guess maybe I was after a little petty revenge. I was angry. I'm still angry. Maybe I wanted you to suffer a little for the worry you put so many people through. I didn't think about the physical toll it might take on you. It was small of me and I'm sorry."

She closed her eyes to block out both his anger and the guilt she could hear threading through his voice.

"I'm the one who's sorry for deceiving you all those weeks."

"You should have told me the truth." His voice was flinty hard again.

"I didn't dare, Gage." She opened her eyes and pulled herself up a little on the couch so she wouldn't feel at such a disadvantage. "I was so frightened of losing the girls. I suppose you know all about the custody fight with Jaime's parents."

"I know they were awarded joint custody because the judge in the case said your condition put you at greater health risk than most single mothers. I guess what I don't understand is why that made you run.''

How could she explain the complicated dynamics of the situation? She sighed again. ''My husband and his parents didn't have a very easy relationship. Irena and Joaquin came from great wealth in Venezuela and tried to control their son with it. They never approved of me for various reasons—because I'm an American and because I'm not Hispanic and because of my…my diabetes.''

That had been their root objection—they hadn't wanted a flawed daughter-in-law, one who had to constantly deal with blood draws and insulin and the potential for greater health risks down the road. Their dislike had been tough on her, she had to admit. She winced now, remembering how desperately she had sought their approval in the first few years of her marriage.

''A few weeks after they were awarded joint custody,'' she went on, ''Gaby let slip that Irena had taken them to get passport photos. I was afraid they would take them to Caracas and I would never see them again. It was definitely something they would try, and they had the wealth and power to get away with it. I was so frightened. I didn't know what else to do.''

''So you ran.''

''What else could I have done?''

Gage thought of the loving bond between Allie and her daughters. Losing them in an international custody battle would have destroyed her.

If the in-laws were as ruthless as she claimed, maybe she had been justified in what she had done to protect the girls—taking Gaby and Anna out of harm's way before her husband's wealthy parents could steal them away from her.

But the risks she had taken, the heavy burden she had shouldered alone still angered him. "You should have told me," he said again.

"I couldn't. Oh, Gage. I wanted to, but I was so afraid. At first, when I didn't know you, I was afraid you would have me arrested and take the girls. And then I was just so frightened you would hate me if you knew the truth, that I kidnapped my own children. Especially with what happened to your sister. I couldn't bear it if you hated me."

Her voice broke a little on the last two words, and he fought the urge to gather her into his arms and comfort her.

"I tried to hate you after I found out the truth," he admitted. "I *wanted* to hate you for deceiving me all those weeks we spent together. But you know something, Alicia?"

"Allie," she whispered. "Nearly everyone calls me Allie."

"Allie." The name rolled off his tongue much easier than Alicia or even Lisa. It seemed to fit her, somehow.

"You know," he went on, "as much as I wanted to hate you, somehow no matter how I tried, I couldn't force myself to do it. You're a tough person to hate."

"Why? I kidnapped my own children. Even if what Twila says is true and it wasn't technically a crime, in my mind I thought I was breaking all kinds of laws. To be honest, if I thought it was the only way to protect the girls, I would do it all over again."

With her words, a lifetime of conviction seemed to go fuzzy, like he was seeing it through wavy glass. He saw now that one single, terrible moment in his life—his sister's abduction—had given him a strict black-and-white moral compass.

He had relied on it, had used it to become a damn good FBI agent, dedicated to his career.

He thought he knew what was clearly right and what was undeniably wrong. Now for the first time, as he listened to Allie talk about why she had taken her children, he started to see in shades of gray. He still didn't agree with her decision to run away from what she saw as a threat. But maybe he was beginning to understand it a little.

He knew he had to make one thing clear to her, though. "You don't have to protect the girls by yourself anymore."

Confusion furrowed her brow. "Why not?"

"You have friends who will help you. I would like to think you would turn to them. And to me. I hope you know I would do whatever it took to make sure nothing happened to Anna and Gaby."

She gazed at him, her eyes huge, then those blue depths started to fill. "Oh, Gage."

This time he couldn't resist her tears. With a muffled groan, he shifted to the couch and pulled her into his arms. "Please don't cry, sweetheart. Whatever I said, I'm sorry."

For some reason that only made her sob harder. She clung to him, her arms around him and her head nestled under his chin.

Just where she belonged.

"I missed you so much," she whispered in midsob. "It ripped my heart out to leave Park City behind. To leave you. I thought I would never see you again."

"Crazy woman." He squeezed her tighter. "You should have known I would come after you."

She gave a watery, disbelieving laugh. "Why would I think that? I was just your next-door neighbor with the noisy kids and the bossy attitude. The annoying creature who nagged you endlessly and butted in where she wasn't wanted and who never left you alone for two minutes so your broken legs could heal in peace. If anything, I figured you would be glad to see the last of me."

"You were also the woman I couldn't get out of my mind," he admitted, the last of his anger dissipating like puddles on the sidewalk in a hot July sun. "The one whose kisses I couldn't live without, who along with her daughters brought love and laughter and joy into a life that has been dark and cold and empty for far too long."

She stiffened in his arms and drew in a swift, shaky breath. Her head tilted up, and she stared at him, incredulity in those tear-soaked columbine eyes.

"You should have known I would come after you," he said again, cupping her cheek in his hand, their gazes locked. "What other choice did I have but to go searching for the bossy, interfering, *incredible* woman I'm in love with?"

Shock widened those eyes further. "Are you trying to make me pass out again? You can't just throw that out there like that with no warning!"

He couldn't contain himself any longer. Through his laughter, he kissed her. She melted against him and returned his kiss with an eagerness that took his breath.

"I love you, Gage," she murmured after several moments. "I think I fell in love with you that first day before your accident, when you came over to warn me to be more careful with the girls. I knew for certain the day a big, macho FBI agent surrendered his dignity to let my daughters play beauty shop."

He winced. "That was a one-time deal. Believe me, it's not going to happen again."

"Don't be so sure. Hurricane Gaby can be pretty persuasive."

"I'll just have to work on my powers of resistance, then."

"Resistance is futile. Haven't you figured that out by now?"

"I'm beginning to." He pressed a soft, tender kiss to her mouth. "I love you, Allie. And I love your daughters. I don't want you to ever feel like you have to take on the world by yourself again. You're not alone anymore. I want a future with you. I'd like to spend the rest of my life with you and Gaby and Anna—protecting you and watching over you and loving you."

She closed her eyes at the rush of emotions pouring through her at his tenderness. When she opened them, she spied the juice box on the end table and she sobered.

"Are you sure you know what you would be getting into?"

She unclipped her insulin pump from the loop of her jeans and offered it to him on her palm. "If you take me, you have to take all this, too. Package deal, here. It's part of who I am."

He studied her solemnly for a moment, then his big hand wrapped around her fingers and the insulin pump, completely enveloping them, and he gave her a hard, close-mouthed kiss.

"I know. It's part of what I love about you, Allie—the courage and strength inside you that helps you cope."

"I don't always cope well. You should know that up front. You haven't seen it yet but sometimes I have major-league tantrums where I get angry and bitter and rail against fate for giving me this damn disease. Sometimes I get so frightened about what the future might hold for me—kidney failure, blindness, or worse—that I have a tendency to forget I need to live in the present.''

''When that happens, I'll just have to be right there to remind you what you have now, and what you will always have—two beautiful daughters who need their mother. And a man who is crazy about you.''

As he kissed her again with sweet tenderness, Allie finally let herself imagine a future with him—one filled with all the things he promised and so much more.

* * * * *

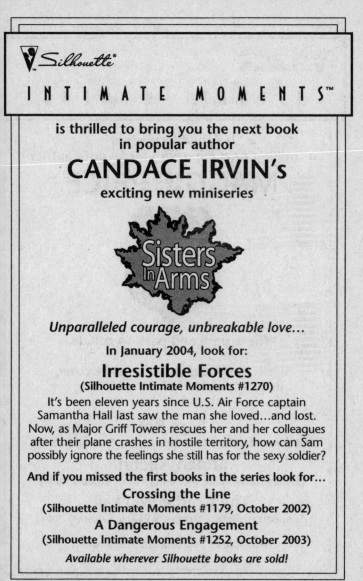

Silhouette®
INTIMATE MOMENTS™
is proud to present
a thrilling new miniseries by favorite author
MAGGIE PRICE
LINE OF DUTY
Where peril and passion collide.
When the McCall sisters go undercover,
they are prepared to risk everything—
except their hearts!
Sure Bet
(Silhouette Intimate Moments #1263, December 2003)
Hidden Agenda
(Silhouette Intimate Moments #1269, January 2004)
The Cradle Will Fall
(Silhouette Intimate Moments #1276, February 2004)
Available at your favorite retail outlet.

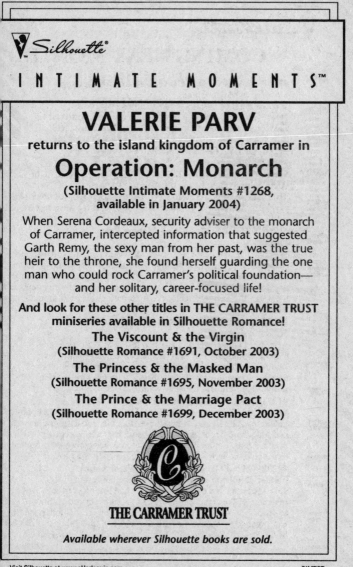

identity? Well, Mr. O. O. Brown would wish he had! "Well, I intend to get him out of my life quickly."

Two beats of silence followed her announcement, and then he said, "Is that so! You ought to give him more of a chance before you come to a conclusion."

"I've given him enough chances for a lifetime. He just doesn't have what you do, Rory. He doesn't tell me how he feels."

"Well, it's hard sometimes, Charity, for guys to put their feelings into words. Sometimes they do things that make them feel guilty later and then it's hard to talk about it."

"You mean this guy feels guilty because he kissed me, so now he wishes he hadn't, but he can't admit he has regrets?"

"No! He couldn't have any regrets—Dammit, the record's over. Call me again."

He sounded frantic. Not one bit like his usual laid-back self. She smiled and listened as he changed to the familiar slow drawl. "There, darlin'. Everyone should be wide awake now. Darlin', call me again tonight, will you?"

"Sure, Rory."

"Good. Let's settle down with the next tune. Put your head back on a soft pillow, close your eyes, think of that special person, someone you want to be close to. Think of that certain someone in your life and listen to this next tune. It will help you relax. Here's 'Kisses Sweeter than Wine.' "

The music came on, and as she listened, her thoughts were on Oregon's smile, his green-and-gold-flecked eyes. Floating in a cloud of bliss, she listened to two more songs, a commercial done in Oregon's husky voice, which could sell furnaces in the Amazon, another request by a sultry-voiced fe-

male named Samantha, and more songs. Time ticked past. Samantha called in again. Charity didn't care for her deep, breathless voice at all. Finally the last chance for a request came over the air. Determined to beat Samantha, she dialed hastily and was gratified to hear the ring, then Oregon's husky voice. She was aching with longing for him. She wanted his kisses, his big strong arms, his loving. She wanted him to tell her he was Oregon Brown!

"Rory, this is Charity again."

"Charity, darlin', you stayed up until the end of the program. What do you want to hear?"

" 'All Alone Tonight.' "

" 'All Alone Tonight' it is. I wish you were here with me, darlin', so I could hold you close. Here's your song."

The music started and Oregon's voice came over the phone. "Charity?"

"Yes. I'm lonesome, Rory."

"Oh, darlin', if you only knew how lonely I am. I wish we could be together. I get so lonely . . ."

"Rory, isn't there anyone in your life?"

"No, darlin'. Except you."

"You tell everyone that."

"No, I don't. Charity, darlin', you don't know how lonesome I've been. I feel like a rolling stone. I don't belong any place, no one belongs to me."

He sounded sincere. Heartbreakingly sincere. She wondered about Oregon. How could anyone who seemed so self-assured, who had worked for one of the largest newspapers in the U.S., who had a nice house and so few apparent worries, be lonesome? There should be a flock of women in his life. The thought startled her. Oregon was appealing, sexy, intelligent, and such a magnificent lover!

"Charity, don't go away. Maybe you should give this guy a little time, a chance to talk to you."

"You don't want to be the one man in my life?"

"Oh, yeah, darlin'."

"Rory, there must be some woman in your life."

"Just you, darlin'. I think I'm falling in love with you."

"I might be falling in love with you." Was she?

"What about the guy who kisses so well?"

"He simply doesn't have what you do. We don't talk things over, we don't feel the same about life, the way you and I do. He doesn't have your . . . voice."

"Charity, we're going to have to meet."

She looked at the phone, then returned it to her ear. "Tomorrow?"

He chuckled softly. "Soon, darlin'. Real, real soon."

"I can't wait until tomorrow night."

Another tiny pause, then he asked, "Charity, are you going to listen to 'Nighttime' tomorrow night?"

"I wouldn't miss it for anything."

"Darlin', I won't—well—Hell, the music's over."

Now, what had he been about to say? She listened to his closing.

"Well, that wraps it up at station KKZF for tonight. Sleep well, darlin'. Nii-aight."

She melted. Then she turned off the radio, climbed out of bed, pulled on a robe, and stepped out onto the back porch. While she sat in the dark, staring at Oregon's house to watch for his light to come on, she wondered about him. Was he really so lonesome, or was that a line? Crickets chirped a shrill melody in the quiet night, while moonlight splashed over the flowers and yard. Finally Charity saw a light

flicker on upstairs in Oregon's house, then off again. His room was downstairs, hidden by the board fence, but for a few seconds he had been in the bedroom where she had slept last night. She wished she were there again and was shocked at her feelings. How could she fall for Oregon so completely and quickly, when she had been so cautious with men in the past? There was no logical answer. Reluctantly she rose and went inside to bed.

Thursday morning the ringing of the phone woke her from a sound sleep. "Charity?"

It was Oregon, and he sounded just like Rory. If she hadn't known before, she would now. " 'Morning, Oregon."

"Darlin', you're in bed!" His voice lowered. "I can just picture you there, your curls all tangled, your blue eyes sleepy, your long, pale lashes curling over your eyes. Your mouth so inviting . . . I want you to wake me up, so we can love again."

He sure wasn't at a loss for words when he had a phone in his hand. His seductive voice stroked her, and she stretched sinuously in bed. "Enough of that!"

"You don't like it?"

She heard the hint of laughter in his voice. "Not now. It's disturbing."

"That's exactly what I want it to be, hon."

"Oregon!"

"My attorney says you've decided to sell the paper."

"That's right. I don't know anything about a newspaper. Aunt Mattie doesn't either. So I want to sell it. Yesterday I talked to our lawyer, Mr. Oppenheim, about selling."

"Well, I'm interested in buying. I want a paper. I can't get the ink out of my blood."

"I think we can work out a sale. I'd like you to have the paper. That would please Aunt Mattie. She sings your praises rather high."

"She's sweet. I'd like to hear someone else sing my praises."

She laughed. "You're cute."

"Oh, my. I don't care to be called 'cute.' I'll have to repair my image tonight."

"That was a compliment, not a challenge."

"Yeah, sure. Cute." He sounded disgusted. "Charity . . ."

"Yes?"

"It was better to wake up yesterday, with you in my arms." His voice was intimate and husky, sending dancing sparks cascading down her spine. She was breathless, yearning for him.

"Hmmm."

"Charity, I want to kiss you, to really kiss you."

"Hmmm."

His voice held a smile. "See you in a little while, darlin'."

"Hmmm." The receiver clicked in her ear. Bemused, she lay in bed while memories played through her mind like a kaleidoscope. Finally she dressed in cutoffs, a white cotton shirt, and sandals, and went to work to help clean the house thoroughly.

At about three in the afternoon, when she was in Aunt Mattie's hot attic above the garage, Oregon's head thrust through the opening in the attic floor and he grinned at her. "Hi. Want some help?"

Eight

She straightened, suddenly aware of the smudges of dust on her face and hands, of a sheen of perspiration on her brow, tangled locks curling over her forehead. She smiled. "You're just in time."

"Charity, is Mattie moving away?"

"I don't know what we'll do, so I'm trying to sort through things and get rid of what she doesn't want or need. She can't stay alone, but we haven't reached a decision about the future." She glanced around. "I don't know what to do with all this stuff. There are some heavy things that should go to the Salvation Army and I've been wondering how I would get them down out of the attic."

"At your service, darlin'." He scrambled up with ease and crouched slightly to avoid hitting his head on the sloping roof. Then, without hesitation, he reached for her.

"Oregon, it's too hot up here . . ."

"It sure is," he murmured as he leaned down to kiss her. His kiss was more overwhelming than the last had been, and it turned the attic into an inferno. Dimly she heard Aunt Mattie calling her name.

Oregon released her, and she answered. "Yes?"

"You're wanted on the phone. It's long distance, Charity. It's Ziza."

"I'm coming." She sounded as if she had run a mile. She pointed to Uncle Hubert's golf bag and clubs and a screen door, propped against the attic wall. "Can you bring those down, please?"

"Sure thing."

She hurried down the steps and discovered Aunt Mattie had pulled the phone around the corner from the kitchen counter to the garage. It rested on the washing machine. When Charity answered, Ziza's voice came over the crackling wire.

"Charity, sweetie, this is Ziza." Charity could picture Ziza's wild tangle of black curls, her big blue eyes, and the slender figure that made people think she was ten years younger than her age. "Sweetie, I'm married to the most adorable man! This is finally it, Charity, forever! Bernard. I just can't wait for you to meet him." She didn't pause for a remark from Charity, but continued breathlessly, with laughter punctuating her sentences. "Sweetie, you're not married yet, are you?"

"No, Ziza."

"Are you in love?"

"No . . ."

"Well, sweetie, it's high time we changed that! You're too cute and too old to live without a man. And I have just the one for you. Mr. Perfect."

"Ziza, I don't need to meet any men." She saw a long black boot emerge from the attic and rest on

the top step. She picked up the phone to step inside the kitchen, but the cord got twisted and she couldn't untangle it without dropping the phone.

"Don't be ridiculous! You need a man in your life more than anything else, and I'd be remiss in my duty if I didn't see to it that you got one."

Charity felt as if she were standing in quicksand. Sinking in quicksand. Mired to her waist in oozing trouble. Both boots came down a step and long, jeaned legs began to appear. She knew Oregon could hear every word she said.

"Ziza, please, I'm living the way I want to."

"I can't hear you. We have a damn poor connection. You'll love him. It's Bernard's brother, Rolf. He's a dreamboat. Who's your favorite actor?"

"I don't have one. Ziza, don't bring him to meet me. I can't go out with him."

"Why not? There is someone else!"

Charity was aware of Oregon standing behind her. "No, there isn't!"

"Then you'll love Rolf and you need to meet him."

"Ziza, I don't have time to date. I have to take care of Mattie." She glanced around. Oregon was investigating Uncle Hubert's golf clubs, studying them intently.

"That's all the more reason to get you out. Rolf looks just like . . . hold your breath . . . Christopher Reeve!"

Charity's patience snapped. "If he looks so damned much like Christopher Reeve, why does he need you to introduce him to a woman?"

The minute she said it, she wanted to clamp her hand over her mouth. Oregon's head raised, and he stopped all pretense of studying anything except her.

He grinned. She felt her cheeks burning beneath his gaze.

"I had to do some arm twisting," Ziza answered, unperturbed. "You'll faint when you see him. If I weren't so in love with Bernard . . . and a teensy bit older than Rolf . . . well, you wouldn't lay eyes on him!" Ziza laughed.

"Don't invite him to meet me, Ziza. When will you and Bernard get here?"

"We're in Houston now, and we'll get in about noon Saturday. We'll stay at a motel, sweetie, but Rolf will stay with you, and don't protest. Mattie has already said he can stay. And you have a date Saturday night."

"No, I don't."

"Why not? Sweetie, are you in love? I think you're in love! Don't deny it, I can tell. Charity, who is he?"

A silence ensued while Charity mulled over the best answer to give her aunt. "I'm not alone, Ziza."

"Mattie's there?"

"Well, no. A neighbor is."

"Charity, you sound different. It won't hurt you to tell me who the lucky man is. Mattie and her neighbor will be delighted."

"I can't talk about it now."

Oregon had folded his arms across his chest and planted his feet apart while he gazed at her thoughtfully.

Ziza laughed uproariously. "Prim and proper Charity. Come on, I can imagine your blush and the little ladies' giggles. Tell me who the man is or I'll have to ask Mattie."

"You're right, Ziza, I'm prim. Let's discuss it later. Just visit Rolf in Oklahoma City on your way

home and forget about introducing us." She was on fire. Damn Oregon anyway!

"Charity, come on. I won't be satisfied until you tell me who he is."

Now she had put herself between a slab of marble and a block of concrete. Either way she was up against solid trouble. She didn't want to meet Rolf, to have him for a houseguest, yet she didn't dare tell Ziza that she was in love with Oregon. She raised her chin and faced Oregon defiantly. "Ziza, there isn't anyone I'm in love with, but I don't want a blind date with Rolf!"

And she knew that the moment she'd declared she wasn't in love, she had flung a challenge at Oregon. He started toward her with a gleam in his eye that told her exactly what he intended. Her heart thudded against her rib cage and her pulse went into high gear.

And Ziza's happy voice came over the wire loudly enough for Oregon to hear. "Oh, Charity, I wonder! I can imagine your blush. Are the ladies giggling?"

Oregon pushed the phone away from her mouth, bent down, and kissed her. His arms went around her waist and he pulled her to him, kissing her as passionately and as hard as possible.

She fought, but there was no way to combat arms like steel bands, a chest like granite, and a kiss like a roaring fire.

She did the only thing she could think to do under the circumstances. She hung up on Ziza. And Oregon kept right on kissing her until she felt she would faint. She trembled, she ached, she struggled, and she couldn't resist—she kissed him in return. Fervently. She forgot Ziza, Rolf, her anger, every-

thing in the world except Oregon Brown. Adorable, sexy, tongue-tied Oregon Oliver Brown.

The phone rang. And rang and rang. Finally she realized it and reached behind her, struggling again to pull free of Oregon's embrace.

He relented, raising his head. She brought the phone to her ear while she stared into his burning eyes.

"Hello? Charity? What happened?"

Charity tried to wriggle free. Oregon grinned and leaned down to nibble her earlobe. "We . . . got cut off. Oh, don't!"

"Don't what? What's the matter with you? You sound breathless."

"It's a . . . poor connection." She couldn't think. She felt tingles coursing through her. Oregon's tongue touched her ear as she struggled to get away from him.

"Now, Charity, it's all set. You have a dinner date Saturday night with Rolf. Is there a good restaurant in Enid?"

"Red Lobster," Oregon said.

"Charity, is there a man with you?"

"A man? Whatever makes you think that?"

"I can't hear you."

"I said, Red Lobster is a good place to eat." She covered the mouthpiece of the phone and whispered frantically, "Get away! Stop that, Oregon!"

"Go out to dinner with me Saturday night." His chin thrust forward slightly, and his green eyes glinted with determination.

"I can't, Oregon," she whispered. She couldn't let Ziza get hold of Oregon. There wouldn't be a minute's peace, and Ziza would ruin their relationship. What relationship? an inner voice scoffed.

"I can't, Oregon," she whispered.

"Charity, sweetie, is someone with you?"

"Go out with me."

"No." She said it to both of them, speaking into the phone while she looked Oregon in the eye.

He folded his arms across his chest and rocked on his heels.

"You sound different, sweetheart."

"It's the connection."

Suddenly Oregon's fingers closed over the phone, and he took it from her so swiftly, she couldn't stop him. While his eyes warned her to leave him alone, his deep voice said, "Hi, Ziza, this is Oregon."

Charity felt as if the quicksand had closed over her head. There went Rolf, peace of mind, Oregon, the weekend, her life. When Ziza got her teeth into a man, she didn't let go.

"I'm a neighbor of Mattie's and I have a date with Charity Saturday night."

Charity couldn't hear Ziza's reply, but she saw Oregon grin. An eyelid dropped over one eye in a quick wink that didn't do anything to soothe her anger.

"That's right, Ziza. Why don't you save old Rolf the trip if you can see him in Oklahoma City?" Another pause, a wider grin appeared, with dimples, and then he said, "Sure thing. See you Saturday. I'll tell Charity and give her a kiss for you." He replaced the receiver and smiled smugly at Charity.

"You just did the lowest, sneakiest—"

That one damned eyebrow climbed into an arch, and his eyes were filled with devilish glitter as he interrupted her. "I'm not about to let you go out with a guy named Rolf who looks like Christopher Reeve. You didn't want to go anyway. Come here. I'm supposed to give you a kiss for Ziza."

She flung her hands up to forestall him. "I didn't want to tell Ziza about you either!"

"So I noticed. Not in love, huh?"

"Now, Oregon, you don't know my aunt, but you will by Saturday night. Oh, brother, you will!" Charity was tempted to add that Ziza was probably planning a wedding right now. Heat burned up from her toes as Oregon pulled her to him and kissed her again. Kissed her as thoroughly and as fantastically as before. When he released her, she stared at him for long, long seconds until she remembered what she had been doing. "I've got work to do," she said.

"I came along just in time to save you from disaster and I'm not worried about your Aunt Ziza. And you're not in love, huh?"

"I had to tell her that." She was blushing furiously and felt aggravated by his high-handed tactics.

He brushed her nose with his finger and drawled, "Well, we'll see about that, darlin'. And we have a dinner date Saturday night."

"I have to clean the attic, and I can get along without your help, Oregon."

He grinned. "Now, don't get in a huff with me. I didn't come over here for that."

"I'm not in a huff. I'm going back to work, and I don't need any help."

His grin widened. "That isn't what you said a few minutes ago."

"I'm saying it now." She climbed the steps to the attic, aware that he was probably watching every movement. She thrust her head through the opening and saw the screen door lying on the floor, blocking her way. She couldn't climb up unless she stepped on the screen or lifted it down. And damned if she would ask for his help. She pulled the door toward

her and lifted one end. The door was heavy and awkward to handle.

She heard a deep chuckle; then an arm closed around her waist. Oregon was standing on the steps as he reached up and lifted her off. For an instant, as he swung her around, she thought they'd fall. Then he settled back against the steps, holding her against his big, long body. She rested her hands on his shoulders and looked into his eyes, and knew she had lost the battle completely.

"My, are you a dirty fighter," she murmured.

"We weren't fighting. Not for one second." He leaned forward and kissed her. His arm held her tightly against him while his other hand cupped the back of her head.

He spread his legs slightly, and her toes rested on a step. It was higher than the one on which Oregon stood, and put her face on the same level as his. And fitted her body to his seductively. Held so tightly against him, she felt his arousal, his growing need for her. His tongue met hers in a delicious tangle that sent her heart flying for an eternity before she reluctantly pushed away. They looked into each other's eyes, and she wondered what he was thinking. She thought he was marvelous. And she refused to think about what would happen when Ziza discovered him. "I'd better go," she whispered.

"For now," he answered, and released her, helping her down before turning and easily lifting down the screen door.

"When will Ziza arrive?" he asked.

"Saturday." The mere thought made her nervous. "Oregon, we've gotten rid of Rolf. Let's postpone our date until Ziza and Bernard are gone."

He grinned at her, and her heart sank. He was go-

ing to be as devilish as Old Nick himself. "She's part of your family, darlin'. I might as well meet her now."

Meet her now? What did Oregon mean by that? "Oregon . . . Never mind. Before you go, will you carry that door to the front? I need to take down the storm door and put up the screen."

"I'll do it."

He left, whistling a jolly tune, and she sat down on the bottom step. She felt as if she were lost in a fog. She couldn't handle Oregon at all. He had caused mountains of trouble in her life. And Ziza would come into their lives like Hurricane Hilda. And what would happen tonight with Oregon? What did she want to happen? One thing would occur—Oregon would be forced to admit he was Rory Runyon. Tonight he would have to explain his reasons for going to the station.

Five hours later, seated in Oregon's living room, Charity wondered what had happened to her plans. Nothing had gone the way she'd expected. She had dressed in a pale blue cotton sundress and sandals and been thrilled by Oregon's reaction when he opened the door. His green eyes had devoured her, drifting slowly down to her toes, up again over her hips and breasts, and down. She realized it was the first time he had seen her in a dress. Then he had helped Aunt Mattie inside and they had settled in the living room for a cocktail.

Dinner was served in the dining room by a maid, who left shortly after the dishes were done. Charity then expected Aunt Mattie to go home to bed and Oregon to go to work. Neither happened.

Aunt Mattie had napped all afternoon after the phone call from Ziza and was ready to enjoy the evening out. Oregon seemed in no hurry to go anywhere. Charity had a suspicion Oregon also had expected Aunt Mattie to go home early.

They chatted about first one thing, then another, while Oregon, looking too appealing for words, in navy slacks and a white shirt, lounged in a large, comfortable armchair. Aunt Mattie told them about her early childhood in Alva, Oklahoma, then about moving to Enid in the early days after statehood.

Charity couldn't believe that Aunt Mattie was so alert. It was the first night since her arrival that her aunt had stayed up past eight o'clock. Charity glanced continually at the clock over the mantel, watching it grow later and later. Still Oregon made no move to go to the station.

Eleven o'clock came, unheard-of for Aunt Mattie, yet the eyes behind the trifocals were as bright as ever. By eleven-thirty Charity knew it was too late for Oregon to get to the station. She rose. "Aunt Mattie, it'll be midnight soon. . . ."

"Midnight! Imagine that! You sweet children have been so entertaining. I haven't been up this late in years. Oh, dear, we've kept you up late, Oregon."

He grinned. "That's all right, Mattie. I don't turn in early, and I can catch forty winks tomorrow." He looked at Charity. "How's your insomnia, Charity? Have you slept any better the past few nights?"

"I don't have insomnia." She blushed and hated it.

"She just stays up all hours and rises with the sun," Mattie said.

"That so?" His green eyes started to twinkle. "The last sunrise I saw was the best I've ever seen."

Charity headed for the door, hoping Oregon would stop. "Wait a minute, Mattie," he said. "You forgot your purse." He handed it to her.

"Oh, my. I'd leave my head if it weren't attached. Charity is so good to remind me about things. Isn't she sweet, Oregon?"

"She's adorable."

Charity felt another wave of heat rush up from her throat. As she looked up at Oregon, her heart was throbbing and it was difficult to speak. "Thank you. That's nice."

He smiled and gave her a quick wink. "Sweet Charity. It's almost time for the radio program you like."

"So it is. Do you always listen to 'Nighttime'?"

"No, but I catch it now and then."

They each took one of Mattie's elbows to help her down the steps to the car. Oregon closed the door after she was seated. As they started around the back of the car, Oregon's hand closed on Charity's arm.

"I thought we'd be alone a little while tonight," he whispered.

"She took a nap today so she could stay awake and visit with you." They stopped behind the back fender of the passenger side of the car, and Oregon slipped his arm around her waist, leaning down to kiss her.

It was a kiss that made her want dozens more. As she pushed away, she felt the intense longing that he stirred so easily.

"Oregon, Aunt Mattie will look for me."

"She won't mind if she sees me kiss you."

"Well, I don't want a bunch of questions."

"I'll be happy to answer them for you," he said complacently. "We kiss because we're falling in love."

"You know, you have moments when you're so damned arrogant, it's revolting!"

Suddenly he yanked her to his chest and kissed her again. Kissed her soundly until she returned it with just as much abandon. And, just as abruptly as he had reached for her, he released her. As she almost fell against the car, he said, "I rest my case."

"Damned arrogance!" she snapped, making him laugh softly.

He dropped his arm across her shoulders and walked her around the car, then reached for her door. For an instant before he opened it, he leaned close to her ear. "I wish you were stretched out on my black satin sheets. You were meant for them and for me, Charity Jane Webster!"

"Oregon, stop that!" she said, but her protest was too breathless to sound sincere. Trying to speak firmly, she said, "Thank you for the dinner." She tried again, hoping the breathy quality would vanish. "It was marvelous."

"You're welcome. Saturday night there'll be just the two of us and it'll be better."

"You may be jumping to the wrong conclusion."

"We need to be alone to talk, Charity."

"Well, I can't now. I better go. Aunt Mattie's waiting."

" 'Night, darlin'." There went her pulse. What a voice the man had!

" 'Night, Oregon." She climbed into the car and drove around the corner to Aunt Mattie's, her thoughts on Oregon's dynamite kisses, his sexy, sexy voice.

As soon as they were in the house, she went to her room to turn on 'Nighttime.' And, right on cue, Oregon's husky voice came over the air. She gazed at

the radio and guessed the program was prerecorded. While she listened, she undressed, pulled on her nightgown and lay frowning in the darkness, missing Rory/Oregon's chatter and phone conversations, worried about Ziza, about Oregon. What did she feel for Oregon? Was it mere lust because of loneliness? Or was it deeper? And did it matter to him? Was it casual, a one-night stand, or had he spoken the truth on the phone when he'd said he was lonely and falling in love with her?

"Dammit," she whispered. Why didn't Oregon discuss things with her instead of teasing and aggravating her, and making her melt? He wasn't at a loss for words as Rory Runyon!

She turned off the radio and flounced onto her side. She lay facing a south window, and through it she saw a light blink in Oregon's house, on, then off. What was he doing? Was he lonesome now?

She groaned and turned onto the other side, squeezing her eyes closed, determined to put Oregon Oliver Brown out of her thoughts.

She failed miserably and slept only a few hours before sunshine awakened her to a bright Friday morning.

She dressed, cooked breakfast, then left to spend an hour with Mr. Oppenheim, going over papers and talking about the sale of the newspaper.

Then she had errands to run. Go to the County Health Department for a death certificate, go to the bank, buy groceries, fill the car with gas, get Aunt Mattie's prescription filled, and take Aunt Mattie to the doctor. She spent the entire day away from home and didn't see Oregon at all. And missed him terribly. It was five o'clock when she and Aunt Mattie returned home for dinner and found a note from

Oregon tucked into the door. He had come over during the afternoon to see if he could help with anything. Charity was very disappointed that she had missed him.

Aunt Mattie was exhausted after their hectic day, so they ate an early dinner, and then Aunt Mattie went to bed.

Charity cleaned the house, then baked a cake and made a lime-Jell-O salad for Zizi and Bernard's visit. Finally she bathed and settled in bed to listen to "Nighttime."

Oregon's baritone came over the air, floating in the dark, bringing his presence into the bedroom. She could see green-gold eyes, imagine his big hands holding a record, see his long body relaxed in the chair, his tight jeans molding his strong legs.

She groaned softly and turned to stare at the radio. Tomorrow night they had a real, bona fide date. Would Oregon reveal his double identity then? The thought of a whole evening alone with Oregon was tantalizing.

"Hello, there, darlin'. I'm so glad you tuned in. This is Rory Craig Runyon at station KKZF bringing you 'Nii-aighttime.' Settle back, darlin'. For the next two hours you'll listen to slow, easy music, old favorites for late hours."

After a commercial, Oregon played "One Love in My Lifetime." Well, now, she didn't believe that was a message to her! No man like Oregon could have lived in a vacuum all these years. She checked over her list of carefully chosen requests: "Blue for You," "Say the Words," "Amazed and Confused," "I've Never Been a Woman Before." As she listened to the music she debated which song to request first.

The song ended, and Oregon's voice filled the

room and her senses like an intoxicating sweet wine. She closed her eyes and thought of lying in Oregon's strong arms, of his gorgeous body so warm against hers. He played "Someday We'll Be Together," then asked for requests. Charity dialed quickly, but received a busy signal. Aggravated, she listened to Samantha's breathless voice, the same Samantha who had called in before! She requested "The Voice of Love," a song Charity didn't know but wished she had found first. She flounced down on the pillows to listen to the music and wonder if Oregon was talking to Samantha while the music played. Her eyes narrowed. She licked her lips and dialed the station. A recording came on the line. "Good evening. This is station KKZF, broadcasting to you at one thousand on your dial. If you wish to talk to someone at the station, you may leave a message at the sound of the beep. We will be open at eight o'clock in the morning. Thank you for calling KKZF."

Charity replaced the receiver without waiting to hear the beep. They must put the calls through to Oregon when he asked for requests, then switch back to the recording. She bit her lip. Was Oregon chatting with Samantha?

The song ended, and she let out her breath. "Good-bye, Samantha," she whispered, and listened carefully to Oregon's farewell.

"There you are, Samantha, a late-night song to soothe away the worries of the day. You call again, you hear?"

"I will, Rory," came the whispery female voice.

Well, he hadn't called Samantha "darlin'." "Here's our next, 'Only You.' " he said. "It's for you, darlin'. I'll listen and think about you, about

your tempting lips and your big, beautiful eyes. Listen to the song."

Charity did. Was Oregon thinking about her? She wriggled in the bed and thought about him, about his strength, his tenderness and passion. The cockeyed, crooked smile and arch of brow that could be so devilish or so delightful. "Oregon!" she whispered. Tomorrow night—what would happen? At the thought her pulse jerked and rattled like an overheated motor. Then Oregon was on again. "How's that? Nice song, wasn't it? Darlin', here's something else nice. Remember Henrietta's Pie Mix? Well, now we have Henrietta's Batter. You talk about yummy, scru-umptious, mouth-waterin' biscuits . . ."

Each word dropped on Charity's trembling nerves like sizzling oil. What a voice the man had! What a voice, and body, and kisses . . . "Oregon!" She wished she could conjure him up out of the darkness.

She listened raptly while he described biscuits in adjectives that made her quiver.

"Now let's get back to some music. What would you like to hear? You call and tell me, darlin' . . ."

Charity did, as rapidly as possible. She let out her breath with satisfaction as she listened to the ring, then heard Oregon's voice continue its magic.

"Rory, it's Charity."

"Darlin', I'm glad you called. Are you all right?"

"Fine," she lied. What would he do if she answered honestly?

"What song would you like to hear, darlin'?"

She blushed with such intensity she felt she must be glowing like the red dial on the radio. " 'I've Never Been a Woman Before,' " she said.

" 'I've Never Been a Woman Before,' " he re-

peated, sounding thoughtful. "That's an interesting title. Here it is, darlin'. Just for you."

The music began, then Oregon said, "Charity?"

"Yes."

"Darlin', I've been waiting for you to call me. 'I've Never Been a Woman Before'—did the guy you like to kiss cause this request?"

"He might have."

"I'm green with jealousy."

"You don't need to be. Not at all."

"I do if he's the reason you requested this song. Are . . . Charity, are you in love with him?"

"No. I can't love him, because he won't talk to me like you do. Not at all. I don't think he really likes me. I think he's just amusing himself."

"You're wrong. Oh, Charity, have you really talked to this guy?"

"Yes, I have." She glared into the darkness and glanced out the window at Oregon's dark house.

"Charity, I'll bet he's falling in love with you. He can't resist. He wouldn't want to resist."

"He doesn't act like it!"

"He doesn't act like it?" Shock and disbelief came through clearly.

"I guess he acts like it, but he doesn't *say* anything!"

"Give him time."

"Time! Rory, you wouldn't need time. You say the nicest . . ." She hesitated. What was good for the goose . . . Lowering her voice, she said breathlessly, "You say the sexiest things, really sexy, that excite me so much . . ."

"Dammit, Charity. How can I do a show when you say things like that in a voice that makes me turn into a bonfire?"

Elation tweaked her nerves. Score another for me, Oregon Brown! "Serves you right."

"Darlin', I just go home to an empty house. I don't have anyone to love. I don't have anybody to talk to either."

"You have a goat—" The instant Charity said it, two things happened at once.

Nine

First, she clamped her hand over her mouth. Second, the record ended.

"Charity, you know!"

"Oregon, you're on the air, or you should be!"

"All that damned talk about—How long have you known?"

" 'Nighttime' isn't broadcasting?"

"Dammit, answer me!"

"We can't talk now!"

"Dammit!" And the last "dammit" was broadcast by "Nighttime." It came out clearly in Rory Runyon/Oregon Brown's voice. There was a screech, the jarring screech of a needle slipping across a record, and then "La Cucaracha" in all its snapping glory came blaring into the bedroom. Charity hung up. She didn't want to talk to Oregon right now. It did serve him right, but she wished she hadn't blurted the truth out over the phone! She

would have preferred to discuss it with him in person, but it was too late now. Curiosity wracked her. Would he ask for another request when "La Cucaracha" finished? He must have snatched up the first record he could find.

She waited to see what would happen. Without a word from Rory Runyon another song, "Cuanto Le Gusta," followed. Charity bit her lip. Was he not talking because he was so angry? What was he doing? The music ended and another Spanish song started. Charity sat up. Had she wiped out Rory Runyon's career as a disc jockey? What was Oregon doing?

The music finally ended and a male voice came over the air. A male voice that was pleasant, but a pitch higher than and definitely not Rory Runyon's!

"There, did you like that touch from south of the border? A little bit of Spanish? This is Bill Foster, filling in for Rory Runyon. Rory will be back tomorrow night, folks, with his usual patter. . . ."

Charity blinked. Where was Oregon? Her eyes widened. There was only one place he could be! He was on his way to her house! She threw aside the covers and scrambled out of bed to find her robe. She pulled it on with shaking fingers, trying to figure how much time had lapsed since she had talked with him.

Something thumped against the window. In shock she stared at the window a second, then rushed to open it. Moonlight bathed Oregon in a silvery glow. He stood beyond the patio, his fists on his hips, his feet spread apart, golden curls tumbling over his forehead.

"Charity, come out here."

She went. He sounded as if he would come right through the window if she argued.

As she hurried through the house, she tied her belt securely around her waist and buttoned the collar to her chin. Her pulse raced and she felt alternately hot and cold. He sounded angry, but he didn't have any more right to anger than she did. He was the one who had hidden his identity!

She closed the door behind her and found him on the patio. It was dark beneath the sloping roof and difficult at first to see his eyes.

"How long have you known?" he asked gruffly.

"Why didn't you admit it to me?" she countered.

"Dammit, you've just been leading me along!"

"Listen here, Oregon Brown! Talk about 'leading me along'! You're the one who started the deception! Why didn't you tell me the truth right away?"

"Because you sounded so convinced that Rory Runyon was nicer than Oregon Brown."

Stunned, she peered at him, leaning closer to try to see his green eyes. "I don't believe you for a second!" She remembered that night at his house. "You wouldn't tell me because you deliberately tried to get me ready and aching for you so you could come home and seduce me! Deny it, Oregon!"

He shuffled his feet and gently grasped her shoulders. "Charity . . ."

It was true. She had known it all along, but it hurt to hear him hesitate. Her eyes had adjusted to the darkness, and she detected a flush creeping over his cheeks.

"Charity, I did, honey, but I can't say I'm sorry, because I'm not. Then I was afraid you'd be angry with me if I told you. When did you guess?"

"That night."

"You knew that night. . . . Well, damn!" He let go

of her. "You've been stringing me along on the show."

"It wasn't as bad as what you did!"

His voice changed completely. The embarrassment vanished to be replaced by a cocky self-assurance that was becoming more and more familiar to her. "You really like the way I kiss?"

"Now, Oregon, I said some of that to get revenge." It was her turn to blush.

"Oh, sure. Let's see, what did you request? You wanted 'I've Never Been a Woman Before,' 'Touch Me in the Morning' . . ."

"I know what songs I requested!" she snapped.

"And you like the way I kiss. You like to talk to Rory. You're falling in love with Rory. You know, you have a little sneakiness yourself. You really had me going!"

"Oregon, I'd better go inside." She was beginning to get signals of danger ahead. Big danger.

He leaned back against the door, facing her, and ran his hands slightly up and down her arms. Her alarm system rang and clanged in a flurry of warnings, but it was too late. Much too late. Her gaze drifted down over his blue cotton shirt and his tight jeans, stretched taut by his arousal. She swallowed with difficulty and raised her eyes to find him watching her intently. His big fingers slipped up her arms, over her shoulders, to her throat.

His husky voice lowered, and she started to melt. "You like the way I kiss, you like to talk to me. Well, it's mutual. I like to talk to you. I like to kiss you. Darlin', I really like to kiss you. Miss Charity Jane Webster, I'm in love with you!" Wrapping his arms around her, he pulled her close and kissed her. And she thawed like snow before a fire, anger dis-

solving into eagerness. His tongue slipped into her mouth, touching hers in wave after wave of stormy, scalding surges, exploring her textures, the moistness beneath her tongue, the yielding softness of her inner lips.

She was dimly aware when he scooped her into his arms and entered the house. His footsteps were muffled by the thick carpet as he carried her to her room. He pushed the door closed behind them and set her on her feet, continuing to kiss her until all her fragmented thoughts and doubts had disappeared and all she knew was how badly she wanted him. His kisses were heady, sweet wine, intoxicating and delicious, sending her senses on a spiral of desire.

She locked her arms around his neck and clung to him, twining her fingers in his hair, feeling his hard maleness press against her as if there were no clothing between them. One hand slipped across his broad, firm shoulders down to the buttons of his shirt. She twisted the button free, slipping her fingers beneath the smooth cotton to his furred chest.

He caught her face in his hands. His voice was hoarse, so low and breathless she felt as if each word was a physical contact. "Charity, I love you."

"Oh, Oregon!" Her heart pounded fiercely. She loved hearing him say the words, yet it threw her into a turmoil. Then her thoughts faded like fog on an Oklahoma spring morning, melted away by the sunlight in his green-gold eyes.

He stepped back and slowly untied her belt, tugging it free. The belt slipped from her waist and dropped. Then he started on the buttons. His knuckles brushed her flesh, his eyes holding her imprisoned. As tension built, making her quiver like a young willow in a windstorm, Oregon slowly unbut-

toned the blue robe and finally pushed it over her shoulders and let it drop around her ankles on the floor.

"You're mine, Charity," he said in his sexy, husky voice, which gloved a note of steel. "Mine forever. I won't let you go."

Charity lay sprawled on Oregon's big, warm body, her cheek on his chest, her legs pressed against his. She listened to his heart thump, to his breath gradually slow, while his hands stroked her bare back, trailing lightly, comfortably down over the rise and fall of her curves, over her buttocks, to the back of her legs, then up again to her shoulders. And at last, Oregon Brown could talk as well as Rory Runyon!

"Charity, darlin', how I've wanted to do that, to hold you again and love you. Darlin', that first night . . . after we made love I couldn't admit I was Rory. And I couldn't apologize, because I wasn't sorry. Not one damn bit! There weren't any regrets. Charity, you and I were meant to be. We just are. There's a chemistry between us, isn't there, darlin'?"

"Hmmm, Oregon." She couldn't talk. She was exhausted, floating in a cotton-candy euphoria, in a sweet world of frothy pink that blanked out everything else. Oregon, Oregon, Oregon! Rory Runyon! Rory Runyon wasn't as important as Oregon Brown. Oregon Brown was the world. Completely. She sighed with contentment.

"Charity, you're mighty quiet."

"Hmmmm." Satisfaction oozed in her response.

His fingertips drifted down, down lightly as feathers to touch her intimately.

She stirred. "Hmmmm, Oregon!"

"I thought I might get a response. What happened to your conversation?" He sounded amused, but she felt too filled with lethargy to move and look at him. She twined chest curls around her fingers, then blew at them. "Oregon, I can't talk now. I can't talk when I'm very passionate—or when I'm exhausted." She felt doubly exhausted after the effort to explain.

He chuckled, a deep, throaty sound that always made her tingle. "I love you, little Charity. Love you terribly. You're all I want." He shifted, then looked down at her. His fingers tangled in her curly hair, twisting it lightly.

"Charity, marry me."

Ten

Her eyes opened wide, her heart started thudding, and her breath stopped.

"Darlin', marry me. Charity Jane Webster, I want you to share my life forever. To have and to hold from this day forward. Will you marry me?"

Her euphoria vanished. She was stunned, blinded by his dazzling proposal. And at the same time frightened.

He sounded so confident, so absolutely sure of himself as he said, "You're all I want."

"Oregon . . ." She didn't know what to say. His eyes, such a deep, deep emerald green, focused intently on her. He blinked, and his brows drew together.

"What is it, darlin'?"

"Oregon, I'm falling in love with you. I *do* love you, but let's not rush into marriage."

"Oh, my lord. Charity Jane Webster, you look like

the kind of woman who would want nothing but marriage. What's the hang-up?"

"It's Ziza," she answered, totally alert now.

"Well, she doesn't have to live with us. She doesn't have to give you permission, either!"

"Oregon, try to understand. My mother died when I was fifteen years old. Dad lived just eight months longer and was killed in an accident at a railroad crossing. His car was hit by a train. I was sent to live with Ziza for a year, then spent the next three years with Aunt Mattie and Uncle Hubert. That year with Ziza was so terrible. She divorced her fifth husband, began to date, and married the sixth. Bernard is husband number eight."

Oregon's mouth curled up in a grin. "Darlin', you aren't going to have eight."

"It's not funny, Oregon. I don't want to rush into marriage. I really didn't want to rush into an affair. I promised myself when I was sixteen that I'd never live like Ziza. She dotes on men and attracts them like cherry blossoms attract bees. I hated that year. She went with three men before she married again. She and my mother were sisters, but they were as different as sugar and salt."

He sobered and brushed the curls off her damp forehead. "Hon, you were young, hurt over the loss of your parents, suffering growing pains. That made everything worse. Charity, you won't be like your aunt. You won't have eight husbands."

"No, I certainly won't! I want one. One and only." She focused on Oregon again. "I just don't want to rush into something. Give me time, Oregon." As he gazed down at her in silence, something tightened inside Charity. She felt torn between years of promising herself to be careful, to be very sure,

and a desperate longing to accept his proposal now. She twined her arms around his neck. "Don't be angry. I love you, Oregon, but we haven't known each other any time at all!"

"Time isn't what counts," he said solemnly. "Charity, I love to hear you say you love me. I want to hear it every day."

"Just give us a little time. It counts some. You don't know me at all and I don't know you."

"You mean you don't know me as well as you want to. I know you, darlin'. Remember, your aunt and uncle talked about you a lot. I know that you won a drama award your junior year in college; I know you hurt your ankle once when you were a cheerleader; I know your first contract in the landscaping business was with Char-burg Drive-in; I know you have hay fever—"

"Well, I don't know anything about you! For all I know, you've had three wives."

"Nope. None."

"Were you ever engaged?"

"Yep, once."

"Why didn't you get married?"

"I guess I didn't want to because I kept thinking of reasons to put it off, until she finally gave me an ultimatum and we broke up."

She narrowed her eyes and stared at him intently. "How long had you known her when you proposed?"

"Four years." She thought she detected a twinkle in his eyes.

"Dammit, Oregon, you take advantage of me!" she said without anger.

"Oh, sure. Maybe I did once."

"There are so many problems. You don't know . . ." Her voice trailed away.

He leaned down to kiss her forehead, her cheek, her ear. He whispered, "What don't I know?"

"Well, I have to decide what to do about Aunt Mattie. I don't think she can live alone. She forgets too many things. And there's my business. Oregon, my landscape business failed and I have debts up to my chin."

"I have money up to my chin." He pulled back a little and grinned.

"My, what modesty!" Her smile vanished, and she frowned. "Seriously, you're not going to pay my debts."

"Oh, lord. I've fallen in love with an independent woman."

"Too bad, buster," she said flippantly, then sobered. "Really, Oregon, I have to get a job and pay off the debts. I don't know what kind of employment I can find. I have a degree in landscape architecture."

His dimples deepened and his green eyes glinted as he said, "Darlin', you worry too much. Way too much. Your problems aren't that big and I'm happy to share them."

"Wait until you have to share Ziza," she said darkly, while her thoughts seethed. Oregon wanted to marry her! To be with her forever. She stroked his broad shoulder. "Oregon, don't push. I can't resist much pressure, but we haven't known each other long and I'm trying to keep my promise to myself. I'm trying to be sensible."

He kissed her throat, then drifted to her ear again. "Okay, darlin'. Be sensible, take your time, but don't ask me to dally long. I want you, Charity, and I'm

going to have you. You'll be Mrs. Oregon Brown someday. And not in the distant future!"

His words came out in a breathy warmth over her ear, words said in his sexiest voice. She tingled and tightened her arms around him.

"This wasn't something taken lightly, Charity." Suddenly Oregon sounded vulnerable, almost pained.

"Are you really lonesome?"

"Darlin', you're what I need in my life." He leaned forward, his arms slipping beneath her to hold her.

"Now, Oregon, I think you have a gleam in your eye."

"Darn right I do. Come here, darlin'. I'll fill your thoughts until all you know is me. Absolutely. I want to hold you and kiss you and touch your beautiful body. To feel you respond, to feel you tremble in my arms, to listen to your heart pound for me." His voice was Rory Runyon's seductive best. And it worked its sensual magic on her ready and all too willing body. She raised her mouth for his kiss and closed her eyes to everything but this golden man.

And it was marvelous. His hands traveled over her, starting the insidious need that made her cling to him desperately.

It was a night of love, and she woke the next morning in Oregon's arms, in the dusky light of Saturday's dawn. She sat up and looked down at him. Long, thick lashes shadowed his broad cheekbones, and his bare chest rose and fell in regular rhythm.

"Oregon! You have to go home. Aunt Mattie will see you." He opened his eyes and focused on her. One corner of his mouth lifted in a crooked smile. "My intentions are honorable. I want to marry you."

She tugged the sheet to her chin and tried to avoid looking at Oregon's enticing chest or inviting mouth. She overcame the temptation to lean down and brush his lips with hers.

"Oregon, will you get up and go home?"

He chuckled and pulled her down. "Come here, darlin'. I'll go, and the world won't be scandalized."

She summoned her stiffest resolve and sat up again. "You need to go now."

"Darlin' . . ."

"Don't you start that 'darlin' ' business in your sexy voice. You know what it does to me!"

He sat up, his face inches from hers, his green eyes flashing with golden promises. He wrapped his fingers in her curls. "What does my voice do, darlin'?" Their faces were inches apart. And his words were suggestive, his mouth irresistible.

"Oh, Oregon!" And then she was in his arms, with his mouth on hers, and she never knew who made the first move. An hour later, dazed, aware of sunlight really streaming through the windows, she sat up and tried again.

"Oregon, please go home."

He chuckled and got up without argument. She watched the powerful muscles in his legs, his sleek, trim buttocks flex as he walked, and she almost called him back. Almost. He picked up the black briefs and snapped them on, then turned and caught her staring. He winked, a lusty, leering wink as he drawled, "It's all yours, darlin'."

"You are tempting, Oregon."

"Oh, darlin'." He headed toward the bed, dropping his jeans.

"Oregon, get dressed!"

With a grin he reversed direction and stepped into his pants. And she happily returned to watching him. He was fascinating. The muscles in his back rippled as he sucked in his flat stomach and zipped his jeans, buttoned the waistband, then bent down to pick up the brown leather belt and slide it around his lean hips. Once again she marveled at the width of his shoulders in relation to the narrowness of his waist and hips. As he shrugged into his shirt, he smiled, asking with innocence, "Aren't you getting dressed, darlin'?"

"Yes, after you're gone and it's safe."

"Safe? There's something dangerous about me?"

"Everything is dangerous about you!"

He grinned. "That's good. I'd hate to be safe." He crossed the room and dropped a kiss on her forehead, looked into her eyes, and then sat down to pull her into his arms and really kiss her.

His tongue met hers, confirmed what they had found before, demanded more, and gave delight before he released her. "Darlin', think about a wedding date. Soon."

"Oregon, I don't know you. A week ago I didn't know you existed."

"That so? Well, we'll take care of the little details, getting to know me, the paper, Mattie. Charity, marry me and we'll live just yards away from her. And the landscape business—how much are the debts, hon?"

"I won't let you get involved." She raised her chin, and he grinned as he rose to his feet.

"What time does Ziza arrive?"

"Late this afternoon. Oregon, don't misunderstand, but I'd . . ." She hesitated. It was difficult to put her feelings into words.

He quirked an eyebrow questioningly. "What is it, hon?"

"Well, Ziza tends to take over, and—I guess it's a hang-up from childhood, but she makes me nervous." She looked out the window. "Money means more to her than men. And my father didn't make a lot of money. She wasn't happy to have me live with her."

"Charity, that's over now. Let it go," he said forcefully.

She met his solemn gaze and continued. "By three I'll probably have a headache."

"If you weren't that close, why's she coming to see you? Is Mattie important to her?"

Charity took a deep breath and tried to keep her voice level, unaware of Oregon's gaze dropping to the sheet as she clenched it in her fists. "No, they hardly know each other. They're on opposite sides of the family. She's coming because I inherited some of Uncle Hubert's money and I'll inherit everything when Aunt Mattie . . . later. I'll be worth noticing then."

"Well, hell's bells. Send her packing."

"No, she's my aunt. That's something else. She taught me to never call her aunt or acknowledge the relationship. She had a date with a college guy once and made me double-date with his little brother, and I wasn't supposed to tell that she was over twenty-five."

Oregon swore softly. Ignoring him, she added, "She's my mother's sister. I can't be unkind, but I dread her visit. As I said, I'll probably get a headache. Oregon, I don't want her to know you've proposed, and it really would be easier if you weren't here. She's very forceful."

"How long since you've seen her?"

"It's been a long time. I was in high school."

"You might not get a headache now," he said dryly. "You've probably changed a lot since then. And I'm not worried about forceful women."

Suddenly she felt better and grinned at him. "I'll bet not. You know you can turn them to putty."

"Putty, huh? Maybe I should stay a little longer. . . ."

"Oregon!"

"I'm going. Some putty!"

"You don't know this one!"

He leaned down, placing his hands on her shoulders and looking into her eyes. "Darlin', this is the fourteenth of May. Let's have a May wedding."

"Oregon, I don't know you that well!"

"You know me better than you do any other man on earth," he said with a smugness that aggravated her and made her blush.

"Let me make up my mind without interference, Oregon!"

"Darlin', you made up your mind a while back, whether you want to admit it or not." He winked, then opened her screen window.

"Talk about forceful people . . ."

He grinned. "This is different, and you know it."

"Suppose Aunt Mattie sees you leave?"

"It won't matter. I'll be part of the family soon. She'll think I'm in the yard looking for Billy."

"Billy! Dammit, Oregon, I can't live with that goat!"

Oregon's grin widened, the dimples punctuating it. "Darlin', I'll take you over a goat any day. Billy can live on the farm. Now, get dressed and I'll think about you, think about you getting out of bed, in a

tub of hot, sudsy water . . ." He spoke in Rory Runyon's intimate, husky drawl, and she burned.

"Oregon, go!"

He grinned, waved, and stepped through the window to the patio. Flopping back onto the pillow she gazed dreamily out the window and watched Oregon stroll across the yard as if he owned it. Sometimes he acted as if he owned the world. And then there were moments . . . She remembered how vulnerable and solemn he had sounded when he'd said, "This wasn't something taken lightly . . ." Did Oregon really need her as badly as he indicated? He wanted to marry her! Oregon Brown/Rory Runyon had proposed! The idea made her tingle like a reverberating bell. Marriage! Did she need to get to know him better? Wisdom said yes and her heart screamed no. She would try to listen to wisdom today.

And today Ziza would arrive. Ziza. "Oh, lordy," she breathed aloud, and threw back the covers.

Just before noon, after fixing Aunt Mattie's breakfast and finishing the housecleaning, Charity studied her reflection in the dresser mirror, smoothed the straps of her white sundress, then glanced around the room. Her gaze drifted to the bed, and in her mind she could clearly see Oregon's big golden body stretched out on it, remember how he had kissed her as no other man had . . .

She burned with the memory, and tingled and ached. "Dammit, Oregon! Get out of my mind."

The doorbell rang. With a lift of her chin, Charity walked grimly down the hall. Her palms felt damp, her nerves strained, and her cheeks were burning as she flung open the door. Determined to present a

positive, relaxed front, she exclaimed, "Come in! Come—"

Oregon grinned and stepped forward to take her into his arms. "Thanks, darlin'. It's good to be here." He leaned down to kiss her.

"Oregon!" She wriggled away and glared at him. "What are you doing here?"

He extended a bouquet of red roses and white carnations. "I thought you might like some flowers for the festive occasion."

"Thank you. They're beautiful."

"You sound as if I'd presented you with a bundle of weeds."

"These will be a red flag under Ziza's nose. She'll have a thousand questions about who sent them and why."

"Want me to throw them out?"

"No!" She smelled them. "They're lovely. I'll put them in the living room."

"Good."

Acutely aware of Oregon's watchful eyes, she placed them on a table. She wished he would go. It made her nervous to think about facing Ziza with Oregon present. She straightened and saw Oregon settle on the sofa.

"Oregon, I'm expecting Ziza any time now."

"Yeah, I know."

She hated to ask him to leave, but she didn't want him to stay. They stared at each other while the seconds ticked past and then, outside, she heard a car motor grow louder and louder.

"Here she is. Oregon, you're going to complicate things," she said as she started toward the door. He followed and stood on the porch beside her.

"She might as well get to know me. I intend to be around for a long time."

How could she stay angry after that? She watched the sleek black Lincoln Continental whip into the drive. Oregon asked lightly, "You have a headache?"

"No, I don't." She met a satisfied gaze.

"I didn't think you would."

A scream interrupted their conversation and a woman jumped out of the car and, arms outstretched, rushed toward them. "Charity!"

Eleven

"She's the age your mother would have been?" Oregon asked softly, and Charity knew why. Ziza was slim, carefully fed, with a figure that was exercised and groomed for hours each day. With a wild tangle of black curls, heavy makeup, and a simple black dress that probably had had a staggering price tag, Ziza Feathers hurried up the walk to them. As a handsome, brown-haired man climbed out from behind the wheel, Oregon muttered, "My goodness, I do believe she robbed the cradle."

The man was young; he had to be close to Charity's age. Then Charity momentarily forgot him as Ziza flung her arms around Charity while big blue eyes sized up Oregon Brown.

"Charity, love! It's simply been ages. And you'll have to introduce me right now!"

She released Charity, who said, "Ziza, this is

Mattie's neighbor, Oregon Brown. Oregon, this is Ziza."

Oregon accepted Ziza's extended hand for a brief shake. "Glad to meet you, Ziza," he said blandly.

"Oh, my goodness. That delectable voice! You just have to be the man I talked to on the phone."

Charity felt as if she had stepped back into quicksand. Why hadn't Oregon let sleeping dogs lie and stayed home?

"I'm the very one."

"And you have a date with Charity tonight . . ."

"That's right."

At the foot of the porch steps the tall, slender man paused. Charity glanced at him. He was handsome, with blue eyes and brown, wavy hair, but he couldn't be a day over twenty-six, which made Ziza twice his age.

She clasped Charity and Oregon by the arms. "Well, you two will meet Rolf anyway. Bernard, my precious Bernard, got sick in Dallas and flew home, and Rolf came down to drive me back so I wouldn't have to travel alone. Isn't that the sweetest thing!" As if on cue, in a scene that had been rehearsed a hundred times, she turned. "Rolf, darling, come here and meet these nice people."

He climbed the steps, his blue eyes fastened on Charity as if she were a long-sought-after gem, and suddenly Charity knew it wasn't simply a matter of Bernard's becoming ill. Ziza had planned this just as surely as there was a sun in the sky. Ziza linked her arm through Rolf's. "This, darlings, is Rolf Feathers. Rolf, here's Charity Jane . . ."

Rolf picked up her hand, holding it too long between his, while his eyes seemed to devour her. "I've heard so much about you, Charity."

"And this is her neighbor, Oregon Brown," Ziza continued happily.

Reluctantly Rolf pulled his gaze from Charity and shook hands briefly with Oregon.

"Now, where's Mattie? Let's go inside." Ziza linked her arm through Oregon's, gazing up at him with wide eyes, while Rolf took Charity's arm. And Charity knew absolutely that Ziza was up to one of her games.

Oregon held the door, shifting his arm to take Ziza's. In his coaxing, melting baritone, he said, "Ziza, you greet Mattie. I'll be right along." And he winked at Ziza.

For just an instant Ziza looked startled, then she smiled and sailed inside. Oregon looked the soul of innocence as he turned to Charity and Rolf.

"Charity, I want to show Rolf the flowers." Oregon motioned with a jerk of his head. "Come here, Rolf."

Oregon looked guileless, but Charity had a feeling she was throwing Rolf to the wolves. Since when was Oregon interested in flowers? There wasn't so much as a dandelion blooming in his yard. And he couldn't be interested in Rolf either. Oregon led Rolf away, and Charity went inside. She found Ziza in the living room.

"Where is everyone?"

"Aunt Mattie," Charity called, "Ziza's here." She turned to her aunt. "Ziza, why did you bring Rolf?"

"I told you, sweetie, to drive me home." She winked. "Besides, Charity, it will do you good to throw a little jealousy into Oregon Brown. Charity, that man is a hunk! I wouldn't have guessed. He is luscious, and what a voice! When you said you had a date, I could just imagine some sweet little college

boy, not Mr. Muscle. And dimples too!" Her blue eyes drifted over Charity. "You've grown up."

"That happens," Charity murmured, her thoughts elsewhere. What was Oregon doing? *Showing the flowers to Rolf?*

Ziza continued blithely. "Well, Rolf will give him some competition. It never hurts, Charity. Take it from someone who knows. Darling, if you need any help with investments—I know you'll inherit the—Mattie! It's so nice to see you again."

Ziza kissed Mattie's cheek, and they sat down while Ziza explained Bernard's absence and Rolf's presence. Then she announced, "Now, I'm taking us all to dinner tonight. No arguments. I know you and Oregon Brown have a date, Charity, but you can run along after dinner."

Charity grimaced inwardly. Ziza hadn't been there half an hour and things were in an uproar, plans were changed, and the rest of the day and night were looking grim. Then Rolf and Oregon appeared, and Charity straightened in shock. Rolf looked ashen beneath his tan, while Oregon was smiling innocently as he settled in a chair near hers. Ziza's eyes narrowed, constantly darting back and forth between the two men, while she introduced Rolf to Mattie.

Mattie smiled. "How nice of you to drive Ziza to Enid."

Rolf shifted nervously, shooting one quick glance at Oregon. "I'm glad . . ." His voice cracked. He swallowed and tried again. "I'm glad to do it." Then, almost as an afterthought, he said, "When we get to Oklahoma City, I want Ziza to meet the woman I'm in love with."

It was Ziza's turn to look startled. "Silly thing! He's joking." She cast steely eyes on Rolf. "You

know you told me there's no woman in your life right now."

"I forgot about her."

All eyes in the room focused on Rolf, and he giggled nervously. "Just a joke," he muttered.

Charity looked intently at Oregon. He looked too, too pleased. His gaze shifted to hers, and, as if he saw the question in her eyes, he shrugged one broad shoulder.

Undaunted, Ziza wriggled in her chair, zeroed in on Charity and Oregon, and said, "Darlings, I just have to know how you two met."

"Over the fence, you might say," Charity replied. "We're neighbors."

"And what is your line of work, Oregon?"

Charity waited to see what he would say. Oregon smiled, placing one booted ankle on his knee and resting a hand on it. "I'm a disc jockey."

Ziza frowned. Charity knew that each of Ziza's past seven husbands had had more than average-sized bank accounts. She looked at Oregon's happy smile and realized he knew exactly what he was doing.

"A disc jockey." Ziza pronounced it like a death sentence. "Well, of course, Mattie now owns the paper here. Even though dear Hubert is gone, I'm sure you can find a nice job at the paper. Something with a little more future in it."

"Oh, I like being a DJ. I enjoy my days at home. Just Billy and me. My kid, Billy." He gave Ziza another dimpled smile, and Charity left it alone. She wasn't going to explain Billy either. Oregon continued cheerfully, "I can stretch out in my hammock while Billy frolicks in the yard."

Ziza looked stricken. Mattie unknowingly added

fuel to the blaze. "Oh, Ziza, Billy is so cute. That's how Oregon and Charity met. That naughty little Billy came through the fence and ruined some of Charity's plants."

"Kids will be kids," Oregon said with a smile.

Ziza glanced at Charity. "Sweetie, I need to freshen up. Will you show me the way?"

Charity rose and walked down the hall. Before they reached the bathroom, Ziza took her arm and pulled her into a bedroom, closing the door after them.

"My dear, I didn't come a moment too soon." She shivered. "That man is gorgeous! He's a hunk and so-o-o sexy, but, sweetie, he's not the man for you. I mean it, dearie. Don't get tied up with a divorced man who won't work, who has no ambition. He wants to stay home and play with his kid. There's no future in that!"

"Well, Ziza, I'll have to make up my own mind."

"Sweetie, looks aren't everything. A disc jockey who doesn't want to work during the day!"

"That's the same reaction I had when I met him. About working during the day. The disc jockey part is just fine."

"Oh, my God. Charity, I don't know what happened to Rolf. You don't suppose that Brown punched him one, do you?"

"Oregon? Rolf doesn't have any bruises that show."

"No, but he's acted damned strange since he stayed outside to look at the flowers. There's no woman in his life. Sweetie, I'll see about Rolf. You dump Oregon and try an evening with Rolf. He's in stocks and bonds and he has a brilliant future."

"Thanks anyway, Ziza. I'll take my chances with Oregon."

"You're not serious about him, are you?"

"I am," Charity answered happily. "I'm in love with him." It felt good to say it and it sounded so right!

"Oh, my God. Oh, sweetie, you're just looking at his gorgeous body. The man is a bum! Living out here in the sticks, too!"

"It's pretty nice here, Ziza."

"And he has Billy."

"I'll admit I don't like Billy, but if I marry Oregon, he's promised to send Billy away." Charity was beginning to enjoy herself.

Ziza's eyes widened. "Oh, my God, it gets worse! He'll get rid of his kid to have you as his wife. Charity, the man's after your money. Or Aunt Mattie's money."

"I don't think so."

"He is! Get rid of him. And for heaven's sake, give Rolf a chance. Take my advice. Rolf's a whiz with investments."

"Thanks, Ziza. Shall we go back?"

"I hope you do what I say. You're just like your mother, looking at the world with wide-eyed innocence. The first handsome devil to throw the charm at you, and you fall for him. A gorgeous body and sexy voice are fine, but money is what counts! Now, you take your aunt's advice—give Rolf a chance. Dear, his future is marvelous. Get rid of this lazy Oregon bum!"

"He's not really a bum!" Charity laughed, while Ziza's brow furrowed in a frown.

"Charity, I see my duty. I want you to come back to Kansas City with me."

Charity felt a knot tighten in her stomach. "I can't leave Mattie. There are a thousand things to do here, but thanks." Charity smiled and relaxed. Ziza wasn't as formidable as she remembered. Or time had changed her reaction to her aunt. "Shall we go back to the living room?"

Ziza stared at her. "You know, you have grown up."

"It's been a long time," Charity said gently. The past was over and done. And some old hurts were laid to rest. Without waiting for Ziza, Charity turned away. Ziza caught up with her, and together they returned to the living room.

To a silent living room. Mattie was rocking gently, Oregon was gazing out the front window with a smile on his face, and Rolf looked as if he were sitting on a tack. The moment they entered, Ziza said, "I told Charity and Mattie, and now I'll tell you boys: I'm taking everyone to dinner tonight." Her gaze rested on Oregon. "No arguments. I know you two have a date, but you can put it off one night. I haven't seen Charity in years." She turned to face Mattie. "I was just telling Charity, I want you to come home with me, both of you." She rummaged in her purse for a cigarette, and placed it between her lips. "It would be so nice to have you for a week."

"Thank you, Ziza," Aunt Mattie began.

Suddenly Oregon leaned forward with a lighter in his hand, holding it for Ziza. Charity stared at him in amazement. She hadn't seen him smoke one cigarette. Ziza leaned forward, inhaled, and, while she was close to Oregon, looked up into his eyes. Her full dark lips curved in a tempting smile. Oregon smiled in return as she said a throaty, "Thank you,

Oregon." She straightened and waved her cigarette in the air, not allowing Aunt Mattie to continue.

"Don't say it, Mattie. Don't decline yet. You and Charity think it over."

"That's nice, Ziza," Mattie replied. "Charity can go, but I don't travel so well any longer."

"I could put you two on a plane! Mattie, you'd love it." And suddenly Charity's sinking feeling returned. Ziza knew where the defenses were down. To get Charity away from Oregon, Ziza would work on Mattie.

"Ziza." Oregon cut in in a husky baritone that stopped Ziza's chatter instantly. "I can't wait any longer. I want to have a little chat with you about Charity." Charity closed her eyes briefly, merciful blackness shutting out everyone. What was he up to now? Oregon didn't know Ziza. "The rest of you will excuse us, won't you?" While he spoke lightly, his gaze rested on Rolf, who paled visibly. What had Oregon done to the man? As Oregon took Ziza's arm, Charity wondered if Ziza had met her match. Or vice-versa. Ziza could twist most men around her finger with ease.

As soon as Oregon and Ziza were out of sight, Aunt Mattie sat forward, her gnarled fingers gripping the arms of the rocker. "You two sit and talk while I get us some tea."

"Let me do it, Aunt Mattie." Charity jumped up and went to the kitchen. She was in time to see Oregon stroll across the yard with his arm across Ziza's shoulders. Beneath the shade of the elm he turned Ziza to face him. He looked relaxed, his hands slipping into his back pockets while he talked. Ziza seemed to draw herself up, and Charity wondered what Oregon was saying. Whatever he had said to

Rolf had finished the man off. She couldn't imagine anything that would faze Ziza. Charity carried a tray of glasses of iced tea back to the living room. She offered one to Mattie, then one to Rolf, who shot her a quizzical glance, snatched a glass, and quickly mumbled his thanks.

"What business are you in, Rolf?" she asked.

"Investments," he said shortly, and turned to Mattie. "That's an interesting painting over the mantel."

Mattie thanked him, and they launched into a discussion of the picture and of how Mattie and Hubert had bought it in Oklahoma City. Charity glanced at the print of Gainsborough's *Blue Boy.* Rolf had surely seen it a dozen times before. What had Oregon done to him? She studied him openly. There wasn't a mark on him.

As if aware of her observation, he flicked a nervous glance at her, then back to the picture. He rose and moved to sit by Mattie, across the room from Charity. Oh, Oregon had done something, all right!

And then she heard Oregon's voice, his marvelous baritone, talking about the weather and the Plaza in Kansas City. Ziza and Oregon entered the room. Spots of color marked Ziza's cheeks, and her blue eyes were flinty. Oregon looked relaxed and happy as a lark.

And within ten minutes Charity realized that Oregon, Mattie, and she were carrying the conversation. Ziza and Rolf sat in grim silence until Ziza suddenly rose to her feet. "Charity, Mattie, I'm dreadfully sorry, but suddenly I feel ill. I think we'll be on our way to Oklahoma City now so I can take a plane home if I get worse."

Everyone rose and drifted to the door, while

Mattie offered to let them stay at her house. As Ziza put her arms around Charity to hug her farewell, she whispered, "Keep in touch. I wish you all the happiness in the world."

Charity wondered what had brought that on. Ziza rushed to the car and climbed in beside Rolf. They waved good-bye as the black car drove out of sight.

"I'm so sorry Ziza became ill," Mattie said. "It's a shame, when you haven't seen each other for so many years. Ziza's always tied up in her own interests, though. She should've come to see you those years when you were in high school."

Charity put her arm around Mattie's thin shoulders. "I had you and Uncle Hubert, and that was better."

"You're a sweet girl, Charity," Aunt Mattie said, and if she had left it at that, Charity would have felt a warm glow, but Mattie went right on. "Don't you think so, Oregon?"

"She's sweet as chocolate candy." He winked at Charity, and she blushed.

"Hubert and I were so worried about raising a young girl, and that prom night you stayed out until five A.M., Charity, you'll never know what that did to your uncle!"

"That was a long time ago," Charity said emphatically to Oregon.

With one of his smug smiles that made her feel as if a slow-burning fuse had been ignited beneath her feet, he said, "Oh, yes, the time when Jack Mullins ran out of gas."

Charity wanted to explode. Was there anything Mattie and Hubert hadn't told Oregon? "My, what a memory you have about things that don't concern you!" she snapped, and his dimples appeared.

"If you two will excuse me," Mattie said, "I think I need a little nap."

Oregon held the door for Charity and Mattie, then followed them inside. Charity began picking up glasses and napkins while Mattie went into her bedroom. Oregon, with glasses in each hand, followed Charity into the sunny kitchen. She set down the tray and turned to face him.

"All right. What did you do to them?"

His brows arched. "Who, me?"

"Come on, Oregon. I've never seen Ziza like that in my life."

He grinned, his green eyes as devilish as that old goat of his. "You have to fight fire with fire, and all that. She resorted to dirty tricks to get you separated from me for a week and I couldn't let her get away with it." He hooked his thumbs in his belt. "If Mattie wants to go to Kansas City, you and I will take her this summer."

As aggravated and curious as Charity was, she was also thrilled by his words. But she wasn't going to let it drop. "You aren't off the hook. What did you do?"

"Hon, you said Ziza understands money, and she's easy to handle." He looked down at her with a heavy-lidded gaze. "She's not an independent woman. She's easy to manipulate, whereas you, darlin', are like moving the Rock of Gibraltar."

"Oregon, that's ridiculous! It's the other way around. Ziza? Easy to handle?"

"Sure. You were holding your own just fine. I simply speeded things up for you." A very steely note came into his voice. It was a tone she had heard only once, when he had waited in the yard the night before and told her to come outside. "I just explained

to her that she mustn't interfere in your life or mine."

"That's all?"

"Well, I told her my finances were sufficient to support you comfortably."

"You must have been very convincing." She was beginning to get the drift of the conversation she had witnessed beneath the elm.

"I have my persuasive moments." He pulled his thumbs out of his belt and reached for her. "Come here." He leaned close and whispered, "Darlin', I hope to hell to get my way. I want you, Charity Jane, and I'm going to fight for all I'm worth . . ."

Her pulse was drumming so loudly she couldn't hear the rest of his words. She gazed into his hungry eyes. "I'm like the Rock of Gibraltar? Really, Oregon, when it comes to you, I'm mush. Soppy, gooey mush."

"You don't say!" he replied, and kissed her.

She returned the kiss, wrapping her arms around his neck and clinging to him until he raised his head. "Charity, I did run them off. Are you sorry?"

She shook her head. "Not really. Ziza never did care about me. I was a nuisance."

"Darlin', forget that time. I wish I could wipe that year out of your life, but it's over and gone."

"I know. It doesn't matter now. Life improved when I came to live with Aunt Mattie and Uncle Hubert. They were good to me, and I loved them, but then, I guess you know all about that. Oregon, have they told you everything about me?"

"Everything!" he said with a wide grin.

"I hope you're wrong! Do you smoke?"

"Nope. Don't smoke, don't chew tobacco . . ."

"Why do you carry a lighter?"

"Oh. I thought Ziza might smoke. Sometimes it's handy to have a lighter."

"And what did you do to Rolf? Did you hit him?"

"Hit him?" His green eyes gazed guilelessly at her. "Darlin', I wouldn't just up and hit a man. I showed him Mattie's roses."

"Oregon . . ."

"Well, maybe I said a few things, but I didn't hit him. I told him I belonged to the Enid Mafia . . ."

"The Enid Mafia! Oh, dammit, Oregon."

". . . and if he so much as looked at you, I'd put out a contract on him."

"That's ridiculous and terrible!"

"I don't like competition for my girl."

She couldn't help but smile. He kissed her temple, murmuring softly, "Charity, have you reached a decision yet?"

"I can't be like Ziza. I can't rush into marriage when I don't know you."

"It isn't time that's important. Don't you feel something special?"

"Yes. But I still won't rush into a lifetime commitment."

He moved away. "I'll be back in a little while."

"All right, Oregon." He had yielded too easily, and she had a suspicion he was up to something again.

"I'll just go out through the back."

She followed him to the patio. "Oregon . . ." He paused at the door. "Thanks. Ziza isn't really that fond of me."

She expected one of his light, quick replies, but instead he turned back to her and cupped her face in his hands. "Darlin', you'll get to know me. I can wait a little. But, Charity, you'll never be another

Ziza, and I'm going to be your one and only as long as I draw breath."

She trembled and wrapped her arms around him, standing on tiptoe to kiss him. Finally she pulled away and said shakily, "How can I keep my wits about me when you say things like that?"

"There's something else. If I buy the paper, I'll have to go to work during the day."

"That's all right," she answered. "I'll have to work during the day too."

"Not necessarily. I know, don't protest. I can see it coming in your blue eyes. Darlin', if I work during the day, I want the nights with you. I'll retire Rory Runyon."

She smiled, her full lips curving sweetly as she trailed her fingers along his cheek. "I won't mind, because I'll have Rory Runyon all to myself. I went through agony while you talked to Samantha."

"Samantha? Oh, on the program."

For a long moment they gazed into each other's eyes, wordless messages passing between them, confirmation, desire. Oregon turned abruptly. "I'll be back in a little while."

And he was. As Charity peeled a potato for Mattie's dinner, she looked out the kitchen window and saw Oregon step out from behind the crepe myrtle. She saw his hair, his eyes, and his long legs, but between eyes and legs he was hidden behind an armload of boxes and books.

She hurried to get the potato on to boil, rinsed her hands, and rushed to the back door as Oregon called, "Charity!"

"What on earth?" she asked when she stepped outside.

"Have you got a minute?" He put everything down in a chair and straightened.

"Sure. Until I get ready for an important dinner date."

"Good. Come here." He took her hand and sat her down on the porch swing beside him, then pulled the chair filled with books and boxes close beside them. He put a scrapbook in her lap, opened it, and said, "Now, darlin', here's my past."

She looked down at pictures of Oregon at an early age. "Oregon, I'm glad to look at these, but this isn't what I meant about knowing you!"

He could look so damned innocent and amazed. "It isn't? Darlin', here's my whole past." He rummaged in the stack and withdrew a fat book. "Here's my baby book. You can read when I got my first tooth, when I crawled, what my first word was . . ."

"Dammit, there's more to it than that."

"How can you swear over a baby book? Come on, darlin', let's read, and pretty soon you'll know me."

"I'm getting to know you pretty well right now." She didn't know whether to laugh or swear. So she didn't do either. For the next hour she looked at Oregon's scrapbooks, photo albums, boxes of mementos his mother had saved. He gave her the lock of hair from his first haircut, and she tucked it away to keep.

Mattie joined them for a time, then left while they continued, until Oregon rose. "I have to go now. You keep them, Charity. I'll get everything later. Darlin', I'm sorry, but I have to do 'Nighttime.' We'll have several hours first."

"That's all right. I love 'Nighttime.' "

"I want to hear you say you love something else."

She smiled up at him as he leaned down to drop

a kiss on her cheek. She stayed on the swing and watched as he lithely bounded over the fence. She was tempted to tell Mattie about his proposal, but it sounded ridiculous to think about marrying him when she had known him such a short time. She looked at the album spread open on her lap, at snapshots of a lanky young Oregon in a high-school football uniform. The cocky grin hadn't changed. But she couldn't marry someone just because she had seen all his old photos. She thumbed through a box of articles by Oregon, forgetting the time while she read. Finally she closed the box and went into the house.

Two hours later Charity was ready to go out. Smoothing her yellow sleeveless dress, she walked to the kitchen to get Mattie's dinner on the table. As soon as it was ready she called her aunt. "Aunt Mattie, dinner."

Glancing at the clock, she saw it was five minutes until Oregon was due. Her pulse hummed along eagerly, and she felt trembly with anticipation. "Aunt Mattie," she called again.

When she didn't get an answer, she decided her aunt had taken off her hearing aid. She went to Mattie's room, but it was empty. Puzzled, she tried the bathroom. One by one, she went through each room in the house, only to find them all empty. When the doorbell rang, she opened it swiftly and faced Oregon.

One hand was resting on his waist, pushing his gray coat back and revealing a white shirt above charcoal slacks. His gaze heated her as it drifted down over her yellow dress, down to her yellow pumps, and up again. And she did the same thing in return to Oregon, her heart beating rapidly as she drank in

the sight of him. How handsome he looked! Their eyes met, and she wanted to step into his arms—until she remembered Mattie.

"Have you seen Aunt Mattie?" she asked.

"No. I can't see anyone except a gorgeous curly-haired blonde. Y-u-m, yum!" He reached for her, but she sidestepped him and held his hands.

"Oregon, I can't find Aunt Mattie. Come in and let me call the neighbors."

Oregon followed her into the kitchen and lounged casually against the door, looking so disturbing, marvelous, and distracting that she finally turned her back on him while she discussed Mattie's whereabouts with the neighbors.

In fifteen minutes Charity was frantic. She hung up the phone after talking to the last person on Mattie's phone list. "No one has seen her. Where can she be?"

He crossed the room and put his hands on her shoulders. "Now, don't worry. Enid's a pretty safe place to wander around in, and sometimes she just likes to take a walk. She's done this before, and I've helped Hubert find her. I'll call the police—I know someone down there—and just alert them. Then you and I'll look around the neighborhood."

After he made the call, they climbed into separate cars to drive in opposite directions, agreeing to meet again in thirty minutes. When they met after half an hour, Charity waited nervously while Oregon parked and climbed into the car beside her. "I haven't seen her, but Billy's gone," he said.

"She took Billy with her?"

"I think so. He has a leash that usually hangs on the back porch. It's gone and the gate was closed."

"I feel a little better to think that goat might be with her. I'll look some more. Where can she be?"

"I called the police and they're making an all-out effort. It's getting dark. Why don't we go together now? I'll drive."

Charity was getting so edgy, she was glad to let him. As Oregon drove, she twisted her hands together. "I can imagine so many terrible things. She isn't wearing her hearing aid, and she can't hear a car honk or the motor—"

"Charity." Pulling to the curb, he turned and cupped her face in his hands, and his voice was gentle and calm. "Don't imagine anything bad. She's with Billy. They're probably sitting somewhere while he chews up the flowers. Now, come on, don't worry until you have to."

"I'll try," she said grimly. "This is why I can't leave her alone. I don't know what I'll do, Oregon. I can't take her to Tulsa to live with me and I can't move in with her and give up my life."

A strange look flickered over his face, one almost of pain. In a deep, solemn voice that sounded so vulnerable, he said, "Darlin', I've asked you to marry me. Isn't that in your choices?"

"Of course it is! I was talking about the immediate future."

"So am I."

"I'll still have to figure out what to do about Mattie. She can't live alone."

"Hon, you'll work it out, but remember, this happened while you were living with her."

"That just makes me feel worse."

"No. What I'm trying to tell you is that there is just so much you can do and no more. Hon, when we're married, we'll live by her and you can hire a

companion for her, someone to stay all the time. We'll talk about it later. Let's try the park by the zoo." He backed the car down the driveway.

"That's miles away!"

"Not impossible, though."

They found Mattie sitting in the park, just as Oregon had guessed. Billy was tethered nearby, chomping on grass beneath one of the tall yellow lights that shed a glow over the entire park. Charity was so relieved she could scarcely speak, but Mattie seemed to feel nothing was wrong. She simply remarked on what a nice stroll she and Billy had had.

By the time Oregon and Charity had gotten Mattie home and called the police and neighbors, only an hour remained before Oregon had to go to the station. So Charity grilled hamburgers, they ate with Mattie, and then Charity walked to the door to say good-bye to Oregon.

After a long, heated kiss, Oregon gazed down at her. "I'll tell Bob to hold the line for your requests. No one will get through except you."

"Can you do that?"

"Sure." He grinned. "Have any big requests like 'I've Never Been a Woman Before'?"

She blushed and was grateful they stood on the darkened porch. "Enough from you! I didn't think you'd remember."

"I can tell you exactly. 'The Men in My Life, 'Touch—' "

"Now, stop! Did you play any of those pieces particularly for me?"

"Don't tell me you didn't know!"

"Well, how could I be sure?"

His voice shifted down to the low hum of an idling motor. "When I kiss you like this and then play

'You Do Something to Me'—hon, it's only for you!" He pulled her to him and kissed her in such a manner that Charity's system underwent a major upheaval. When Oregon released her, she stood in his arms, dazed, gazing up at him with wide, befuddled eyes. And she almost lost her wits and threw over the traces, almost cast aside her long-standing, firm promises to herself not to rush into marriage. She almost said yes. "Oregon . . ."

His eyes narrowed, and he waited. And while he waited, Charity's wits settled down, like a bird on a branch, from the flight caused by his kiss. Settled down enough that she said simply, "I'll listen to 'Nighttime.' "

"Something tells me that wasn't what you started to say."

"Just give me a little time. T-i-m-e!"

"I am. Want to go to church with me tomorrow? I'll take Mattie too."

"Oregon, I mean, give me months of time."

"Months, huh?"

She didn't like the way he said that word. "You're going to be late for the show."

" 'Night, darlin'." He hurried down the walk.

In a daze Charity undressed for bed and settled down to listen to "Nighttime." The music filled the darkened bedroom, and then Oregon's voice came on, husky, sexier than ever.

"Hi, darlin'. Here's 'Nighttime,' on station KKZF. This is Rory Craig Runyon, darlin', I'll be playing some night songs"—his voice lowered, sliding down the scale to another octave—"night songs only for you."

Charity felt on fire. "Darlin', it's a gorgeous night, a night for love. My empty arms need you,

want you. Here's a song for you: 'Black Satin Sheets.' "

Charity felt sure she must be glowing in the dark like the radio dial. Thank goodness she was alone! She hadn't heard the instrumental song before, the scratches on the record and the style of music made her think it was old, but the message was clearly Oregon Brown's! If she married Oregon—if! If they married, what would she do about Mattie?

Married to Oregon. The thought almost levitated Charity off the bed. She could picture Oregon down to the smallest detail, his big fingers on the records, his lively green-gold eyes, his charcoal slacks molding muscular legs . . .

The music ended and his voice lazed into the room, as tantalizing as his presence. "Darlin', that's for you. Now here's something else—Captain Nemo's Fudge Bars. Fudge as te-empting and dee-licious"—his voice dropped again—"as your . . ." Pause. A pause that put Charity's whole system on hold. What was he about to say? Her imagination was the only thing that functioned, and it worked furiously. "Oh, no, Oregon," she whispered to the empty room, squeezing her eyes closed and bracing herself for the rest of his sentence.

It came in syrupy tones. ". . . as your momma made."

Charity felt as if she had just narrowly escaped getting run down by a truck. Maybe she should turn 'Nighttime' off and save her heart considerable strain. But, then again, it would be under a strain if she couldn't hear Oregon. Suddenly, getting to know Oregon far better didn't seem half so important. And wisdom whispered, "This is the one and only!"

She sat up in bed and peered at the radio. Did she want to marry Oregon?

His voice swirled around her like sweet spring water.

"Darlin', there's a big moon out now, a million stars, a night for love, for you in my arms. Here's another song for you, darlin'," and "What Are You Doing the Rest of Your Life?" came on.

Charity smiled, leaned back in bed, closed her eyes, and thought about Oregon Brown. Charity Brown. Mrs. Oregon Brown. "Mrs. Charity Brown." She said it out loud and decided it had a very nice ring to it. She didn't have any particular songs to request and tried to think of something. Her eyes flew open. She threw back the covers, rushed to the closet, turned on the lights, and pulled out her album collection. She'd send a message back to Oregon. She rummaged through the albums, selected three, turned off the lights, and settled back in bed as Oregon came over the radio.

"Did you like that one, darlin'? Let me hear from you. What song would you like? I'll play another and you call me when it's over. Here's an oldie from me to you. 'Full Moon and Empty Arms.' "

Charity listened, then dialed as soon as the music stopped. One ring, and a man answered, "KKZF 'Nighttime.' "

"This is Charity."

"Hi, Charity. Oregon said to put you through. Here goes . . ."

A ring came over the radio, and then Oregon's special voice. "Hi, there."

"Hi. This is Charity."

"Darlin', I've been waiting for your call."

She curled her toes and wished he were with her. He asked, "What do you want to request?"

" 'I Honestly Love You,' " she said.

" 'I Honestly Love You.' Sure, darlin'. Hang on while I put the record on to play." Music came on, faded, and then Oregon's sexy voice burned through the line into her soul. "It's been forever since I left you. Darlin', I need you."

She thrilled to his words, and she poured out her thoughts to him. "Oregon, I've looked at the scrapbooks, but I don't know anything about the past year in your life. I don't know about two weeks ago."

"I moved back here when my Dad died. I don't want to live on the farm. He didn't either. I have someone who runs it for me. I moved into the house. I've dated first one person, then another, and they didn't mean anything to me. Charity, we can build a new house if you'd like. You don't have to move into my old house."

"It's lovely, but let's take one thing at a time. Let's worry about that much later."

"I hope not much later."

"Oregon, why me?"

His voice lowered, dropping to depths below the surface, down to a molten heat that poured out sensuously. "There's something special about you. There's a chemistry between us. You're fun."

"I just don't know you. And aren't you rushing into marriage rapidly, after avoiding it for years?"

"I've been alone, Charity. Really alone. I left home when I was eighteen to go away to school and I didn't come back here to live until my parents were gone. I've traveled, I've devoted a lot of time and energy to—"

"Now, Oregon, I know there have been women."

"Can't deny it, hon, but it never held a lot of meaning. There never has been anybody I wanted to spend the rest of my life . . ." He paused, then said, "Uh-oh, darlin', the song's going to end. Call me later, darlin'. I love you."

Then Oregon's voice came over the air, but Charity was drifting from Oregon's last words, sailing like a bird on air currents, carried higher and higher in widening circles by Oregon's *I love you* and *There never has been anybody I wanted to spend the rest of my life* . . . The lingering recollection of his words, his sexy voice, billowed around her.

"There. 'I Honestly Love You,' darlin', for only you and my listeners. I'm so grateful to my audience. Y'all have been great, so *responsive* . . ." Oregon's voice dropped on "responsive," drawing it out, the sound sliding down Charity's spine like his big fingers.

"Hmmm," she murmured aloud, and wriggled, a smile curving her lips.

"I can't tell you how much I've liked talking to you in the late hours on 'Nighttime.' Night time is a special time, a very special time."

Charity felt on fire. My, she wanted Oregon! She was burning with the need for his big, strong arms, his sensational kisses.

"So, to all of my loyal listeners, I want to tell you, I've fallen in love. I mean to tell you, I'm in love with the sweetest, sexiest little gal this side of the Atlantic and Pacific oceans . . ."

Charity felt as if her eyes would pop out of her head. Her body became rigid. She went cold, then hot. Her breath stopped. "No," she whispered. "Oregon, no . . . !"

She grabbed the radio and shook it. "No!" But it didn't stop the husky, golden voice.

"I'm in love. I want to get married if and when she'll have me. I need her. And, in a way, while we didn't meet through 'Nighttime,' we came to know each other better because of 'Nighttime.' You never know where love will appear. So, I want to dedicate this next song to her, to my sweet . . ."

"Oregon!" Charity shook the radio again. "Don't announce me on 'Nighttime'!" She plunked the radio on the table and snatched up the phone to dial furiously.

". . . sweet little gal. Here's 'Be Mine Tonight,' dedicated to my darlin'."

The recorded voice came through the phone. "Good evening. This is station KKZF, broadcasting to you at one thousand on your dial. If you wish to talk to someone at the station, you may leave a message at the sound of the beep. We will be open at eight o'clock in the morning. Thank you for calling KKZF." There was a shrill beep, and Charity left her message. "Oregon Brown/Rory Runyon, will you stop! Call me—"

There was a click, and Oregon's deep voice came on. "Darlin' . . ."

"Oregon Brown, that is the lowest thing you have done! Don't pressure me into marriage! Don't announce me to the world! Don't—"

"Charity."

The word was said with the same quiet, steely authority he had used outside her window and with Ziza. And it stopped her instantly. Vaguely she wondered how anyone who was as nonchalant as Oregon could suddenly become so commanding, but he managed it with amazing ease.

He sounded solemn as he said, "Charity, I get a lot of calls from women. I wanted to explain my coolness. I needed to put a stop to them. It isn't personal, it's just Rory Runyon's chatter that touches lonely hearts—Dammit, I have to put on another record. Hang on, darlin'."

She listened to Oregon come over the air again. What he'd said made sense. She could imagine the lonely women who called him. Maybe he did have a good reason to declare his love and he hadn't said her name. Part of her mind worried over his remarks while another part listened to him say, "How was that, darlin'? Here's another for you and all—"

There was a bang, a rattle, the sound of something scraping in a jarring dissonance against the microphone, and she heard Oregon snap, "What the hell—"

Another male voice cut in above the background racket. "All right, mister, don't move. You bastard! I'm gonna blow your head off. I know you're in love with my woman!"

Twelve

Charity felt as if she had been struck by lightning. She sprang up, landing on her hands and knees, glaring at the radio, as she yelled, "No, he's not! He's in love with me!"

More scuffling sounds came, then, "Don't either one of you move. Get back against the wall, and you, Runyon, get your hands over your head."

"Look, we're on the air. Let me throw the switch—"

"You ain't throwing no switch, lover boy! I know all about you and Marlene."

"I don't know Marlene."

"He doesn't!" Charity shouted, her fingers trembling as she dialed information. "Give me the number of the police station!" Charity gasped, repeating it to herself as she dialed hastily. "He's in love with me!" she told the radio.

"Enid Police Department."

"This is Charity Webster, and I'm calling for a disc jockey at station KKZF. A man is threatening to kill him."

"At station KKZF? That's been reported, and a car is en route."

"En route? Thanks." Charity hung up and dialed KKZF and got the recording, while she heard over the radio, "You and Marlene. You've been saying all that garbage to her over the radio, thinking you could fool me. Well, you can't! She left me tonight just to listen to you."

"Look, my girl's not named Marlene. Call her and ask her."

"Huh!"

"She's not!" Charity shouted, shaking the radio. "I'm his girl, Charity Webster, you monster!"

A knock sounded. "Charity, are you all right?" Mattie asked.

"I'm fine. Someone is trying to kill Oregon!"

She flung the radio on the bed and pulled on her jeans and a shirt. The door opened, and Mattie thrust her head inside. "Someone wants to kill Oregon?" She looked around. "Where is Oregon?"

"He's at the radio station. At KKZF. A man is threatening his life! I'm going—"

"Oh, Charity, that's nice of you to rush to Oregon's rescue, but let's call the police."

"I did, and they're on their way." Charity snatched up her car keys. "I'll be right back."

"Charity, you might get hurt."

"No, I won't. The man isn't mad at me."

"I'll worry about you."

"Aunt Mattie, I'm the only one who can save Oregon. I've got to go."

"Oh, dear me." Mattie wrung her hands as she

followed Charity through the house to the door to the garage.

"Now, lock up and don't leave. I'll call you!"

"Oh, dear! A man with a gun. Oh, I do dislike violence! Charity, be careful and don't aggravate him. . . ."

Charity flung herself behind the wheel of the car and closed the door. While she sped out of the garage and down the driveway, she fumbled with the radio dial until she caught Oregon's voice. He sounded as calm as if he were talking to Billy.

"Mister, I don't know Marlene. Not any Marlene. I'm in love with a woman named Jane."

The man said a rude word. There was a shout in the background, a clatter, the mike squawked, and then he heard the man's voice again. "Get back or I shoot him now! He's dead if you come closer."

"Do as he says," Oregon said quietly. "There's been a misunderstanding. Let me talk to him. You guys get back."

"Damn right, get back."

Charity's palms were wet, her brow felt damp, and her heart was a roller coaster. She honked and raced across an empty intersection as the light turned green. And into the commotion on the radio came a woman's scream. "Let me in! I'm his girlfriend! Rory! Cedric, what you are doing? Are you nuts? Cedric, I love you!" The woman screamed again. Suddenly the station went off the air. Charity swore and spun the dial, then grabbed the steering wheel to turn a corner with a squeal of tires. She ran a yellow light, racing toward station KKZF.

When she turned the corner, she saw the blinking red lights of police cars. Her heart pounded against her rib cage at the sight of an ambulance and a fire

truck, their red and yellow lights flashing and casting eerie reflections on the building. There wasn't anyplace to park, so she stopped beside a police car, jumped out, and ran to the door.

A uniformed policeman blocked her path. "Sorry, miss, you can't go in."

Charity felt like sobbing, as she gasped, "I have to. I can save Rory Runyon's life!"

The man gazed at her impassively. "That's what three other women have just told me. How many women are in love with that guy?"

"I don't know about that!" Charity snapped, trying to draw herself up to her full five feet three and wishing she had pulled on something besides jeans and a white shirt. "But I'm the one he's in love with!"

The policeman leaned forward. "Good for you, honey bunch! Now, if you'll just join Runyon's fan club forming over there by the parking lot, you can sympathize with the other ladies."

"You have to let me in! I can tell that maniac that Rory loves me, not Marlene!"

"Yeah, sure, but if I let you in, I'd have to let Irene and Nancy and Ginger in. Sorry, toots, no dice."

"Dammit, his life is in your hands!"

The policeman shrugged. "I'd like to know how he does it," he mumbled. "I bet you don't know what he looks like."

"I do! He has blondish-red hair."

"That's a new one! So far I have two Tom Selleck look-alikes and one Richard Gere."

"Dammit, go look at him! He's big and blondish-redheaded and owns a goat."

"No kiddin'! Owns a goat! Honey bunch, that's a

good one! Nice try. A lot more original than the other three."

Charity wanted to plant her tiny fist on his big square jaw. While she fumed and felt like crying at the same time, a woman dressed in high heels and a red satin dress came rushing up the walk.

"Officer, I'm the woman Rory Runyon loves," she said in a throaty voice.

"You don't say! I'll tell you what, that Runyon is one busy man!"

Charity stepped back. Next to a red satin dress, her sneakers and jeans would have little influence. Suddenly a shot shattered the night and everyone froze.

Charity looked up at the lighted second-story windows. Had the man shot Oregon? For another ten seconds no one moved; then a woman screamed and pandemonium broke loose.

"Let me in to him," the woman in satin gasped, and tried to shoulder past the policeman, who put out an arm and blocked her.

"Sorry, lady. You can join the others over there."

"But he may be shot!"

"Probably just a shot into the air. There'd be more commotion otherwise."

Charity hoped he was right. She looked up at the windows again, at the expanse of grass between the building and the parking lot. While the woman argued with the lawman, Charity moved away toward a tall pine that stood beside the front corner of the building. She glanced around. A group of women waited in the parking lot. A television van slowed and stopped in front. Clusters of policemen stood in the front. She searched the ground until she found a brick, put it in her shoulder bag, and began to climb

the pine. She reached the second floor, opposite a window, before she was discovered.

"Hey, you!"

Charity scooted closer to the window and ignored the voice below.

"Lady, you up there in the tree!"

She looked down and saw another burly policeman standing below, hands on his hips. "Who, me?"

"Get down."

"Yes, sir," she answered politely, and shifted toward the window. She picked up the brick, then held out her bag.

"Ooops! Look out!" She dropped the bag on his head.

"Hey! Dammit, get down here."

Charity gauged the distance, drew back, and lobbed the brick through the window.

Glass shattered, leaving jagged pieces, while the policeman blew a shrill whistle and started up the pine after her. She pulled off her shoe, knocked out the pieces of glass, and climbed over the sill, oblivious of the shards that cut her hands.

As her feet hit the floor, she heard the policeman yell. "Lady, you're in trouble! You're obstructing justice. Come here!"

She ran through a darkened room, then stepped into an empty hall. For an instant she was lost. Then she heard voices coming from her right. Thankful she could move quietly in her sneakers, she hurried around a corner.

Ahead the hall was filled with police with their weapons drawn. A man in a gray suit was talking on a radio while the broad-shouldered policeman stood beside him, their backs to Charity.

How would she ever get through them? She

walked as quietly as possible until she heard a clatter behind her and knew the policeman had climbed through the window.

She ran, hoping to burst through the men surrounding the room where Oregon was. Behind her the policeman yelled, "Stop her!"

A uniformed man reached out and caught her. Instead of fighting, she looked steadily at the man in the suit.

"I'm Rory Runyon's fiancée. If you'll let me in there, I can save him."

The policeman who had been chasing her caught up with them. "She climbed a tree and broke in. I warned her to stop."

She continued to gaze at the man in the suit. "Please, give me a chance. He doesn't know Marlene. Maybe the man will listen to me!"

"I can't take a chance of your getting hurt."

"You're taking a chance standing out here in the hall. Let me go in there."

No one moved for an instant, and then the man nodded. "All right. We'll go to the door of the control room and you can tell the guy who you are. We'll see if he believes you." Cold, dark eyes looked into hers. "Are you sure you want to? That's not a toy gun."

"I'm sure. Please . . ."

He held her arm and moved through the line of policemen. They went into the small, darkened studio, then paused at the door to the control room. Dressed in a brown shirt and brown slacks, his black hair standing up like spikes, the man with the gun, Cedric, was backed into a corner. He held a rifle, aimed at Oregon. A woman, wearing a pink bathrobe, and her brown hair in curlers, stood a few feet

away, crying loudly. Another man, Bob, Charity assumed, was standing behind Oregon. Oregon himself was sitting back in his chair, his feet on the floor, hands on his hips. He was facing the gunman, his back to the turntables. His eyes shifted to the door, and Charity saw him stiffen. "No! Get her out of here!" he yelled.

"Wait a minute!" Cedric said. "Don't move. Who's she?"

"I'm the woman he loves!" Charity said. "He loves me, not Marlene!" She looked into Oregon's green eyes. "And I love him."

Never taking his eyes off Oregon, Cedric asked, "Are you two married?"

"No, but we're going to get married," Charity answered, and Oregon's brows drew together over the bridge of his nose.

"Gonna get married, huh? Let her in here."

"No!" Oregon shouted.

The rifle lowered a fraction. "Shut up, Runyon! Let her in here. Get over there by Runyon, where I can see you!"

"Charity, don't come in here!"

Charity looked up at the man who held her arm, saw the silent question in his eyes, and nodded. He released her, and she crossed the room to Oregon.

"Thought you said her name was Jane," the gunman snapped.

"It is," Charity answered. "Charity Jane Webster."

"And you're going to marry him, huh? You hear that, Marlene?"

Marlene burst into fresh sobs, her shoulders shaking as she buried her face in her hands.

"Can I give her the chair?" Oregon asked.

"Hell, no. You sit right there, Runyon. So you love this woman and you're going to marry her."

"That's right, if she'll have me."

"Someone get a preacher," Cedric ordered.

"Hey, now, wait—" Oregon began.

"Shut up!" The eye of the rifle wavered a fraction, then trained on Charity. She felt as if she had turned to ice. "She'll get it first, so you sit real still and tell them cops to get a preacher."

"Now, look, you can't force her to marry me!"

"He won't!" Charity gasped. "I want to, Oregon."

"You do?"

"Dammit to hell, get a preacher or you won't have her to marry!"

"Charity . . ." Oregon looked at the man with the gun. "Can I stand up and put my arm around her?"

"Sure thing. Look at that, Marlene!"

"Oh, Cedric, you imbecile!" Marlene burst into more loud sobs while Oregon rose and folded Charity against his chest. He leaned down to whisper in her ear on the side away from the gunman. "Darlin', you shouldn't have come. We can have it annulled. You don't have to marry me under force."

She looked up at him. "I want to, Oregon."

He focused intently on her. "You do?"

"Yes. I'd already decided to say yes."

"Oh, Charity . . ." He looked at Cedric. "Listen, we're going to get married, but I want her to have a pretty dress and a church wedding and her relatives—"

"You want a hole blown in your head?"

"No."

"Then you just shut up and marry the girl. Someone better get a preacher!"

"Get a priest," Oregon said as he pulled Charity to him again. "I want you to have a church wedding," he whispered. "A dress. Mattie will want to see you get married . . ."

"Cedric, you're going to go to jail!" Marlene wailed.

"Marlene, why didn't you care what happened to me an hour ago! Tellin' me you had to hear Rory Runyon!"

"I'm sorry, Cedie!"

"Well, in a few minutes Mr. Rory Runyon will no longer be single! He'll have a good-looking wife."

Oregon winked at Charity, and she smiled up at him.

"Where the hell is that priest?"

"Someone's gone for him," a deep voice announced from the studio.

"When did you decide to accept?" Oregon asked her.

"Tonight. Today. Yesterday. I don't know. Maybe when I saw you in the hammock!"

He grinned.

"Well, look at the lovebirds, Marlene."

"Cedie, you're a jackass! You can't force people to marry. They can get it annulled."

"We don't want it annulled," both Charity and Oregon said at once, then laughed.

"Huh! Don't give a damn what they do later. Just want you to see that the man isn't in love with you, Marlene."

"Cedric, you're the limit!"

"Here's a priest," the deep voice said loudly. "Priest coming in."

A balding priest paused at the door, taking in the occupants of the room. "I'm Father—"

"Can the idle chitchat, Father. Marry these two."

"My son—"

"We want to get married," Oregon said quietly.

Through glasses perched on his nose, the priest's brown eyes peered first at Oregon, then at Charity. "This is irregular. . . ."

"We know," Oregon said, his arm around Charity's waist. "We'll do it again the right way, but can you marry us now?"

"Well, we need a blood test and a few formalities, you know . . ." He looked over his shoulder at the policeman standing in the doorway behind him. The man in the gray suit nodded to him. "But I suppose we can get to those later. Very well. It's highly irregular—"

"Do it, Father," Cedric said flatly. "Marlene, you better watch. In a few minutes Rory Runyon won't be single. Hey!" he shouted. "Are there TV cameras out there? Get 'em in here to take pictures. I want all of Enid to see Rory Runyon get married."

There was a flurry of movement, and then a man appeared with a camera.

"Keep that light out of my eyes," Cedric said, waving the gun a fraction. "Stand over there and get every second of the wedding on film." Marlene began to unroll her hair.

"Your names, please," the priest said.

"Charity Jane Webster."

"Oregon Oliver Brown."

And they were married beneath the glare of a television camera, the dark scope of a rifle, the tearful sobs of Marlene, and the satisfied smirk of Cedric, with the Enid police force, station KKZF employees, and the crew of Channel Three news as an audience.

"I now pronounce you man and wife," the priest declared, as the camera whirred.

In the other room someone put on a record of the "wedding march." Oregon smiled, his dimples appearing as he pulled Charity into his arms and leaned down to kiss her, to kiss her as if they were alone and there were no audience, no gun, no camera, only the two of them.

And while Oregon kissed her, she dimly heard Cedric say, "I surrender."

Pandemonium broke loose around them. There were shouts, Marlene commenced sobbing again, the cameras whirred, and someone hugged Charity and Oregon at the same time.

Oregon released her, glanced at the chaos around them, put his arm across her shoulders, and said, "Let's get out of here, Mrs. Brown."

Epilogue

Charity stood at the kitchen stove, putting a cake in the oven. Voices carried from the family room. Kevin said clearly in his high voice, "Want to see how Mom and Dad got married the first time?"

Charity frowned as Scottie Barnes asked, "How many times did they get married?"

"Two!"

She pushed the cake into the oven and straightened. Why hadn't she put that tape of their wedding away!

"They had to get married. A guy with a gun made them. Dad said he wanted to anyway."

Clamping her jaw closed, Charity started toward the family room. As she passed the door to the utility room an arm shot out and circled her waist, capturing her.

"Hey!" she said softly as Oregon pulled her into the utility room and closed the door.

"Aha, me lovely, got you now!" Above wheat jeans and a bare chest, green-gold eyes smiled at her.

She laughed and tried to wriggle away. "Oregon, let go. Kevin is about to show the video tape of our first wedding."

"So? It'll keep him occupied until the cartoons come on. And I'll keep you occupied." He pushed the lock on the door and said, "There's a soft bundle of laundry here. Come here, darlin' . . ."

His voice could still melt her into squishy jelly. She tried one more protest as he leaned down to kiss her throat. "I just don't . . . like the whole neighborhood . . . Oregon . . . to see pictures of that wedding. Why doesn't he show the church wed—" She forgot what she had intended to say. She bent her head forward while Oregon kissed the back of her neck. Before she closed her eyes she glanced out the window. Kevin's new pet, a small brown goat, was chewing happily on a blooming rose bush. For an instant Charity focused on what was happening outside. "Oregon, that goat—"

"Mmmm, you smell so nice, Charity. Charity Brown, I love you. I mean, darlin', I am head over heels in love with you," he said, his voice dropping down to that deep level that vibrated his chest and turned Charity to mush. "Darlin' . . ." He pushed her white blouse aside and kissed the curve between her neck and shoulder, his lips trailing lower, starting scalding tingles.

"Oregon, Bonzo is eating my Sunrise rose. . . ."

"Hmmm. It can't taste half so good as you, darlin'," he murmured, and swung her down on a pile of clothes.

"Oregon! I'll have to wash these again if you . . . scatter them all . . ."

"Darlin', shhh. Charity Jane, don't you like this?" His big fingers slipped beneath the blouse to cup a full breast, to ease away the white lace.

"Oregon, I love you!" she gasped, winding her arms around his neck, threading her fingers in his soft red-gold hair.

"That's good to hear, darlin'," he murmured. "I love you and I'm going to kiss you until you stop talking to me about weddings and goats and roses. Until you melt and whimper and moan and want me, if it takes all day and all nii-aight."

And each word dropped down on her like scorching oil, oozing over her trembling nerves, burning into her like fire until he reached the word "night," said in his most adorable drawl. And Oregon Brown's two-syllable *nii-aight* wrapped around Charity's heart.

With that last word, all Charity Jane Webster Brown's attention flew into a rosy sky and was burned into oblivion by a red-gold sun called Oregon Oliver Brown.

ABOUT THE AUTHOR

SARA ORWIG has six million copies in print of forty published books, including Regency, contemporary romance, historical and mainstream fiction. She is a graduate of Oklahoma State University and writes and teaches in Oklahoma City.